To those who taught me that
right and wrong aren't simply rules to learn,
but decisions to consider day after day.

ALSO BY ANGELA M. SANDERS

The Joanna Hayworth Vintage Clothing mysteries:

The Lanvin Murders
Dior or Die
Slain in Schiaparelli

THE
BOOSTER
CLUB

Chapter One

S he'd be so glad to be through with all this. Claudine Dupin turned down a darkened side street, the slender bag with her tools snug across her back, her footsteps soundless. The last of the summer's crickets chirped from velvet-napped lawns. By Thanksgiving, she'd be drinking vintage Bordeaux in Geneva. She'd have enough money to last the rest of her life. But tonight it was the same old boring grind: Break in, steal the goods as arranged. Oh, and try not to be too messy about it.

Her dark hair was twisted tightly at the back of her head, and she was dressed all in black. Likely, no one would see her in the shadows of the trees, but if they did, she'd look like any thirty-something woman on her way to a dinner date.

The house's owner had instructed Claudine—working through Larry the Fence, as usual—that they'd be gone until midnight, and they'd set the alarm. The safe was upstairs in a bedroom. She was to steal the jewelry and only the jewelry. Larry would have explained to them that such a targeted theft wouldn't look natural if there were other valuables lying around. Hopefully they'd stowed everything else away. Just a few months ago she'd had to leave a job hauling twenty pounds of sterling flatware. Larry was thrilled, but her shoulder had ached for days.

She double-checked the address, then slipped up the driveway to disable the alarm. She rolled on a pair of gloves. A quick clip of her wire cutters ensured she'd be able to get the job done without a security outfit checking in.

The French doors at the rear of the house were a cinch. A pug came bounding down the hall toward her, but didn't even bark. Claudine knelt and scratched him behind the ears. So far, this was as easy a job as she'd ever done. She pulled a flashlight from her pack. The light's focused beam passed over a white couch and mid-century furniture. The abstract painting dominating one wall of the living room was almost a duplicate to one she'd seen a few months before on a job a mile away. Probably used the same decorator. She wondered if they knew.

She headed to the refrigerator. She wasn't really hungry, but every client seemed to expect a "real" robbery, and for some reason that included eating and scattering wrappers everywhere. She sighed. She lifted a pint of ice cream from the freezer and scooped some into the garbage disposal before tossing the half-empty container on the floor. On second thought, she didn't need the pug getting sick. She retrieved the carton and left it on its side on the faux-mod buffet. Better. She gave the dog a slice of lunchmeat and stuffed the rest down the disposal, too. She'd leave a few other wrappers in the hall.

Upstairs, she found the safe where they'd said it would be. The wall safe was an old, square-front number that probably came with the house. It didn't even have a combination wheel but operated with a key. She could pick the lock in a second, but on a hunch, she checked the top drawer of the nearby desk. Yep. People were dummies about security.

She unlocked the safe and pushed aside papers to reach for the stacked velvet boxes. She cracked them open quickly to glance inside, then halted. The second box contained a Victorian parure in onyx glimmering with diamond chips, as rich and dark as a bottomless lake against its satin setting. Mourning jewelry, likely inherited. They were crazy to get rid of it. Sure, it didn't go with their minimalist-everything decor, but so what? Tiffany necklaces were a dime a dozen. You didn't often find treasures like this.

People. She slipped the boxes into her pack and left the safe open to show that the job was done. After a half-hearted wander through the house looking for other easy-to-nab valuables, she petted the dog once again and let herself out the back door.

Easy job. Uneventful. Easy money. Lord, she couldn't wait for these to end.

As she rounded the back of the house, car lights swung into the street, then filled the driveway. Claudine swore under her breath and flattened her back against the wall, just out of the beams' path. The car idled, blocking the sidewalk. The driver wasn't coming all the way into the driveway, but neither did he back out as if he were only using the driveway to turn around. A gray sedan. A Taurus, she thought. Not the kind of car the couple who owned the house would drive. The car's engine cut, but its headlights remained on.

Damn. He couldn't see her. A moment passed, then another. She steadied her breathing to the calm meditation she'd studied. Think, Claudine. As she prepared to inch toward the rear, the car engine started again. The sedan backed into the street and disappeared.

***

An hour later, after occasional glances in the rearview mirror for the gray sedan, Claudine pulled her Honda Accord into the parking lot of the Villa Saint Nicholas retirement home. At any other retirement home, ten at night would have been too late to drop by. Not here. The Villa's residents were just getting started.

She pushed open the double glass doors to a hall of fake plants and worn linoleum squares. The stridently cheerful aroma of a supermarket air deodorizer wafted from the office.

"Hey, Claudine," a heavily tattooed man said from the office just off the hall. A thick book dangled from one hand. *Gone With the Wind.* Warren always did like a romantic potboiler. "Hank's in the cafeteria."

"Thanks."

The cafeteria doubled as the Villa's social room. Hank was just inside the door playing cards. At the sound of his daughter's voice, he wheeled his wheelchair toward her. "Hi, honey. Just getting ready for a game of crazy eights with Bobby." He waved at her all-black outfit. "You come off a job?"

Claudine relaxed. Despite the dingy walls and institutional tables, the Villa felt like home and its residents family. "Yeah. Another insurance racket. Easy money."

"Why do you take those? You could do a lot better, you know. Like you used to."

She could explain that the thrill of pulling off a big heist had dissipated years ago, and that the money didn't mean much. Unless it was really big money, big enough to put an end to the life completely.

She lowered her voice. "I came tonight because I want to

talk to you about something I've got planned. Something big."

"Hey, Deanie," Bobby said from across the table, using Claudine's childhood nickname. He tossed down a card. "Spades." Since Bobby quit as a card shark, he seemed to have shrunk within his clothes to the size of a twelve-year-old. A twelve-year-old with white hair and a knack for pulling aces out of nowhere, that is.

"Come join us," Hank said, wheeling his chair to Bobby's table.

Claudine peered over her father's shoulder. The theme song to *Practical Hospital* blared from the TV room across the hall, where the home's oldest resident, Grady, watched reruns with his hearing aid turned off. "How much are you in for this time? You should know better than to play with Bobby."

Hank smiled patiently. "Oh, honey. I only play to keep Bobby's brain working good. It's easy to get senile around this place."

A redhead pulled up a chair and set her orthopedic cane next to her. As usual, she hiked up her dress to showcase her still remarkable legs and feet tucked into gold mules. She went by Gilda, but her birth certificate likely said differently.

"Claudine, baby." Gilda twirled a hennaed strand of hair. "Your father was telling us this hilarious story about one of his old gang, a box man."

"I wouldn't call him one of my old gang. I mean, the guy only lasted one job."

"Hank said he spent the night in the house drilling out the safe's hinges." Gilda slapped her knee and guffawed. Bobby and Hank chortled with her.

"Idiot." Hank shook his head. "You should have seen the look on his face when he found the safe still as locked as ever. Some people are just too dumb for crime."

"Listen to this one. Maybe Claudine can figure it out," Bobby said.

They loved to give her crime puzzles. Comfort-wise, their rundown nursing home was no palace. Talking about old times seemed to be the one thing that kept them going. Besides, her father had trained her for this since she was old enough to walk. He used to lull her to sleep with Sherlock Holmes and Nero Wolfe stories, pointing out how the criminal could have avoided getting caught.

"So, we broke into this fancy house, right?" Bobby said.

Claudine drew up a chair. "What were you doing on a break-in? I thought you stuck to cards."

"I was a lookout for my brother's operation sometimes back in the fifties."

A tall, gaunt man wearing a priest's collar and robes joined the group. "You must be Hank's daughter," he said and held out a hand. "I don't believe we've met. I'm Father Vincent."

"Nice to meet you." What kind of crook was a man of the cloth?

"Just arrived at the Villa last week. So far I'm really enjoying it. Great community."

"Not much of a card player, though," Bobby said.

"I'm better with cars. Mechanically minded," Father Vincent said.

Claudine nodded. He was either a driver, or he stole cars. Or both. "But you've kept your vestment."

"After so many years in skirts, I can't give them up. So much more comfortable."

"I could lend you a couple of my old hostess skirts," Gilda said.

"Anyway," Bobby said, "I was just telling Claudine a story. Seeing what she would do." He laid his cards on the table to better gesture with his hands. "So, we broke into this fancy house, and they got a safe in the bedroom wall behind a portrait of a dog."

"What make?" Hank asked.

"Cocker Spaniel."

Hank snorted.

"Mosler 357. Dual combination," Bobby said.

Hank whistled. "A tough one."

"You knew there was something in it, right?" Gilda asked. Claudine didn't know what Gilda's background was, but suspected she might have been a small-time blackmailer. She'd worked in the clubs after World War II and no doubt picked up information certain husbands wouldn't want shared.

"Oh, sure. A contact at the bank told us the wife had just been to her safe deposit box that morning for her diamonds. There was a big shindig that week."

"How much time did you have?" Hank said.

"About forty-five minutes. We had a tail on the husband, still at work, and one on the wife, getting her nails done."

"Two locks? Can't be done," Hank said. "No less than an hour to crack, and four hours minimum to peel."

"Unless—" Claudine cut in, "You said it was a bedroom wall, right?"

Bobby nodded.

"Standard two-by-four construction?"

"She got it," Bobby said with admiration. "You're good. And that's exactly what happened. My brother cut the safe right out of the wall. We spent the evening in the cellar at home cracking it."

Hank patted Claudine on the hand. "She's the smart one in the bunch. Takes after her great-great-grandpa."

Claude Dupin was a famous jewel thief at the turn of the

twentieth century in Paris, and her namesake. People said the fictional gentleman-thief, Arsène Lupin, was inspired by him. Hank crowed about their shared blood, even if his own brand of housebreaking had been a tad less glamorous.

"Maybe she can figure out what to do about Wanda's kids," Gilda said.

"Wanda Rizzio?" Claudine asked. Wanda was a slip-and-fall artist a decade or so older than she with skill that would have made Buster Keaton envious. "Last I heard, she was in Sacramento."

"Came back to Carsonville last month. Got picked up down at the mall. Seems one of the security guards saw her spill her cola," Bobby said.

Part of Wanda's ploy was to dump soda, then pretend to fall and break an arm. She'd show up later threatening to sue. Once she'd shown Claudine her impressive selection of neck braces and casts.

"What about her kids?" Claudine said.

Hank and Gilda looked at each other. "That's the problem," Gilda said. "On her way to be booked, Wanda fell. I mean, for real. Broke her arm, banged her head. They took her to the emergency room right away, but she didn't make it."

"Died," Hank said. "Almost like she couldn't bear the shame of a real tumble."

"The kids—all four of them—were farmed out to foster families. But they couldn't stand being apart, and they ran away. Their dad's long gone. Larry the Fence says they're living in a squat. He's trying to get together a group to help them out."

Grady slumped in from the television room and took a chair.

"Do they know how Wanda earned her paycheck?" Claudine said.

"Larry says they've been sheltered. He's surprised they had the gumption to buck social services."

Warren wandered in from his office, a finger holding his place in his novel. Six faces watched her expectantly. They wanted something from her.

"What?" Claudine said. "Why are you looking at me like that?"

"We can't do anything about the kids, honey," Bobby said. "You know the rules. Besides, we're all broke."

"No joke," Father Vincent said. "That vow of poverty was a real buzz kill."

Claudine pursed her lips. Larry was not only a clearinghouse for stolen goods, he was a locus for information. If he said he'd get the word out to help Wanda's kids, they could count on a tidy collection of money. "Money shouldn't be a problem." Even as she said it, she knew the kids needed a lot more than that.

Putting Claudine's thoughts into words, Gilda said, "The kids need a home."

"Why don't you take them in here?"

"What?" Grady said, fiddling with his hearing aid.

"We don't have the room," Hank said.

Not only that, the Villa Saint Nicholas didn't need to draw attention to itself, as Claudine knew. Hosting a group of runaways was asking for trouble. "I'm no social worker. I'm sure Larry will figure something out."

Bobby tossed the deck of cards aside. "When your mother died, who was around to make sure you and André got to school?"

"The community." Her father answered before she could. "I owe a lot to you guys."

It was true. She told her schoolmates that Hank worked the

graveyard shift, and that's why Art Weinstein made breakfast and took her and André to school most mornings. Art was an embezzlement consultant, so his hours were flexible.

"And didn't I take you shopping for school clothes?" Gilda asked.

She had. Gilda had even buckled to Claudine's insistence on blue jeans instead of skirts. They'd pick out Claudine's wardrobe for the year, then send Mary Rose back to boost it for them.

"Look how well you turned out. We got to look out for each other," her father said.

"Oh, guys," Claudine said. "I'm grateful to you, I really am. But what am I supposed to do? Leave the Rizzio kids in my tiny apartment while I rob rich people?"

"You don't have to take them in, just help the folks Larry pulls together figure out what to do next," Bobby said.

They really knew how to pluck at the heartstrings. She was sorry, but it just wasn't good timing, not with the Cabrini heist coming up. "I'll kick in a couple hundred bucks, how's that? I'm afraid that's all I can do right now."

The residents' disappointment was palpable. "What'd she say?" Grady asked.

Father Vincent cupped his hands to his mouth and shouted, "No dice."

"Told you," Gilda said.

Claudine took her place behind her father's wheelchair. She felt bad about the kids, and she'd contribute to Larry's kitty, but that was all she could do. "Dad, can we go upstairs? It's about the job I mentioned. The big one."

"Sure, Deanie. See you later, guys."

"Heard from André?" Claudine asked as the wheelchair rolled across linoleum, then lumpy carpet.

"He's in Mexico City. Got himself a job starring in a telenovela. Grady's going to line it up for us on the computer this
week." He shook his head. "I wish your brother would use his
skills for something more useful. Or at least come help you at
the shop. He asked if you'd send him some Acqua di Parma, by
the way. The cologne, not the aftershave."

"No problem." The Scent Shoppe had been the family's
cover for three decades.

Once they were in the elevator, Hank said, "Since you're
coming up, I got something to show you."

Her father's studio apartment was as small and drab as the
others she'd seen in the retirement home, with a bed pushed up
against the wall, a couch facing a television set in a cabinet, and
an electric burner and under-counter refrigerator occupying the
make-shift kitchen on the remaining wall. What set his apartment apart was the view. Up on the second floor, his window
looked out on the learning garden of the elementary school next
door. In the summer, the voices of children yelling and playing
filled the air.

Hank lifted himself from his wheelchair and grabbed a nearby cane.

"You need help, Dad?" He seemed so much older these
days.

"No, honey. I'm fine. I got a postcard here somewhere.
Where is it?" He slowly made his way to the table next to his
bed.

Claudine wandered to the television cabinet and picked up a
photo of herself as an eight-year-old. Even at that tender age,
her father had her picking locks on the dining room table.

"Let me see," Hank said, now seated on the bed with a stack
of magazines and scraps he'd clipped from the paper. "I set it
aside for you. Ah, here it is."

Claudine examined the front of a postcard, a photo of New York City with the Statue of Liberty in the foreground. She flipped the card to look at the reverse side. "Oh, Dad."

"What? He's getting out. He asked about you."

She put the postcard down and folded her arms in front of her chest. "It's been over between me and Oz for a long time."

"They say he's going into his brother's business. He has a big janitorial contract, and Oz is going to help him get new accounts."

"Oswald's a con man, remember? You really want to take anything he says seriously?"

"Oh, come on, Deanie. You kids were so happy together. It's not like you're seeing anyone else, are you?" He felt for his cane. "Besides, with both your skills, you could really clean up."

"It's not going to happen, so just forget it." Sure, Oswald, better known as Oz, or even "the Great Oz" in certain circles, was charming. He had a way of leaning against the doorframe and capturing your glance. Then he'd start to smile, as slow and sweet as warm honey. He used that trick on any pretty woman who crossed his path. And any stooge. Somehow, everyone around Oz ended up doing the work while he counted the loot and stuffed his own pockets. She'd never told her father the details of her breakup with Oz. She'd simply told him they didn't get along.

Hank shifted to the couch and sat down again. "Sweetie, I'm an old man. I'm not going to be around forever. I don't want to see you end up alone."

"I'm not alone. I have friends." That was a bit of a fudge. Who could she trust in the straight world, anyway?

"I don't want to make you mad. I only say it because I love you."

Claudine's face softened. "I know, Dad." She parted the few

strands of hair stretched across his scalp and kissed the top of his head.

"You should think about making more friends or joining some kind of group. I know you're getting bored with the work, and managing the shop isn't going to satisfy you, either. Our kind of life can get lonely."

"They don't have social clubs for the bent."

"Well," he said, a hint of a smile on his lips. "There's Larry's effort. For the Rizzio kids."

Claudine rolled her eyes. He'd planned this all along, the fink. "Please, Dad."

"Just promise me you'll think about it, okay? He needs someone with your brain."

Claudine only paused a moment. It wouldn't be too long now that she'd be free of this life. She'd do the Cabrini job, then figure out what came next. It wouldn't hurt her to humor her father now, especially if it meant she could sidestep a reunion with Oz. "All right. I'll think about it. Listen. Have you heard about the exhibit of the Rosa Cabrini jewels in San Francisco?"

Eyes sharp, her father leaned forward. "Lay it on Hank, honey."

Claudine began to run through her plans, but as she spoke, her thoughts were on the Rizzio kids. She hoped she wasn't making a mistake by promising to help them. It was risky. After all, who else would be stupid enough to get involved?

Chapter Two

"Lord, I'm an idiot. Why did I ever agree to this?" Ruby Reed pulled her Volvo with its "Chihuahuas on Board" decal into a parking spot a few blocks from Klingle's department store.

A client had insisted on a Chanel 2.55 handbag, and the only store in town tony enough to stock one was Klingle's. The thing with Klingle's was that not only did they have cameras and tag detectors at the door, they had real live security guards. The thought nearly sparked a hot flash.

She shouldn't have taken the job, but it was the only way she could see to get into the Carsonville Women's League. The client had beamed at her offer of a "wholesale" Chanel bag and agreed to nominate Ruby. No guarantees, though. When the singer Taffeta Darling stopped by for her now-famous haircut last year, it was a mixed blessing. A steady stream of society ladies now passed through Ruby's Crafty Cuts, but it had awakened a long-dormant resentment. And a mission.

Ruby tugged her lilac tote bag higher on her shoulder. The cameras at Klingle's could be disregarded as long as she moved quickly without attracting attention. Most of the time the security crew was watching TV in the back room or ducking out for cigarettes at the loading dock. The electronic tag monitors—she had that covered, too. Her Balenciaga bag, purchased legit online, and a bargain because of its torn lining, had a thick layer of tin foil beneath its mended interior.

So much had changed since her short stint at shoplifting as a teen. Of course, back then she stole things she and her sisters needed—school clothes and food, for instance. Did a little pickpocketing, too, but that was—what?—thirty-five years ago. Her heart tugged as she remembered Larry's story about the Rizzio kids, in the same predicament.

Klingle's perfumed air rushed out as she pushed open the glass doors. Ruby pretended to examine a nearby display of calfskin gloves for a moment. Then she pulled herself into a queenly pose and walked toward the in-store Chanel boutique.

"Psst."

She raised an eyebrow. "Come to me my melancholy baby" tinkled near cosmetics. Marcel the Piano Man. She sighed and turned away from the boutique to approach the piano. As the player seamlessly transitioned to "Brother, Can You Spare a Dime," she stuffed a twenty in the oversized brandy glass on the baby grand.

"Thanks, babe." The piano man winked.

Extortion. Still, his services were helpful. She adjusted her bag once again, lifted her chin, and strode off.

The Chanel boutique occupied prime real estate near the front of the store and was separated from the rest of the ground floor by open ebony shelves encased in glass. An Asian man with Clark Gable hair arranged quilted wallets behind the counter. A beefy guard stood, feet at hip's distance, near the entrance.

"May I help you?" the salesman asked.

Ruby smiled and pulled a hand to her cheek, to better display her surprisingly realistic Bulgari ring. Larry the Fence had made her a good deal on it. The salesman smiled. "My husband wants to buy me an anniversary gift, and I'm thinking I'll suggest a Chanel handbag."

"Many of them have a long waiting list, but we might be able to find something for you." He reached behind him for a red tote.

"Oh, I think that one's too large. You know, for my small frame." It had to be the much smaller 2.55 with the chain strap.

The security guard shifted feet, and his shoes creaked. He had a regulation mustache. Probably aiming to be a cop someday. Lucky for her, he didn't appear to be paying much attention. "Everything's Coming Up Roses" tinkled from the piano. So far, so good.

"How about this one?" He placed a small handled bag on the counter.

She pretended to examine it, even slipping it onto the crook of her elbow. "That might work. Do you have anything with a shoulder strap?" She set the bag on the counter. The more distraction she laid out, the better.

"We do have these."

Ah, now this was better. He set two 2.55s on the counter— one small in ballet pink, and a larger one in camel. Her client had specified a black bag, but Ruby left some wiggle room saying she wasn't sure her cousin could get that one wholesale since it was so popular. These were four-thousand-dollar bags, which meant she'd reap half that. A full mortgage payment. But far more important was the possible entrée to the Women's League.

She slung one purse over her shoulder and walked to the full-length mirror. The guard shifted his stance so he could watch her. He let his arms fall. Maybe she'd underestimated him.

Uneasy, Ruby set the bag on the counter and took up the

larger purse. It hit at hip length. The client had specified the small 2.55. It would fit inside her Balenciaga easily, but how could she tuck it away with that oaf of a guard standing over her?

"Do you have the small one in other colors?" she asked.

"I have a powder blue and a nude. There might be a black one in stock in the back. I can go check, if you'd like."

Perfect. "If you don't mind," she said sweetly. The sales associate slipped through a door at the back of the boutique. He'd laid the bags on the counter. All she needed was a moment alone with them.

The security guard's eyes narrowed.

"What?" she said to him.

"I know your gig," he said. His voice rumbled bass.

"I don't know what you're talking about." She clutched her bag close.

"You're going to slip one of those 2.55s in that purple bag, aren't you? Then you'll walk out saying your husband will come back to buy one."

"How dare you." Ruby's voice was low and threatening. She'd never been cornered like this. But he couldn't nail her for anything—yet. She moistened her lips.

"You're not going to do it while I'm around. They hired me to watch the Chanel bags so I watch the Chanel bags."

The piano music abruptly changed to "Stop in the Name of Love." Their signal.

Heart thumping, Ruby whirled around. Her tote knocked a few of the purses off the counter.

The store manager entered the boutique with a pristinely coiffed blonde on his arm. "Here we have our Chanel collection. I'm certain you'll find something you like here."

"Ruby," the blonde said. This was a piece of luck. It was

Jocelyn, one of her hairdressing clients and a lawyer running the go-to divorce center for wealthy wives. She backed up and examined Ruby's face. "What's wrong? You're all flushed."

"That—that brute accused me of being a thief," Ruby said.

"No." She glared at the guard. "Impossible." This comment she aimed at the store manager.

"Did you accuse Miss—uh—" the store manager started.

"Ruby."

"—this lady of being a shoplifter?"

The guard's face froze. "I'm keeping an eye on the merchandise. She was ready to slip one of those little bags into her tote. I could tell."

"What do you mean, 'you could tell'?"

"She's my friend," Jocelyn said.

Ruby's pulse ticked double-time. Thank goodness Jocelyn had a weakness for half-price Jimmy Choos.

"To my office. Now," the store manager said.

The sales associate, unaware of the drama, emerged from the rear. His arms brimmed with boxes. "None in black, although I did find a very nice mint green version."

As the store manager led the security guard out, Ruby knelt next to the fallen purses. "Let me help clean this up." She swept the bags into her arms and placed them on the counter in a jumble.

"It's so nice to see you here," Jocelyn said. "I wonder—"

Ruby tucked her tote closer and smiled. Maybe Jocelyn would ask her to go have a cup of coffee. Or a drink. Just a block from Klingle's was a cocktail lounge where they made everything from scratch, even the tonic water. It was all the rage. She and Jocelyn might become real friends. Maybe she'd even recommend her to the Carsonville Women's League. With Jocelyn's recommendation, too, they'd have to let her in. Then she could clear her mother's name for good. They owed her that.

"—do you think you could fit me in for a root touchup? I mean, if it's not too much trouble. Maybe later this week?"

Ruby's smile faded. "I'm sure I could find time. For you, no problem."

"Thank you so much. I'll give you a call. Too-da-loo." Jocelyn's heels clicked on the terrazzo floor as she left the Chanel boutique. She didn't even look back to wave.

Hurt mingled with disappointment. Damn that Women's League. It's not like they did any actual good, what with their endless flower shows and tea parties. If it wasn't for her mother, she'd say to hell with them all.

Jocelyn was now a small blonde figure in the crowd of shoppers. She stopped and air kissed another blonde with an armload of shopping bags. Ruby's hurt steeled to determination. She'd show them. Ruby would help the kids and do it in a big way. A public way. She'd let them all know just how much they'd underestimated her—and her mother.

Ruby made her way to the exit. The Chanel 2.55 snuggled within her tote didn't even peep as she passed the monitors. What she'd need was someone with real money and class to help out. Real clout. But who in the petty criminal world had that kind of class?

***

Deborah Granzer had told herself she'd stop. She'd promised herself the last time this happened. She had more class than this. She did.

She opened a closet in her lonely mansion and withdrew a form-fitting black cocktail dress. She knelt to pull out the black satin sandals with rhinestone trim, and paused. Behind the carefully lined-up shoes sat a silk-covered box. She poked at its contents. Seven watches—three Rolexes, two Piagets, a Cartier tank, and an ugly Gucci. She replaced the lid and slid the box to the very back of the closet.

She'd sworn she wouldn't do it again, and she was doing it.

Within an hour, she had shed her identity as the meek wife of the owner of a chain of supermarkets and was pulling her car into the parking lot of a hotel out by the airport, one she hadn't visited before. It was a nice hotel—a businessman's hotel.

Swinging her evening bag, she strode to the lobby and followed the din of music and clinking glasses to the lounge. She knew she looked good. The turned heads of a few men, fingers paused over their smartphones, confirmed it. Tonight she had given more attention to makeup than usual and even dabbed on a few drops of a bottle of perfume she'd once felt pressured to buy at Klingle's. Yes, she got attention, but she sure didn't feel like herself. Then again, that was the point.

"What'll you have?" The bartender placed a paper coaster in front of her.

"Cosmopolitan," she answered. A drink her alter ego, Sabine, would choose.

She turned to the main part of the lounge and surveyed its mostly male, mostly suited clientele. She shifted on her bar stool and drew one long leg over the other. Across the lounge, a businessman raised his head from his laptop long enough to catch Deborah's glance. He wore some kind of chunky black watch with a lot of buttons. Probably a C.P.A. She shut off her smile and shifted her gaze elsewhere in the room.

Ah, there was one. And if she wasn't mistaken, that was a

Patek Philipe on his wrist. She'd love to have a closer look. He smiled, slipped his smartphone in his pocket, and rose to join her.

Half an hour later, Sabine had listened to Patek Philipe's business at the sewage treatment plant under construction, laughed at his feeble jokes, and touched his sleeve. He seemed like a nice guy, really. They all did—most of them, anyway—but how could they be when they left their wives all alone?

She leaned forward to whisper something in his ear and gently rested her palm on his knee. She slipped her other hand up his sleeve in a caressing motion. Within seconds, his watch was in her satin clutch.

He flushed and took a sip of Scotch. He glanced behind him, then at Deborah. "I don't usually do anything like this."

Deborah smiled encouragingly. The jerk.

He took another sip. His lips widened to a grin. "But no one would ever know. And it's not every day I meet someone like you."

Got him. "Tell you what," Sabine said in a breathy voice. "Leave your key, and I'll come up in a few minutes. It's more discreet that way." By then, she'd be on the freeway.

He bolted the rest of his drink and let his eyes linger on her chest before rising. "In a few, then."

"In a few," she said, raising her barely-touched Cosmopolitan in a mock toast. The power rushed through her bloodstream. And the guilt.

***

The next day, Deborah dragged herself from the house. Although the watches were shoved far back in the closet and covered with a down jacket and her husband Louie's old hiking boots, she swore she heard them ticking all night.

But she had to go to her hair appointment. Even though he never seemed to be around to appreciate it anymore, Louie liked her to look good. She'd tried Carsonville's elite spa, the Shangri-La, but she wasn't comfortable there. Too much white marble and condescension. This small shop on the east side she'd chosen today, Ruby's Crafty Cuts, was getting a lot of buzz.

At the salon, a middle-aged woman with an elaborate updo and hot pink capris held out her hand. "Hi, honey, you must be Deborah. I'm Ruby."

Deborah's eyes widened as she took in the salon. It had been converted from the house's living room, complete with a yellow-painted fireplace next to the mint green shampoo sink and fluffy powder blue throw rugs everywhere. A baby gate partitioned the salon from the kitchen. Two Chihuahuas raced to the gate and pressed their noses against the slats.

"They're adorable," Deborah said.

"That's Marty and Freda. I foster Chihuahua rescues." She waved a hand toward the kitchen. "Go on, darlings. Mommy has to work."

"Can't we have them in here?"

Ruby smiled. "If you don't mind. Marty's a gentleman. I'm sure he'd love the company." She lifted a honey-hued dog into the salon, where he scampered, nails skittering, around the hardwood floors and came to rest at Deborah's feet. "He wants you to pick him up."

"Hi, little guy," Deborah said in a baby voice, starting to relax. Puppy in lap, she leaned back in the chair.

With deft fingers, Ruby fluffed her hair and lifted a wavy brown hank to the side. "What would you like done?"

"Just a trim."

"It's nice at your shoulders, but you have such delicate features. You'd look terrific in a pixie. It would really bring out your eyes and cheekbones."

"Oh, I couldn't." Eyes and cheekbones? Did she really have eyes worth looking at? "Louie—that's my husband—likes it the way it is."

Ruby dropped her hair and met Deborah's gaze in the mirror. "You're Deborah Granzer, right? From the grocery store chain?"

Please, not again. She'd been having such a nice time, too. Once people heard she was married into the Granzer family, they treated her differently. Some lady was even trying to get her to join the Carsonville Women's League. No way. "Um...that's a lovely purple tote you have."

Ruby's eyes took on a steely look. "It's Balenciaga. The real thing. I could get you one half-price, if you want. My uncle's in the trade."

"Oh, no," Deborah said. "That's not what I meant."

If Deborah wasn't mistaken, Ruby was relieved. "Come over to the sink, and we'll wash your hair. Marty, you'll have to get down."

In a moment, a thick stream of warm water poured over her scalp. Heaven. Even better, the hairdresser seemed to have let go of the Granzer connection.

"Would you like some music? I don't know how you'd feel about it—it's not very high class—but I have some Patsy Cline."

"I love Patsy Cline. Unless you have Loretta Lynn, of course. She's my favorite."

The hairdresser led her back to the chair and fastened a plastic poncho around her neck. At the sound of "Walking After Midnight" crooning from the stereo, Deborah let out a long sigh.

"Anything wrong?" Ruby said.

"No."

"Honey, I'm a hairdresser. It's kind of like a bartender. We see everything, and we keep secrets."

"I'm fine. Really. It's just so comfortable here, that I—" Deborah avoided meeting her gaze in the mirror. "Can I have Marty in my lap again?"

"Sure." Ruby picked up the dog, who rooted under Deborah's plastic poncho, then settled into a soft bundle. Ruby clipped up her hair and combed out the strands at the nape of her neck. "The Granzer family. That's something. How'd you meet your husband?"

"It's kind of boring," she said. "Are you sure you want to know?"

"I know 'boring.' I met my husband a million years ago at the pet food store. But I'm a romantic. Love to hear these stories."

Deborah leaned back, the Chihuahua warm in her lap. "Well, we met at my parents' dry cleaning shop. I used to work there." When they'd first met, he'd been so enamored of her. "Louie had come in with a couple of suits to have cleaned. Over the next couple of months, he brought in every textile in his house—his sleeping bag, curtains, rugs, coats, you name it."

"But he couldn't get up the nerve to ask you out?"

"Finally he did. It happened when I was handing him a set of dry-cleaned hot pads." Louie had paused and opened his mouth. They stared at each other, each still grasping an edge of pot holder. Louie's voice had cracked as he'd stammered out his invitation.

"That's sweet. I hate smooth guys. Where'd you go on your first date?"

"To see that old movie *The Birds* down at the Bijou. Louie likes birds."

And that's how it started. Her parents weren't too wild about her dating Louie until they discovered he was heir to Granzer's Shop 'n Save. She and Louie had been so happy together the first few years of marriage. They moved into Louie's family home, and Deborah even went with him on a few of his birdwatching trips before grass allergies sidelined her. But they never had much to talk about. The phone was the worst. Louie always seemed too stymied to talk. Her throat tightened.

Ruby set down her scissors. "Honey?"

Maybe it was the music, maybe the sympathetic ear, maybe the dog sleeping in her lap, but her lip began to quiver. Then the tears started. The mirror showed a red-faced, sodden-haired girl. No one would have believed she was already twenty-four.

Ruby disappeared into the kitchen and came back a second later with a glass of wine. "Sweetheart," she said and patted her arm. "Drink this. It's from a box, but it's not bad."

Deborah was gulping back the tears now. The wine shimmied in its glass as she drew shuddering breaths. "Thank you," she managed to say.

Ruby pulled up a chair. The Chihuahua appeared from under Deborah's poncho and leapt to Ruby's lap. "Honey, don't you have anyone to talk to?" The hairdresser reached into a nearby drawer and withdrew a folding fan, which she flapped at her face. "Don't mind me. Hot flash."

"Well," Deborah said. "It's Louie. I don't think he loves me anymore."

Ruby dropped the fan to her side. "That can't be. You're a darling."

"He spends so much time away, birdwatching. It's like he can't stand to be with me. Plus, it's not safe to leave me alone. Just a couple of weeks ago, someone broke in and stole all my mother-in-law's jewelry. Plus the sterling."

"Oh, dear."

"Full flatware service for twelve," Deborah said. "The burglar shut off the security system and opened the safe just like he knew all the codes."

Ruby patted her hand. "No wonder you don't feel safe. Why don't you get a dog? Chihuahuas might be tiny, but they bark."

"I do like dogs, but I'm not sure Louie wants one."

"What about a job? Do you work?"

"No, no job."

"Any hobbies? Or kids? It sounds like you have a lot of time on your hands."

"I like to clean house, but it isn't very fulfilling." Deborah bit her lip, then drew a long sip of wine. "I want to have kids. Maybe once Louie is home more, we can try."

"Just how much is he away?"

"This time is the longest so far. It's been three weeks, and I'm not sure when he's coming home."

Ruby's reflection in the mirror was sympathetic. She reached out and lifted a few wet strands of hair. "I'd better finish this while we talk." She shifted the dog back to Deborah's lap, where he settled, this time on top of the poncho. "No kids for me, either. My husband and I wanted them, but the doctor said it wasn't going to happen. We've got the dogs, though."

Deborah leaned back and let the older woman spritz her hair, then comb it out and clip the ends. It was so restful, having someone care for her like this. Ruby stopped clipping to refill her wine glass.

When Louie had been home last, she'd reveled in fixing his dinner, keeping the house tidy, and helping him catalogue his bird photos. The box of watches was left, forgotten, in the back of the closet. Louie had set up a projector in his study, and in the evenings he cycled through the photos from his last birding trip to Peru—the Hooded Tinamu, the Horned Screamer, the Peruvian Booby, and other birds that for Deborah blended into a blur of feathers and beaks—for hours.

"Here's the Andean Cock of the Rock, the national bird of Peru. Isn't its crest stunning? Of course, the female is much less showy," he'd said, clicking to the next photograph.

"Yes, I love that orange head."

"Crest," he corrected. "You should see them at mating time, all the males bobbing and showing off for the females."

"Then what happens?"

"Oh, the female lays eggs, usually under a rocky outcropping, and raises her chicks."

"By herself?"

Louie looked at her incredulously. "Of course."

"Who's that woman?" Deborah had asked one evening while Louie was flipping through the photos again. She'd been mending a tear in the lining of his safari jacket and had looked up in time to catch the image of five people—the woman among them—in an open field. The woman was on the stocky side with a long, blonde ponytail.

"Trixie. Ornithologist," he said.

She set down the jacket. What sort of birdwatcher was named Trixie? "Does she go on a lot of these trips with you?"

"A few. She teaches at Cornell. Does a spot-on imitation of the Eastern Speckled Gnatcatcher. Spectacular."

It wasn't long after that evening that Louie had left for Ecuador. Now that winter was coming in the Northern hemisphere, he said, it would be hatching season in South America.

Deborah shook her head at the memory, causing Ruby to lift her scissors a moment.

"Have you talked to your husband about how much you miss him? Maybe he's hoping you'll join him," Ruby said.

"I have allergies. Louie says birdwatching is no place for someone who can't crouch in a field. He doesn't want me to come."

"Oh, dear. I'm so sorry. It must be awful to stay in that big house all alone. You need to find some interests. Besides cleaning, that is. You can't leave those feelings all bottled up, or they'll sour."

"Or worse," Deb nearly whispered.

Ruby stopped brushing the clipped bits of hair from Deborah's shoulders and looked at her in the mirror. "Darling. You're—you're not having any dark thoughts, are you?"

Deborah clutched the Chihuahua so tightly that he whined and slipped from her lap. "No. Not that. I don't think about hurting myself, but…."

"But what, honey?"

Should she say it? Ruby was so kind and understanding. Maybe she'd have some kind of insight. Maybe she could help. Deborah gulped her wine.

"Honey," the hairdresser said. Patsy Cline launched into "Three Cigarettes and an Ashtray."

Deborah bent her head. "Sometimes I feel compelled…."

The hairdresser seemed to be holding her breath.

"Sometimes I do things to men."

"You don't—"

"No," Deborah said quickly. "I just—I just take their watches." She bit her lip. She hadn't meant to tell Ruby quite that much.

Ruby's fingers froze in Deborah's hair. "You're mad because your husband doesn't spend enough time with you, so you boost men's watches."

Deborah nodded. Blood hummed in her ears. Why had she said that? Would she call the police?

Ruby set down the comb. "Right off the man?"

"You don't think it's awful?"

"I think it shows unusual skill." She shook her head. "Right off the man. Amazing."

"I've always been rather nimble. From mending, probably. In the dry cleaning shop. I can fix a tear in a chiffon skirt so that you'd never know it was there."

"You sell the watches, of course."

"Oh, no," Deborah said. "I couldn't profit from it."

"But presumably you have a number of—"

"Eight."

"Amazing," she repeated. Ruby tipped Deborah's face toward the mirror. Her hair was dry now and fell in cocoa-brown waves to her shoulders. "Look at you. Lovely. Your husband must be nuts. Although I'd still like to see you in a pixie."

Deborah caught Ruby's gaze in the mirror. "You've been so kind. Thank you for listening to me and being so sympathetic." She paused and took a deep breath. "You won't—you won't say anything, will you? I mean, you understand, right?"

"Oh, I understand, all right. More than you'd know." Ruby spun her chair and unsnapped the plastic poncho. "I might have something more interesting for you to do than clean house. You said you like kids?"

Chapter Three

Claudine checked the address. This couldn't be right. Larry the Fence would never have set up a meeting in such a public place. She looked once again up the street. No gray sedan. It had been three days since she'd seen it. Her shoulders relaxed. Must have been a fluke.

She heaved open the tea house door, its handle molded into an Art Nouveau swirl in brass, to velvet banquettes and the scent of jasmine and Darjeeling. The clink of coffee spoons on porcelain underscored the quiet string quartet music playing in the background.

"May I help you?" asked a man who could have buttled for the Queen Mother.

"Uh, yes," Claudine replied. "I'm here to meet friends. I think."

"Do you have a reservation?"

For a tea house? For real? "I'm not sure," she said. She definitely wasn't going to give any names. A middle-aged redhead with an elaborately curled coiffure waved from across the room. Larry had said to look for someone who resembled Shirley MacLaine, but with bigger hair. "Never mind. I think I found her."

"Hi, I'm Ruby," the redhead said. "We're the first to arrive. Have a seat." She moved a bulky lilac tote from the chair next to her.

"Claudine." She held out a hand. "I didn't expect Larry would choose somewhere so—so like this."

"Oh, Larry can't make it, so he put me in charge. I arranged to meet here."

"Usually it's the back room at the Tic-Toc. More private."

Ruby wrinkled her nose. "I don't see why we have to meet in some smelly bar. The Carsonville Women's League comes here, you know."

"I just wonder if we fit in, we—"

"We fit in perfectly fine."

The host returned carrying two leather-bound menus dangling tassels. "How many more will be joining you?"

"I'm not sure. Could be quite a few."

"Quite," the host said with raised eyebrows.

"Jerk," Ruby said when he left. "I don't know where he gets off with that attitude."

Claudine glanced at her watch. It was three o'clock, the time Larry had set. The table could probably seat at least ten people—more if they pulled up a few chairs—but so far it was just the two of them. She glanced over the room. Nothing suspicious. Still, there was always the possibility that the police had found out about their meeting. That would explain Larry's absence.

"How many do you expect?" Claudine asked.

"Don't worry," Ruby said. "Everything is completely fine. I know for sure at least one other person is on her way."

"Great." Not. She should never have let her father wheedle her into this.

"Oh," Ruby said. "Here she is."

A fine-boned woman with wavy shoulder-length hair looked around the room. She had a lost way about her, as if she needed protecting. It was hard to believe she'd be competent at her work—a con, maybe? Hustler? Ruby waved her hand to attract the woman's attention, and the woman's face lit up, transforming her from lost girl to siren.

"Deborah, meet Claudine."

They shook hands. Deborah's hands were cool and her bones thin as a sparrow's.

The host appeared behind her. "Will there be others?"

Ruby challenged his smirk with her own locked-eye gaze. "I believe they couldn't make it."

"Shame about such a large table. Oh, well." He started to walk away.

"We'll order now," Ruby commanded. The host turned at the steel in her voice. "We'll each take a pot of Oolong, and we'll have a tray of macarons to share." She pronounced the word as if it rhymed with "Cameroons."

"The *mah-cah-rohns*, you mean?" the man said.

"That's what I said." She handed the menus to the host and dismissed him by turning her full attention to Claudine and Deborah.

Well. Claudine had been thinking she might want a cappuccino, but that clearly wasn't going to happen. Not as long as Ruby had something to prove. Interesting that she'd chosen the most expensive tea on the menu.

"Deborah," Ruby said and took the young woman's hand. "I'm so glad you made it."

The younger woman smiled shyly.

"Deb is married to Louis Granzer of Granzer's Shop 'n Save."

Claudine felt the blood drain from her face. Shoot. She knew about the Granzers all right and especially about their safe's former contents. An emerald brooch with matching earrings and matinee-length pearl necklace, if she remembered correctly. Plus that blasted sterling. What would the Granzer wife be doing here? This was a trap. She tensed in her chair.

Deborah's expression remained placid. At her husband's name, she slid her phone from her purse and set it on the table. "In case Louie calls. He's out of town, and, you know...."

"I'm sure he'll be in touch soon." Ruby patted her hand.

Deborah leaned forward. "I have some watches I'd like to get rid of, and—"

"Honey," Ruby said to Deborah, "we don't talk about business. I'll introduce you to Larry later." She turned to Claudine. "Deb's new at this. I met her when she came into my salon, and we got to talking." Ruby gave Claudine a meaningful look. "She has skills."

Claudine stifled a groan. This was getting worse and worse. She was stuck in some fancy tea house with a couple of amateurs, one of whom might yet turn her in to the police. If Claudine hadn't promised her father, she'd be out the door.

A waitress arrived with a silver tray laden with teapots and a gilt-edged platter of macarons in Easter egg colors. Claudine lifted the lid of the teapot set in front of her. Fragrant steam escaped. With delicate fingers, Deborah transferred a daffodil-yellow pastry to her plate. Claudine squinted at her in appraisal. The diamond solitaires in her ears were real, and at least a carat each. Apparently they'd made good with the insurance money. If this naif was planning to see Larry the Fence, she'd better bring along someone with experience. She'd be lucky if she made it out of there with cab fare.

"I'm so glad to be here with you," Deborah said. Her smile almost dissolved Claudine's caution. "Why don't we get to know each other? I know we can't talk about that" —she lowered her voice— "but maybe we can share a little bit."

"Or we could talk about Wanda Rizzio's kids," Claudine said. "Which is why we're here."

Ruby shot her a dirty look. "I think that's nice, Deb. I'll start. I grew up down South, but when my dad left us, me and my little sisters, Pearl and Opal, came back to Carsonville, where Mom was from. Mom was president of the Carsonville Women's League." Ruby looked from Deb to Claudine to see if they registered the importance.

"Oh, my," Deborah said.

Something didn't add up. "So you were wealthy," Claudine said.

"For a little while." Ruby dug in her bag for a fan and flapped at her reddening face. "Sorry. Anyway, Mom died when I was fourteen, and I went to beauty school and married Bruce, and here I am," she finished quickly.

"Oh," Deborah said.

There was a lot missing, Claudine thought. She wondered who had taken responsibility for the sisters. Ruby, probably.

"Tell us about you," Ruby said to Deborah.

"I'm an only child. I wish I had sisters like you." Deborah gave the women a melting look. Ruby appeared ready to adopt her. "I went to the state university and started a degree in child development. I wanted to be a teacher. But then I met Louie when I was home during summer break."

"You'd make a lovely teacher," Ruby said. "I did a couple of quarters of community college."

"You've been awfully quiet, Claudine," Deborah said. "What about you? Where did you go to college?"

"Nowhere," she said. Why all the nosiness? They had a job to do. This wasn't a social club.

"Is that all?" Ruby asked.

"Look, we're here to talk about the kids, right? Why don't

we get down to business?"

"All right. Sure," Ruby said. "No harm meant."

"Sorry," Claudine said. "I have somewhere to be, that's all."

"Where are the others?" Deborah asked. Her phone on the table chimed, and her eyes shot to its screen. "My mom." She sounded disappointed. She pushed the phone away a few inches.

"I think it's just us," Claudine said. No one else was foolish enough to meet in a group like this. Now she knew why.

"Larry says Wanda's kids are squatting in an old firehouse in the warehouse district down by the river," Ruby said.

"How many are there?" Deborah asked.

"Four. The oldest is a boy, not quite eighteen. Then there's another boy and two girls."

Claudine remembered the oldest boy, Hugo, from years ago. He'd been chubby and interested in model airplanes. Wanda had been disappointed that he didn't have the physique for slip-and-fall work. "Isn't there a family shelter in town—you know, somewhere they can stay together?"

"Nothing," Ruby said.

"And no families who can take them all?" Deborah asked.

"Apparently not. And now that they've run away—" Ruby started.

"Exactly," Claudine said. It would be juvie for them.

"Oh," Deb said. "Those poor kids. My parents get lots of stuff left behind at the dry cleaner's. Some good sleeping bags and coats. We could put together a care package."

"First we have to see if they'll take our help," Claudine said. "We don't know much about them now, other than what Larry says. And you know Larry." Larry, who'd set her up for this.

"True." Ruby tapped a peony-pink lacquered nail on the table. "We'll visit the firehouse. Check out the situation."

"I know," Deborah said. "We'll have a fundraiser. Then we can help them get the things they need."

"That's a brilliant idea," Ruby said. "The Women's League does them all the time."

Claudine looked from woman to woman. Were they talking something legit? "You mean like a bake sale or car wash or something?"

"No. Not that," Ruby said. "A cocktail party. Or a dinner. We sell tickets and invite a crowd who can donate, you know, get the right people involved."

"But—" Claudine said. Raise money? Straight-like? "Absolutely not. Have you forgotten something?" She leaned forward and whispered with enough force to ruffle the solitary mum adorning their table, "We're crooks." She leaned back and folded her arms over her chest. "I'm sure we can scare up a few donations if we tap into that community."

"I do have a lot of rather expensive watches," Deborah said.

"The Women's League would never sell stuff to raise money," Ruby said.

Claudine arched an eyebrow. "If you like the Women's League so much, why not just join them?"

"I have my reasons." Ruby's icy tone made it clear she didn't want to go down that path. "As for doing this legit, I don't see why we should endanger the kids by pulling them into anything illegal."

"Maybe we could hold it here, at the tea shop," said Deborah.

"My salon is out," Ruby said. "It's too small, and it would agitate the dogs."

"Stop it already. No one agreed to hold a fundraiser, we—" Claudine began.

"I have a big house," Deborah cut in.

THE BOOSTER CLUB   37

Ruby's face lit up. "Of course. The Granzer mansion. People will come just to see it."

"I wouldn't exactly call it a mansion," Deborah said in a small voice. "It's not like we have servants or anything."

"The big stone building up on the bluff, right? The one at the end of the street?" Ruby asked.

Yes, Claudine thought. That'd be the house. They might need to rent silverware, but she had to admit it would be a good spot for an event. Not that she'd have anything to do with it.

"Well, yes."

"Perfect." Looking satisfied, Ruby settled back on her velvet-upholstered chair.

Claudine shook her head involuntarily. This idea of Ruby's was bad news all around. "Look, I'd better be moving on. Why don't we talk about all this next time?" Claudine pushed her chair out and reached for her purse. There'd be no next time for her. She'd send a check to Larry and wash her hands of this.

"Already?" Ruby asked.

Seeing her rise, the host trotted to the table with their bill on a porcelain saucer.

"I'd better get home, too," Deborah said. "Louie's supposed to fly in tonight, and I want to make sure the house is presentable."

"Fine. All right," Ruby said. "Let me get the check."

"Oh, no." Deborah dropped a fifty dollar bill on the saucer, and the host snatched it up. "Keep the change."

"We'll be seeing you again?" the host asked Deborah. "And the rest of you?" he added with less enthusiasm.

Ruby seemed to pick up on his tone immediately. "Why, yes, you will. Regularly."

"I suppose you want the large table again," the host said.

"A more intimate table, better placed, of course, will be

fine." She yanked her bag to her shoulder and, chin up, walked to the door.

Claudine paused, then followed, with Deborah behind her. On the sidewalk, the women faced each other.

"I'll send out an email about going to the firehouse. We can check on the kids, bring them food," Ruby said.

"Fine. I guess I'll see you girls later," Deborah said.

"Wait," Ruby said. "We don't have a name for our group. We have to at least settle that."

"Why do we need a name?" Claudine asked.

"It makes us official," Ruby said.

They moved to the side to let two chattering women enter the tea house. Through the window, the host was smiling broadly and gesturing toward a table.

"How about the Booster Club?" Claudine said. Who cared what the name was? She wasn't going back anyway.

A smile glimmered on Ruby's mouth. "All right. The Booster Club it is."

Deborah looked puzzled.

"Come on, Deb. I'll explain."

Chapter Four

The Booster Club. Claudine shook her head.

She pulled the Accord into the garage behind the Scent Shoppe, the Dupin family business. Well, second business. The Scent Shoppe occupied a rehabbed Victorian house with an apartment upstairs, where Claudine now lived alone since her father had moved to the Villa. The house was on a commercial street, but quiet—perfect for their line of work.

She'd left Sue, a retired bookie, in charge of the shop while she was gone, but the woman's car was nowhere to be seen. The boutique's front door jangled as Claudine entered a miasma of scent underscored by the quiet soundtrack of Fred Astaire's "Putting on the Ritz." "Sue?"

A dark-haired man with a slender mustache glided from the house's old living room, now rimmed with perfume display cases. "Ah, señorita, can I help you?"

André! Claudine hugged her brother. "I almost didn't recognize you with dark hair. What are you doing home? Dad said you were in Mexico City filming a telenovela."

"My evil twin killed me off and went to prison. They said they might write me into the series next year, but I'm not holding my breath." He dropped the Mexican accent. "I sent Sue home. Hope you don't mind." He picked up a bottle. "I see we got in the new Comme des Garçons."

"Heavy on the cedar, but not bad. You want to stay with me?"

"There's a vacancy at the Villa, so I'm staying with Dad." At her look of concern, he added, "Ronny passed. I heard it was peaceful."

"He'd been sick for a while." Strictly speaking, Ronny shouldn't have been a Villa resident since he hadn't broken the law. He'd made his living buying cheap electronic items from China, then reselling them on the street as hot. He didn't have the stomach for crime, but he liked the community.

"Are you sure you'll be all right? I have a roll-a-bed."

"Dad's getting older. I figure I'll stay there until someone makes a stink about me not being retired and kicks me out."

The door rang, and a woman dressed as if she'd just left her yoga class hesitated.

"Señora? May I help you?" The accent reappeared, and her brother once again became the Latin lover.

"I, um—" The woman bit her lip. "I was thinking about getting a signature scent. I'm not sure where to start."

André led the woman to the boutique's showroom. "We're just about to close, but you, with those dazzling eyes, must have a perfume that sings with violets. Let's try Aimez Moi first." Seeing Claudine gesture from the vestibule, he said, "*Un momento, por favor.*"

Claudine lowered her voice. "You don't mind closing up?"

"Not at all. Oh—Oz came by."

Oswald. Her ex. A shiver ran through her. Whether it was dread or anticipation, she didn't know.

"He left this for you." A folded note appeared in André's palm. André had never stopped practicing his illusionist's skills. He'd always been the adventurous Dupin—joining the circus

after high school and training as an acrobat, living for a year on
a cruise boat and performing as a magician, and, along the way,
charming enough well-to-do widows to keep himself in Belgian
loafers. He liked to brag that if he left the widows a touch
lighter in the pocketbook, they were much richer in joie de
vivre. "I'm due at the Villa for dinner after I close up here, but
I'll stop by soon."

Claudine took the interior stairway behind the counter to the
apartment, which had a convenient second entrance from the
outside. An orange tabby cat leapt from an armchair and rubbed
against her legs. "Hi, Petunia. Get enough beauty sleep?"
Petunia was male, but he was a year old before she figured that
out, so his name stuck.

She dumped kibble into the cat's dish and poured herself a
glass of wine. She took Oz's note to her armchair but couldn't
bring herself to open it yet. Oz, damn it. She'd had a long dry
spell as far as men were concerned. No civilian was safe, and
the crooks were, well, crooks.

She clicked on a lamp. It was getting dark so early these
days. Still avoiding the note, Claudine reached for her laptop
and checked her email. She had a new message from "chihua-
hualover." "Let's meet to check out the old firehouse. Monday
at 4 pm," it read. "See you there." Claudine would send her
regrets later.

Petunia, having crunched enough of his dinner to satisfy
him for the moment, jumped into Claudine's lap. With one
hand stroking the cat's head, Claudine ripped open the note at
last.

"Hi Deanie. Hank said he told you I'm out. I hear you have
a big job planned. Would love to see you. How about Monday
afternoon? Oz." Below his name was his phone number.

After three years, she was pretty sure Oz was out of her

system. He'd find some other woman to charm into keeping him in beer and clean laundry until he moved on. But if he knew there was a big job in the works—something he might get a piece of—he'd plague her until he had a piece of it, too.

She tossed the note on the table and picked up her wine glass. This heist was going to be a big one—her biggest—but also her last. She could clear a couple million fairly easily and live off the investments. The San Francisco Museum of Decorative Arts had planned an exhibition of jewels from Rosa Cabrini's estate. Cabrini, an opera singer, had run through five husbands—a sheikh, an oilman, an Argentinian soccer star, a shipping magnate, and the heir to a disposable diapers fortune—before dying in the bed of her chauffeur, a friend from childhood. Along the way she'd amassed a heap of jewelry that made Elizabeth Taylor's collection look like it came from a Cracker Jacks box. The best of it would be on display in San Francisco in less than a month.

Claudine had the building plans encrypted on her laptop, plus three colleagues on tap to help with the heist. An Austrian jeweler was already crafting fakes. She'd break in and whisk past security, both physical and electronic, and swap out the real jewels for the dupes. A dour but whip-smart colleague in St. Louis would do surveillance the night of the heist. A colleague in Geneva was ready to transform the jewels into ready cash to deposit to an offshore bank account. It was a small but crack team, and Oswald had no part in it.

Oz would know if she were lying—con men were good at that. He'd never relent if she flat out told him to get lost. Putting him off and hoping he'd be distracted elsewhere was the best solution. He wanted to meet on Monday. She supposed she could look at the firehouse with the Booster Club Monday afternoon instead—or at least pretend she was.

She punched Oz's number into her phone and sent a text. "Already have plans Monday afternoon. Will be in touch." Yeah, right.

She nudged Petunia off her lap and lowered herself to the floor for her nightly series of stretches. Faint piano music from the house next door drifted through the window. Something by Brahms—a sonata, maybe. Soon the days would be too cold to leave the window open. She could already smell the shift to autumn.

Her father had beamed when he'd heard the details of the San Francisco heist. Finally, he'd said, something worthy of her grandfather, something closer to her old jobs. Dad would be less happy when he heard she was quitting the business. She sat up. Had he told Oswald anything detailed about the heist? Surely he wouldn't be that stupid.

She relaxed again into a hamstring stretch. Then, rising from the floor, she grabbed the top of the doorway and raised her legs, toes pointed, to waist level. Where would she be now if she'd gone to college, as originally planned?

Her face burned as she remembered being called into the high school vice principal's office. In one chair sat her favorite English teacher, hands in lap, and in the other, Ellie Whiteby, one of the most popular girls in school and a gold-plated goody two-shoes.

"Miss Whiteby tells me she saw you shoplifting last weekend," the vice principal had said. Ellie nodded, her Pantene girl hair glinting in the sunlight through the window behind her.

Remembering, Claudine cringed. Yes, she had pocketed a tube of ointment. It was one of two times she'd ever been caught shoplifting. Otherwise, her record was impeccable. The shopkeeper had let her go with a stiff warning when he found out she was only trying to help her father's sprained back. She didn't tell him, of course, that he'd sprained it jumping from the second story window of a house he was burgling.

"We checked with the drugstore, and they confirmed it," the vice principal added.

Her English teacher had seemed genuinely upset. "I'm so sorry, Claudine, but we're going to take back the college scholarship we offered you."

"We're withdrawing our letters of recommendation, as well," the vice principal said.

"I'm so sorry," the English teacher repeated almost in a whisper.

"It can't be helped," Ellie had said. Claudine and Ellie locked gazes. A smile of triumph flashed over Ellie's face.

Ellie would pay, Claudine remembered thinking. How and when, she didn't know, but she'd pay. Yet she never had.

Chapter Five

Monday afternoon, Ruby stared at the firehouse. It had been built as a Works Progress Administration project during the Depression, then abandoned when Carsonville built the big new station eight or nine years ago. The years had not been kind to either the firehouse or the neighborhood. The building's windows were shards, and mortar crumbled from its brick exterior. Beyond the firehouse extended the rail yards, and next door was a graffiti-covered warehouse. Weeds burst through cracks in the sidewalk. It was hard to believe that only a few blocks away were high-end restaurants and glittering condos.

"Are you sure anyone lives here?" Deborah asked. Next to her, Claudine also surveyed the building.

A crow perched on a gutter, its talons scraping the metal. The weather had turned cold overnight, and a brisk wind whipped up the narrow street.

"Larry says this is definitely the place." Ruby shifted her grocery sack to the opposite hip and tried the garage doors where the fire engine would have once been. Locked, of course. In the late afternoon light she could make out nothing but cobwebs and a few boxes on the dusty cement floor inside.

"Maybe they moved on," Claudine said.

"Could be," Ruby said.

"Hold this." Claudine handed her purse to Ruby and set her box on the sidewalk. She grabbed the gutter's drain and shook it.

"What's she doing?" Deborah said.

"Don't know," Ruby replied. Larry the Fence spoke of Claudine so reverently, said she was one of the "elite." Ruby hadn't seen anything particularly elite about her clothing or manners, although she did have the air of having walked from the set of an old film noir. Now it dawned on her. Larry had meant the criminal elite.

With one hand on the drainpipe, Claudine leapt up the firehouse's brick wall, using mortar as toe holds.

"Careful," Ruby couldn't help saying.

"No worries," Claudine said. Within seconds, she was peering into a second story window. She lowered herself a few feet, then dropped to the ground light as a tabby, her hair rustling on her shoulders. She brushed her palms together. "They're up there, all right. In the firemen's bunk room. Quite a set-up, too. Four kids, plus a dog. A big one."

Deborah's mouth had been hanging open. She shut it. "How did they get in there? They didn't climb up like you did. The dog couldn't make it."

"There's got to be another way in," Ruby said. "We could toss pebbles at the window and tell them we have things for them."

"I don't think they're interested in attracting attention." Claudine examined the warehouse next door, which featured gaping windows, most with broken or no glass, and a sagging door. She returned to Ruby and Deborah. "I bet they enter through there." She nodded at the warehouse. "There's some kind of connecting door or window."

"Maybe we should just leave our things on the street," Deborah said. "We could yell up, 'Hey, Rizzio kids, we've got some things for you,' and then push the stuff against the wall."

"No," Ruby said firmly. "We've come this far, and we need to talk to them, tell them we want to help them." She pursed her lips. "We should have brought dog food. Next time."

Claudine shook her head. "They don't want to be bothered. They're probably convinced we want to drag them back to their foster homes."

"But they need homes. They can't live all winter in this place," Deborah said.

"Yes, we can." The voice came from behind them.

A husky boy—Ruby corrected herself, young man—stood behind them. His brown hair was shaggy around his shoulders, and patchy whiskers sprinkled his jaw. He wore a tight gray blazer and matching pants. The combination was part street warrior, part C.P.A.

"What do you want?" he asked.

"Larry the Fence told us about you," Ruby said.

"I don't know what you're talking about."

"We have some things." Deborah pointed to her bulging garbage bag. "Clothes. All dry cleaned and ready to wear. For you and your brother and sisters."

He looked at the bag but made no move toward it.

Claudine stepped forward. "I'm Claudine Dupin. I was so sorry to hear about your mother." The boy continued to stare, but he didn't walk away. "I knew her when I was growing up. Wanda was a little older than me, and I looked up to her. You know how I climbed the building just now?"

The boy nodded. "I saw you."

"I learned my agility routine from your mom. She taught me to how to land."

Absorbed, Ruby watched the exchange. Claudine was full of

surprises.

"So, you're—" he started.

"Yes," Claudine said. "Larry heard through the grapevine that you kids ran off after your mother's accident, and he put out a call for help. That's why we're here."

The boy took in the three women. "I'm Hugo. Uncle Larry told you about us?"

"Well, Hugo, obviously you're not getting everything you need or you wouldn't be living in an abandoned building without heat. If anyone else finds out you're here—and it's likely they will sooner or later—you'll be kicked out," Claudine said.

Ah, now she's taking a harder line. Ruby set down her bag.

"It's county land," he said, defiance in his voice. "Besides, they want to keep us apart."

"All the more reason."

"For what? Are you a lawyer?" the boy asked.

"I know a little bit about the law," Claudine replied.

Like how to break it, Ruby thought.

"We could help raise money for a real lawyer," Deborah said. "We talked about a fundraiser."

"No pressure," Claudine told the boy. "You don't trust us. I get it. Wanda wouldn't want us to force you to do anything." She picked up her box and turned toward the car.

"Wait." Hugo stepped toward Claudine. He stopped. He didn't seem to want them to stay, but he didn't seem to want them to leave, either.

"Look," Ruby said. "It's easy. We think you might be able to use some help, and we want to help. So we brought some clothes and" —Ruby appraised the boy's belly— "food."

"Yeah?" Hugo said.

"Some tuna, peanut butter. And donuts. And a cheesecake,

although it wasn't the smartest idea, not knowing your cutlery situation." Bruce had suggested the donuts and cheesecake. After years working with middle-schoolers, he knew a teen's appetite.

The boy's resolution was wavering. She could tell by the way he swallowed.

"Well?" Claudine said.

They stood sizing each other up. A minute passed.

Claudine turned again toward the car. "Come on. They don't want us here."

"All right," Hugo said. "You can come up."

***

Claudine had been right—the firehouse's entrance was from the adjoining warehouse. Hugo led them through the old building, where they skirted fallen lumber and crumbled bricks before ascending a staircase at the rear. Ruby stumbled, and Deborah grabbed her arm. A thin shaft of light appeared and bounced before them. Claudine had a penlight. Figured, Ruby thought.

On the second floor, planks at a window bridged the few feet between the warehouse and the firehouse. If the kids wanted, they could pull in the planks and shut the window, closing off access to their room.

Hunched over, Hugo scrambled across the planks and dropped into the firehouse. Behind him, Deborah hesitated.

"Go on," Claudine said.

"It doesn't look sturdy." Deborah backed into Ruby.

"It's fine. You just saw Hugo do it."

Deborah didn't move.

Claudine let out a sigh. "Watch me. Keep your center of gravity low—you can crawl, if you want." Claudine crouched slightly and moved purposefully across the planks, making it look effortless even carrying a box. "See? Set your bag on the bridge." In a fluid motion, Claudine picked up the bag and tossed it through the firehouse window. "Now, you."

Deborah bit her lip and gingerly tested the plank. She dropped to all fours and inched across the planks. Once in the firehouse, she broke into a grin. "Come on, Ruby," she said across the gap. "It's easy."

Ruby crossed, more slowly than Claudine but with relative ease. God bless those yoga classes. She dropped her bag on the other side and stood up straight. "Would you look at that."

The bunks firemen had once used lined the back wall, and surprisingly cozy furniture occupied the front of the firehouse's second floor. A dizzying landscape of spray-painted flowers in glorious orange and red covered two of the walls. But it was cold. In the middle, a fire pole dropped to the first floor. Streaky afternoon light filtered through what was left of the dirty windows.

The Rizzio kids sat together on a bunk. The pit bull growled. Lordy, Ruby thought. A pit bull was a damn sight bigger than a Chihuahua.

"Hush, Tinkerbell," Hugo said. Then to the women, "She's protective, but friendly. She won't hurt you."

Ignoring the growls, Deborah was at the dog's side, cooing and stroking her head. Tinkerbell's ears relaxed and her eyes shuttered to half-mast. Ruby made a mental note to try again to see if Deborah would consider a smaller animal.

"Impressive mural," Claudine said, still staring at the walls. Something in her expression seemed to have changed, softened. It sharpened again as she looked around, appearing to make a mental inventory of the room.

"Joanie did that," Hugo said.

A small girl in a hoodie and jeans ducked her head and smiled. Her lank hair was pulled into a ponytail, and a vivid bow clipped its side. She remained silent.

"That's Scotty and Lucy. Twins." Hugo pointed to a boy and girl, maybe about twelve years old. "Team," Hugo addressed the group. "These ladies brought us some things. I wouldn't have let them up here, except that they knew Mom."

"Why do you want to help us? What are you getting from it?" Scotty asked.

Deborah paused petting Tinkerbell long enough to ask, "Do we have to get something from it?" Tinkerbell pawed at her arm.

"It doesn't make sense that you'd want to spend time and money on us unless you stand to gain. We have to protect ourselves."

Ruby looked from face to face. Each child watched her, and so did Deborah and Claudine. Why did she want to help these kids? Sure, she wanted to prove something to the Carsonville Women's League. But it ran deeper than that. A lot deeper. The Rizzio kids could have been her, Pearl, and Opal. They'd only been homeless a few weeks, but she never forgot the fear, the feeling of being unwanted. As for Claudine and Deborah's motives, she couldn't say.

"We are all fortunate in our situations, but we weren't always. Look. I brought groceries." Ruby unloaded her bag. "A can opener," she said and placed it on top of a can.

"As if we don't have one already," Hugo said.

Ruby's patience was waning, and along with it her sympathy. "There's no call to be rude."

None of the children responded.

Damn Larry the Fence. Ruby didn't look forward to crawling over those planks again. "Come on, Deb, Claudine."

Claudine stepped forward. "Listen. You asked why we're here. I told you I knew your mother. I did." She scanned the children's faces. "I'm not sure how familiar you were with her livelihood, but, well, we're part of the same community. We help each other because no one else will."

The children didn't reply.

Claudine continued. "My mother died when my brother and I were little, and the community made sure we had food, got us to school, got us to bed when my dad had to work late. I still consider them family."

"You're crooks," Hugo said.

So he did know, Ruby thought. Did the other children?

"I'll be honest," Claudine said. "When I first heard about your situation, I didn't want to get involved. I still don't think it's a good idea. But to the community, I hold a debt of honor. My responsibility to your mother is to make sure you're okay. But I'm not going to force myself on you. First you don't want us here, then you lead us up, and now you're chasing us out again. Make up your minds. What's it going to be?"

Tinkerbell made a hollow-throated moan and plopped to her side.

Hugo looked to his brother and sisters. One by one, they nodded. "I guess."

"You guess what?" Claudine said.

"Yes. Thank you, yes," Hugo said.

"Yes, what?" Claudine pressed.

"Yes, thank you, we appreciate your help. Is that what you want me to say?" Hugo said.

Deborah anxiously lifted a hanger. "I brought some things from my parents' business. Two down coats—one is a really cute mauve—and a cashmere trench. Plus a wool blanket." She unfolded the blanket on a lower bunk. "There's a little stain up here in the corner. We couldn't get it out. But it's perfectly clean."

Lucy pulled the plastic covering off the mauve down coat and slipped it on. Tinkerbell rolled feet up on the blanket and made happy growling noises.

All eyes shifted to Claudine. She paused, then nodded. "Here's batteries, a couple of flashlights, and books."

"We need those," Hugo said.

She nailed it, Ruby thought. So dismissive of the Booster Club, but she always seemed a step ahead. "What will you do when it gets cold? No electricity here."

Hugo's face turned stony. "We'll figure it out."

"How long have you been here?" Claudine said. "Larry says it's been at least a month since your mother's accident."

"After Mom died, someone from the county found us. They made us go to different families," Scotty said. "But Lucy and I got to stay together."

"We didn't want to be without you," Lucy added from the armchair, looking at Hugo and Joanie.

"So you came here," Claudine said.

"Grandpa was a fireman." Hugo had already finished a do-nut and was rooting in the box for a second one. "He used to work at this station, and he told us stories about it. We made a pact a long time ago that if something happened, we'd all meet here."

"With the dog? You came with the dog?" Deborah asked.

"We found her outside. She didn't have a home either," Scotty said.

"We have to figure out where you can go next," Ruby said. "Winter comes, this old firehouse will be a freezer."

"Oh, no." Hugo stood up. "We said we'd let you help, not take control. We want to stay here."

"We could probably get together enough money to rent a house for you somewhere, a house all of your own. It would be a lot safer. More comfortable, too," Claudine said.

"And then throw us out when you got tired of us? Forget it."

"But you can't stay here," Deborah said. "There's no plumbing. What about rats?"

"There's a faucet downstairs. We haven't seen a single rat," Scotty pointed out.

"Tinkerbell," Ruby said. "Although a dog doesn't have to be big to be a good ratter."

"Fine." Deborah stood, hands on hips. "In the meantime, at least we can make this place a little more comfortable."

Chapter Six

The next morning, Deborah rolled up in front of the firehouse in an old Land Rover, her husband's bird-watching vehicle. She'd stuffed its rear with things she'd found in the Granzer mansion's attic: a rolled-up bearskin rug, an armchair, and serving dishes from the family's third-best china pattern, including a bowl she thought would be perfect for Tinkerbell. On the seat next to her was a bucket of cleaning supplies.

Ruby and Claudine were already at the firehouse. They'd managed to open the firehouse's street-level door and had started to load in a few boxes with the help of the boys, Hugo and Scotty.

Claudine dropped her box and hurried to the Land Rover. Deborah unrolled the window. "We're unloading quickly, then we're going to move our cars so we don't attract too much attention." She turned to the firehouse. "Hugo? Could you give Deborah a hand?"

Deborah watched her stride back to the firehouse, brown hair swinging in a ponytail behind her. What was her story? Ruby had already filled Deborah in on her own past as they sat at Crafty Cuts with Ruby alternately trying to convince her to crop her hair or adopt one of the foster dogs and telling her about her rich father down South who disappeared one day. But this one—Claudine—she was a mystery.

It wasn't anything she could put her finger on, but Deborah had the feeling Claudine didn't approve of her. Probably because her crimes were so small. She remembered Claudine scaling the firehouse as if it were a stepping stool. Maybe she was a hit woman. Deborah didn't see the bulge of a weapon in Claudine's pocket, but she might use a knife. She'd slip it from her ankle strap and—hi-ya!—slice someone's jugular.

Deborah ripped her gaze from Claudine and backed the car to the firehouse door. A quarter of an hour later, Claudine and Hugo pulled the big doors shut and padlocked them.

Deborah grabbed a broom and the bucket of cleaning supplies from the Land Rover's passenger seat and climbed the rickety staircase at the rear. Tinkerbell sniffed around her before abandoning her for a rubber hotdog Ruby must have brought.

Deborah looked from the younger girl, Lucy, to Joanie, the artistic one, before settling on the older girl. "Honey? We need to clean this place up. Do you know where to get water?"

Joanie nodded and lifted an empty bucket. She threaded its handle over her arm and disappeared down the fireman's pole in the corner just as Ruby and Hugo arrived with boxes.

Claudine might be in charge of logistics, but Deborah was well qualified to lead a mini-renovation inside. She handed her broom to Lucy. "You get started sweeping up, and when Joanie gets back we'll swab the floors." They were wooden and scarred but surprisingly not too dirty. Had to be Joanie. Deborah knew a kindred spirit when she saw one.

Lucy obediently took the broom and began work in the room's corner.

"Ruby," Deborah said. "I packed some old sheets in the box right behind you. I thought we could double them up as curtains if we string up some laundry line as a curtain rod.

That's in the box, too. Maybe you could take charge of that project." Remembering the grafitti-ed flowers on the wall, Deborah had tucked in pink and green sheets Louie's mother must have packed away in the 1970s.

"And me?" Claudine stood, hands on hips, a faint smile playing on her mouth.

"You'll help with set-up. I'm envisioning a study area over there" —she pointed to a space to the right of the stairs— "and a reading and relaxing area over there by the side windows so they won't be seen."

"Nobody told us we'd have to study," the younger boy said.

"We'll talk about that later," Deborah said.

Claudine held up a pair of wire cutters. "Why don't I see if I can find electrical service nearby? Maybe we can get the kids light, at least."

Joanie, wide-eyed, returned, her thin arms straining over the bucket of water.

"Do you ever talk, honey?" Deborah asked.

Joanie shook her head while her siblings chorused, "No."

"Do you know how?"

Joanie shook her head again, but Hugo answered, "Yes. She talks sometimes."

"All right," Deborah said, feeling the anxiety rise around her. She'd drop the topic for the moment. "Let's get to work."

By the time night fell, the firehouse's second floor had been transformed into an urban cabin. Claudine hadn't been able to get power, but lanterns splashed warm pools of light against the vibrant flowers and vines on the walls. The bearskin rug lay unfurled in one corner near the velvet armchair, where Tinker-bell had already made herself at home. A camping stove and milk crates of supplies on a card table occupied another corner in the firehouse's old kitchen. Soft sheets with small patched areas billowed softly from the windows. A faint hint of pine-scented cleanser hung in the air.

"Wow," Scotty said.

"It really does look cozy. All we need is a fireplace," Ruby said.

Claudine pushed a lock of hair behind her ear. "It won't be long before it's cold enough to freeze water in here. This is an okay solution—for now."

Deborah's satisfaction at seeing the firehouse transformed slipped away. Claudine was right. They couldn't stay here. They had maybe another month before the windows would frost over.

"We could buy them a propane heater," Ruby said.

A little hope flamed in Deborah's chest, although she saw Claudine bite her lip.

"Sure, but that's just buying time," Claudine said. "The kids can't stay here on their own forever. We need to figure out something more permanent."

***

"So, what are our next steps?" Deborah asked Claudine and Ruby the next day after the waiter deposited the pots of Oolong. Despite yesterday's hard work, she had driven home feeling lighter than ever. Plus, Louie was on his way back—at last.

Claudine sat with her back to the wall and calmly took in the tea house's post-church crowd murmuring above a string quartet.

"I've looked into shelters, and unless Hugo is the kids' legal guardian, the kids wouldn't be able to stay together," Claudine said. "Even then, it's dicey."

"Maybe we should help him get guardianship," Deb said. "He's eighteen. He can take custody, right?"

"Honey," Ruby laid a hand on hers from across the table, "I'd wager Hugo isn't much older than sixteen."

Deb put down the macaron. Her chest felt heavy. "Those poor kids. They need someone to care for them."

"And somewhere to live," Claudine added.

"They're too young to stay alone," Ruby said. "Hon, you're not going to cry, are you?"

Deborah took a deep breath. Thank goodness she had Louie. "No. It's just so sad."

"We'll help them. We'll help them stay together," Ruby said. "Maybe we can convince the shelter at St. Jude's to take them all, together."

"No way," Claudine said. "As soon as social services found out the children were there, they'd plop them in strict foster homes. They have a reputation as runaways, remember."

"Besides," Ruby said, "what about other children like them? Even if we managed to find a place for them now, other kids might end up split up."

"Our job is to deal with the Rizzio kids, not try to save every kid in town," Claudine said.

"She's just saying, we shouldn't forget about the others," Deborah replied. She hoped she didn't sound too defensive.

"Well, what are our options?" Ruby said. "I'd say they could come live with me and Bruce, but all we have is a hide-a-bed in Bruce's office. Plus, Hugo insisted they weren't leaving the firehouse."

The Granzer mansion was gigantic. Each of the kids could have his own bedroom, and Tinkerbell could run in the yard.

But Louie would never go for it. He needed his rest for those early mornings at the wildlife refuge looking at ducks, or whatever he did. She didn't even need to ask him—he'd squelch the idea before she'd got the words out.

It killed Deborah to have to say it. "My husband wouldn't want the kids at home."

Claudine paused, as if she might be considering a possible home, but from her expression, Deborah concluded she'd dismissed the idea. Claudine leaned back in her chair. "The alternative is to buy a new place for them. Or build one."

Ruby shook her head. Her Chihuahua-shaped earrings swung. "That could cost millions. We'd have to buy land, design a building, get all the permits, have it built—"

"There are ways to cut corners if you know the right people," Claudine said.

"No." Deborah was surprised at the insistence in her own voice. "We need to do this all above board. Completely legitimately. We need to give the children a fresh start."

Claudine took a deep breath, and Deborah prepared for her rebuttal. "You're right. I agree."

"Me, too," Ruby said. "Absolutely."

"Well, then," Deborah said, surprised at the lack of resistance. "What if we just fixed up the firehouse? I mean, really fixed it up."

The string quartet chewed over an especially busy baroque number while the women pondered this idea.

"Not a bad idea," Ruby said.

"The structure's there. It's already on public land, and it's close to downtown. You'd have to insulate it and fix up the kitchen," Claudine said.

"The bunks sleep twelve, and there's room for more," Ruby said.

"You could even expand into the space next door over time," Claudine added. "It would be much less expensive than starting from scratch. It would take care of the problem of the kids not wanting to leave, too."

"We'd essentially be starting our own family shelter," Ruby said. "We'd have to hire staff."

"The community would be willing to chip in some, but I'm not sure you could come up with enough to run a full-fledged shelter. At least, legitimately," Claudine said with a glance at Deborah.

"You know who loves firehouses?" Deborah said, ignoring Claudine's persistent use of "you" rather than "we." "Grandpa Granzer. He used to be a volunteer fireman."

"That's nice, honey," Ruby said. "I wonder if the county would transfer the land for a good cause? Or at least sell it at a public charity price?"

"Let's go back to old man Granzer a minute," Claudine said. "What do you think he'd say to helping renovate the fire-house?"

"Wait—you said Grandpa Granzer. The Granzer? The one who started the grocery chain?" Ruby said.

"I could ask. He has buckets of money, you know." Louie's siblings sure knew. They sucked up to him night and day. She was the one he insisted on sitting next to at Thanksgiving dinner, though.

"I could do some research on what it might take to get the land transferred to us. You might have to form a nonprofit," Claudine said.

"We'll need money," Ruby said.

"I have quite a few valuable watches—" Deborah began.

"Hush," Claudine cut her off.

"Besides, we're going to do this right. Straight. We don't

need to get the kids in trouble," Ruby said. "A fundraiser. We'll hold a fundraiser. Remember? We talked about that." She turned cautiously toward Claudine.

"Who will come?" Deborah asked. "I mean, besides Grandpa Granzer."

"Thanks to the rock star whose hair I cut, Taffeta Darling, I have lots of clients I could invite."

Claudine shook her head. "No. Too risky."

"Why not?" Deborah said. "It's just a party."

Claudine leaned forward. "I have, um, customers who run in that set."

"Then they'll be happy to see you."

"It's more complicated than that. They're my customers, but we haven't met."

"I don't understand—" Deb started.

Ruby cut in. "Fine. How about this? Claudine, you can help by managing the kids. If you want to stay undercover, go ahead."

"We'll just say it's the Booster Club hosting the event. We don't have to say who's in it," Deborah added.

"Do you really think it's a good idea to raise our profile. I mean, considering?" Claudine said.

She didn't need to add "considering what," Deborah thought. She got it. "We're doing everything above board, totally legit. We don't have to hide."

Claudine sank into her chair and crossed her arms over her chest. "Sure, I guess. Just leave my name off the invitation." When the women didn't respond, she added, "I can do some research into what you'd need to buy the firehouse. And I have some connections in security. I bet I could get someone to check in on the kids from time to time, make sure there's no trouble until you get this set up."

"Too bad more people can't know about the kids," Deborah said. Claudine looked so much more relaxed now that she didn't have to mingle. Funny.

"It would help drive ticket sales," Ruby said.

They were quiet for a moment. Decent people, if they saw how the kids lived, would want to help them. Deborah knew that. But drawing attention to them could ruin everything.

"I do hair for Brenda, the anchorwoman for Channel Two. What if I told her the story? She could interview Hugo. We'll leave the rest of the kids out of it."

"As long as you didn't let on where they are," Claudine said, "that might work. Or not."

"So then," Ruby said. "Let's get down to business. Does anyone have a calendar handy?"

* * *

Claudine shut the county procedures manual and pushed away from her usual carrel at the library. Thanks to her frequent research on building plans for break-ins, one of the assistant librarians, thinking Claudine an architect, was always ready to pull documents.

Buying the firehouse was simple. The Boosters had to get the county commissioners to agree to sell. There'd be a hearing first, then a vote. If that went well, the commissioners might even grant the land to them outright. They'd done it before, and the firehouse, as it now stood, was a public liability.

Once the vote passed, there would be a second, more perfunctory commission meeting to seal the deal and present plans for the property. In the past, these land transfers had taken up to two years, but in a few cases they'd slid through in as little as six weeks. She'd see if she could get the Boosters on the commissioners' agenda right away. Encouragement from the governor should speed things along. Gilda might cash in on some inside info from a few decades ago to get him to write the commissioners a letter. Sure, the Boosters had promised to do everything above board, but a tiny bit of blackmail didn't count.

She rose from her chair. Six weeks was too long to keep the children at the firehouse. It would be winter by then. They'd have to convince them to move. Plus, the timing wasn't the greatest: Eight weeks was when the Cabrini heist would go down. She wouldn't worry about all that now. They'd figure it out. All the Boosters had to do is raise money and make a strong case to the county commissioners. If Deborah succeeded in getting her grandfather's support, their plan just might work. After that, they'd figure out the details with staff and renovations.

Claudine skipped down the library's marble steps to the street and halted. Idling on the corner was the gray sedan that had surprised her the week before. After a second's hesitation, she resumed walking in the opposite direction. She heard the sedan pull into the street behind her. Damn it. She took a quick right into a narrow alley too choked with dumpsters for the car to pass. The sedan crawled down the street, likely to circle the block and intercept her on the alley's other side. Claudine leaned against the wall, clenching her fists, then releasing them.

The sedan should be at the other end of the alley by now. She glanced back toward where she'd come just as a bus rumbled in front of the library. Within seconds she was wedged into a rush-hour crammed bench. As the bus pulled away, the sedan paused, then turned the corner. Away. She let out a long breath.

By the time Claudine had negotiated the bus, returned downtown to her car, and—eyes on the rearview mirror—made her way home, pink cloaked the horizon. From her back window, she saw it would be a clear, cold night. The elm tree was beginning to shed its leaves, and a few stars pierced the dusk.

She had one more task today for the Booster Club. She picked up the phone. "Mickey? Claudine here. Listen. I need a favor. You know the old firehouse by the train station?"

She and Mickey went way back. In fact, her father had first pegged Mickey rather than Oswald as her intended when she was in kindergarten. Claudine and Mickey certainly got along better. But Mickey—tough Irish guy he was, with a nose twice broken and inexpertly set, with fists itchy for trouble—had an unwavering crush on Dick Tracy, which he'd eventually transferred to his current partner, an elegant African-American ex-dancer named Maurice. Mickey and Maurice, or "M & M" as they were called, were the best security company in town. They weren't listed in the yellow pages.

Claudine explained the setup with the kids, and Mickey assured her he'd have someone keep an eye on the place.

"No problem," Mickey said. "Mo—" he called into the background "—would you turn down the heat on the stroganoff? Thanks, hon." He returned to Claudine. "Sorry. I put in some tarragon before you called, and it really loses its edge if it's overheated. Anyway, how long you need the patrol?"

"I'm not sure." Once the county commissioners approved the land transfer, they'd be in the clear. First she'd need to get their petition on the agenda. "Two months at the outside." Wind raked the tree's leaves like fingers through hair, wresting more from its branches. "What do you think it will cost?"

"For you, for Wanda's kids, we'll do it for expenses. Mo and

I, we like to do one job a year for charity, you know? I'll talk it over with him, but don't worry your pretty head."

"One more thing. Could you track down a license plate number for me?"

Chapter Seven

Life sure was good when Louie was home. Deborah leapt out of bed early to bring him breakfast, laid in stocks of milk and cola, and mended his safari trousers. While he took day trips to bird sanctuaries or kept his weekly meetings with the Carsonville Warblers Association, she slipped out to the firehouse to bring the children leftovers and check their homework against the home study program she'd started them on. It was hard to believe it had already been a month since they took charge of the Rizzios.

Best of all, Louie had promised to stay through the Booster Club's fundraiser that weekend. She couldn't wait to show him her hard work.

At the sound of the doorbell, she set down the birdwatching binoculars she was polishing. Ruby. They were going to Klingle's to buy a dress for the fundraiser.

Ruby hugged Deborah. "I still can't get over what a fabulous house this is." Her gaze wandered the acres of wood floors, Victorian sofas, and leaded glass windows looking over a wooded lot.

Deborah remembered her own first step into the Granzer mansion, with a shy but loving Louie at her side, and how she'd felt she'd wandered into the Addams Family set by mistake.

"Seen the kids lately?" Ruby asked.

"I dropped off their lessons this morning. They really want to go trick or treating, even Hugo. We're going to work up some costumes."

"I'll come with you." Ruby wiped a finger along a mahogany side table. "Lord, you keep this place spick and span."

"Come in. Let me take your coat."

"The fundraiser will be so perfect. We'll easily get a hundred people in here—maybe more." Ruby walked through the living room to where the dining room opened into the kitchen. "Oh, yes. We set up the buffet here, and the caterers can work from the kitchen. Does that open to the driveway?"

"Yes, on the side," Deborah said.

"They can pull the van up there."

"Don't worry, Ruby. I already worked it out." She patted an envelope on the hall table. "Plus, I've sold about twenty tickets. Mostly to my mother's friends."

"I've already sold almost forty, and one of my clients took another bundle of ten. Everyone wants to see your house." Ruby reached into her purse for a mirror and touched up her fuchsia lipstick. "Ready to go? You're petite. I see you in something form-fitting, just above the knees. Maybe a grayish purple."

"Not too low in the front, though."

"I know, I know. Louie wouldn't like it. I don't think it would suit you, anyway." Ruby narrowed her appraising gaze. "I'd still love to cut your hair. A pixie. Like Audrey Hepburn's."

"I couldn't." Louie loved her long hair. Her hair wasn't thick, but it was silky, the color of the Wedge-Billed Wood-creeper, Louie always said.

Ruby sank back into a chair and flopped an arm along the chair's back. "Is Louie going to be here for the party?"

"Yes." Deborah smiled. "So's Grandpa Granzer."

"I bet I can sell another twenty tickets on that alone. Grandpa's still okay with the firehouse, right?"

Deborah's smile widened. "He's on board, no problem."

Ruby rose and hiked her bag—not the lilac tote this time—up her shoulder. "Good. Let's go get you a knockout dress."

***

At Klingle's, Deborah glided in the big glass doors, a white-gloved man holding them open. "Ruby? You coming?"

Ruby paused just a moment and seemed to glance toward the Chanel boutique. "Right behind you."

They passed a man in tails playing a piano. He smiled at Deborah and winked at Ruby as he launched into "Ain't She Sweet." Ruby shook her head. The piano man segued into "Tomorrow."

"He seems to know you," Deborah said.

"I'll tell you about it sometime."

They rode the escalators to Special Occasions. Ruby froze before they'd even reached the mannequin in the wispy peach dress at the edge of the boutique.

"Ruby? Are you coming?" Deborah scanned the floor for what might have stopped her, but all she saw were racks of frothy dresses, a couple of harmless-looking shoppers, and a beefy security guard with a mustache.

"Let's find you a dress." Eyes straight ahead, Ruby strode to a rack and pulled out a short, sequined dress. "This would make the most of your legs."

"It's a little flashy. What about this?" She held up a gauzy print dress with a fluttering hem.

"Nice, but better for an afternoon function. Plus, you really want something with a waist to make the most of your figure."

"You have such a good eye," Deborah said. Ruby's attention still seemed elsewhere. Deborah followed the line of her gaze. The security guard. She was worried about the guard. But they were going to buy a dress, not steal one. "I have plenty of money," she whispered.

"I know," Ruby said. "You didn't think—?"

"Don't be concerned about him. Look, what about this dress?" She lifted a simple blush pink silk shift from the rack. It had a soft, draping neck. She held it against her body and looked in the mirror. Not bad.

"What are you looking at?" Ruby's voice was firm.

"Well, I—" Deborah whirled around to find Ruby face-to-face with the security guard.

"Just thought I'd keep an eye on you. Although you don't got your booster bag this time. That is what it was, right? The purple tote?"

"We're here to buy a dress, and you're accusing me of stealing?"

"What?" Deborah's eyes widened. She'd never heard that tone from Ruby. "Come on, Ruby. How about if I get this dress? I don't even need to try it on. I'm sure it fits."

A few other customers raised their heads. Ruby made a dismissive motion with one hand and kept her gaze fastened on the guard. "We come in here, paying customers, and you have the gall to insinuate—"

"I'm not insinuating nothing," the guard said. "Just watching. That's my job."

"May I help you?" An elegant man in a gray suit approached. A worried-looking saleswoman stood at his shoulder.

"This—this security guard is accusing us of stealing." Ruby's complexion pinkened, verging on flat-out red. "My friend and I—my friend, Deborah Granzer" —she emphasized "Gran-zer"— "want a dress for a special function. We did not expect to enter Carsonville's finest store and find ourselves treated like common thieves."

The security guard cast a knowing look at the gray-suited gentleman, but the suited man's expression had morphed from concern to a vague fear. "Miss Granzer. And, madame, I believe we met the other day in the Chanel boutique, am I right?"

"Yes, we did."

Ruby appeared calmer now, but Deborah's anxiety lingered. "I'll just go buy this dress."

"Yeah, at the Chanel boutique. When that purse went miss-ing," the security guard said. "Remember? No coincidence."

"I'm going to the cash register now," Deborah said, hoping to break up the party. The saleswoman looked from the suited man to the guard to Ruby and followed Deborah.

"You see what I mean? Impertinent. I've never been so insulted in my life." Even across the floor, Ruby's voice floated angry and shrill.

"Thank you," Deborah said as the saleswoman slipped the dress into a plastic sleeve and lifted it over the counter. She took a breath and made her way back to Ruby, who now stood, victorious, hands on hips.

Just then, her phone rang, the tune of "Baltimore Oriole" rising from her purse. "Louie."

"Take it." Ruby glared after the security guard and store manager, now descending the escalator.

Deborah grabbed the phone just before it went into voice mail. "Hello," she said breathlessly.

"Hi, honey."

She tried to wait a moment before asking but couldn't help

herself. "You'll be home for dinner, right? I'm making taco casserole. Your favorite."

"That's why I'm calling. I'm heading to the airport."

"Again?" Deborah's chest ached. "But you just got home a few weeks ago."

"I know, Deb. But Trixie thinks we'll see an Andean Condor or maybe even a White-Footed Guan if we leave now."

"Oh." The birds' names passed right by her. Only the name "Trixie" stuck. "The event's this Sunday. Remember? The fundraiser for the Booster Club at our house?"

For a few seconds, he didn't respond. "I'm sorry, Deb."

"You promised. You promised you'd be home for it." Now she was whining like a baby. What was happening to her?

"I know. I'm sorry," he repeated. "Maybe you could make a big donation in my name. To the club."

Deborah barely heard him. He was leaving. Again. She stared toward a mannequin in a filmy fringed gown. From downstairs she caught the strains of "Please Release Me" on the piano.

"I have to go now," she said. "Bye."

"Bye, honey. I love you—" Louie's words were cut off as she pushed "end call."

A torrent of emotion flooded her veins. She'd put on that black dress and hit every hotel bar in town. Watches would rain like hail as they slipped from her palms. She bit her trembling lip. No. She didn't want to do that—she'd promised herself. Besides, she needed to stay home and prepare for the fundraiser. The kids. Think of the kids.

"Ruby?" Deborah whirled back to face her. "I've changed my mind. I'd like my hair cut after all."

***

Pushing open the door to her father's room, Claudine found him in bed beside the big plate glass window with the view of the garden. He was chalk-pale, and silvery strands of hair fell over his forehead. His wheelchair was folded up against the wall.

"Dad," she said. "Are you okay?"

"What are you looking at? Get over here and give me a kiss."

Claudine hurried to plant a kiss on his parchment-dry forehead. "You don't look so good. How are you feeling?"

"Not bad, not bad. Just tired, that's all. Might have a touch of the flu."

"Do you want anything? Water? Maybe some coffee?"

"Why don't you help me get this bed a little more upright? Then you can have a seat and tell me what you've been up to."

She adjusted his bed and fluffed his pillows while he sat up.

"Sit," he repeated. "Is Oz helping you out?"

"He left me a note, but I haven't seen him yet," she said. If her father had looked better, she would have given him hell for telling Oswald she had a big heist planned. He knew better than that. Then again, Oz could charm warts off a toad.

"Why not?"

"I told you, he's a liability."

Hank sighed. "Honey, you're too much of a loner. Oswald's like family. He's not going to turn on you. He has skills you don't. You can trust him."

Trust him? Right. Although he wasn't malicious, Oswald's first concern was himself. But her father was correct that he was a skilled con man. If she needed information, he'd get it. "I haven't had time to see Oswald. Remember the Booster Club? For the Rizzio kids?"

"Yeah." His face relaxed. "I knew that was a good idea. How are the kids doing?"

"Not bad. Deborah—"

"The klepto, right?"

"Right. She has the kids on some kind of study program. They're getting three square meals a day. As far as I can tell, they're staying out of trouble."

"Glad to hear it. I'm proud of you, honey," her father said.

"We're going to have something on TV about it tonight."

Alarm crossed Hank's face. "Ah, Deanie. You didn't—"

"No. I'm not in it, no way. It's about the need for a family shelter in town. Thanks to Gilda's help with the governor, we got a spot on the agenda at a hearing a week from Monday."

"Has Larry raised enough money to renovate it?"

"We're holding a fundraiser at the Granzer mansion, remember? Old man Granzer has promised to chip in, too."

"You've been busy," Hank said. He rested back, looking satisfied. "New friends. I'm glad to hear it."

"I haven't had much to do with the fundraiser, really. The Cabrini heist has chewed up most of my time."

"You know there are easier ways. We get Mickey and the boys to—"

"No, Dad. We want to do it the right way. No broken windows or threatening notes."

"They listen to their wallets, though. The commissioners see there's a lot of trouble, they unload the firehouse like it's a barrel of rabid ferrets. Tried and true, I tell you."

"We're doing it legit. It's best for the kids, and I think it's going to work, too."

A knock on the door interrupted them. "Lunch lady," a

voice rang out, and the door burst open. It was Gilda, pushing her walker with a covered dish on top. "Hi, Deanie."

"It's not lunch time," Claudine said.

"So what? It sounded better than 'dinner lady'." She lowered herself into the armchair Claudine had been sitting in and extended her long legs. Rose-painted toenails peeked from gold sandals. "What are we doing?"

"We're going to watch the news," Hank said. "About the Rizzio kids."

"I'm proud of you, hon," Gilda said. "You're doing right by them."

"They're good kids. It could be worse." Claudine clicked on the television set and rummaged in the kitchen nook for silverware and napkins. She uncovered the dishes. Turkey sandwiches.

"There's a little whiskey in that coffee pitcher," Gilda said, eyes on the television. "I always hated that woman's hair. You could pitch quarters off it."

"So how is this TV show going to help you get the firehouse?" Hank asked.

"Public sympathy," Claudine said. With the public on their side, the commissioners would jump to sell them the land.

"Look how the light reflects off that woman's noggin," Gilda said.

A quick rap on the door and André entered. "*Buenos noches, padre.*" His tan hadn't faded a bit since Mexico, and his teeth shone white in contrast. He wore a dressing gown with a fringed belt and monogrammed slippers. He also carried a plate with a gravy-covered pork chop. "I'd have brought you something from the cafeteria, but since the doctor said no more gravy—"

"You've been to the doctor?" Claudine turned to her father.

"What happened?"

Hank and Gilda exchanged glances. Hank spoke. "Your brother's making too much of it. It was just a check-up, no big deal."

"But wasn't Dr. Parisot here just a few months ago for the check-ups?" Just about everyone at the Villa saw a physician who'd done time for smuggling meds from Canada and selling them to his poorer patients at a fraction of their price at home. He'd lost his license to practice, but it didn't keep him from attending conferences and even presenting papers under assumed identities.

"Love the tycoon get-up," Gilda told André, ignoring Claudine's question.

"Thanks. I was feeling a little *Top Hat* tonight."

"Stop ignoring me. Dad, what's wrong?" Claudine asked.

"Honey, that can wait. I think this is it." Hank gestured toward the television.

Claudine inched up the volume. She'd ask André later about her father.

The anchorwoman, a velvet headband clamped on her offending hair, stood in front of a bridge. "Compared with many towns, Carsonville's homeless population might be small, but that's little comfort for those who sleep in places like this" — she gestured toward the bridge, where a fire burned in a barrel— "and especially the children."

"Kids live there?" Gilda said. "That's awful."

"Not Wanda's kids."

The next clip of film was in a small room with Hugo. As agreed, Hugo was the public face of the kids. A crumb hung from Hugo's bottom lip. He wiped it off. The anchorwoman— smart lady—must have figured him out right away. "Our mom died." He dropped his eyes. "They split us up even though all we had was each other. That's not right." He turned his head away and let out a long breath, as if he were holding back tears. The boy had star potential.

"I'm going to cry," Gilda said. "Hank, doesn't that kid look like Ronald's brat? The one who was so good at baseball?"

"Ah, he must be forty by now."

"Still, he was a good eater, too."

Brenda again faced the TV camera. "A group of local women calling themselves the Booster Club want to build a family shelter for children who don't have parents to care for them."

"That's you, honey," Hank said.

"But it's not an open and shut case," Brenda continued. "The Club has in its sights an old firehouse to renovate as a shelter. They say that using the building would be cost effective and would let the firehouse continue to give to the public. Not everyone agrees."

André said, "I don't see—"

What was this? "Shh," Claudine said, leaning forward. "She's not finished."

"A local developer has been looking into purchasing the firehouse, as well. A spokesman for the company had no comment, except to say that Carsonville's families can best be supported by jobs and a healthy economy. Since the company is only exploring the option now, it asked not to be named."

A developer? The firehouse seemed so resolutely abandoned. But someone else wanted it? They hadn't anticipated this. The program switched to a dog food commercial, and Claudine clicked it off. The room fell silent. "I had no idea someone else wanted the land. I didn't see anything on the county's books about it."

"Well," Gilda said. "It's not a bad story. People will go for the kids angle over the money angle."

"I don't know," André said. "Depending on the developer, sounds to me like you've got your work cut out for you. When's this fundraiser?"

"Sunday," Claudine said. Two days from now. They'd better be on top of their game.

Chapter Eight

At last, the big night. Half an hour before the fundraiser was to start, Ruby guided her old Volvo into the Granzer mansion's horseshoe-shaped driveway. She wasn't sure what to expect: how many people would come, if they'd support renovating the firehouse, if this mysterious developer would appear. At the Booster Club's last meeting they'd discussed what to do if they had competition for the firehouse, but in the end they decided their hands were tied as long as they didn't know who it was.

They had everything set to make an impressive show and sway public opinion to their side. On the strength of a promise of a "wholesale" Louis Vuitton wallet, one of Ruby's clients even invited a county commissioner's wife. Who knew? Maybe the commissioner himself would show up.

"Look, honey," she said to Bruce. "Deborah got valet parking."

A white-gloved man stepped out from the front of the house and opened the driver's door. Well. Deborah hadn't mentioned that. Classy.

She cast a worried glance toward Bruce. Good thing she'd convinced him to wear his good shirt, although his hair was flopping around a lot. "Here, Brucie." She smoothed an errant wave behind his ear.

"Quite a place your friend has here."

"You'll like her. She's real down to earth," Ruby said, but she barely paid attention. She didn't remember those gigantic planters at the door filled with birds of paradise and ginger plants. Something was familiar about them, but she couldn't quite put her finger on it.

Another uniformed man opened the door for them and gestured in.

Ruby halted. Her jaw dropped. So that's why the planters out front seemed so familiar. The entire entry hall was a riot of mauve and gold and chartreuse spray-painted flowers—the colors of Joanie's graffiti garden in the firehouse. The music from a string duo drifted into the hall.

Deborah emerged from the dining room. Ruby couldn't remember seeing her so joyful. "Do you like it? I paid Joanie to do it. It was so stuffy in here before."

Ruby shrugged off her coat for the maid. She still couldn't get over the house's transformation. "It's marvelous. I love it. But—"

"He hasn't seen it. He won't be back until the middle of the week." Deborah looked away a moment, before stepping toward Bruce and extending a hand. "You must be Bruce."

Bruce couldn't tear his gaze from Deborah. "Nice to meet you."

Not that Ruby could blame him. When her hair had fallen to the salon floor, Deborah's eyes and elegant jaw moved to the forefront, just as Ruby knew they would. Now her hair curved at her ear and thickened into a wavy cap.

Ruby leaned in. "I asked the anchorwoman, Brenda, about the developer who's interested in the firehouse, but she wouldn't say."

Deborah opened her mouth to respond, but a yell from the

entry hall interrupted.

"Deb?" a man's voice asked.

"Yes, Grandpa?" Deborah turned, her dress swirling around her calves.

A tall, white-haired man stumped into the hall. The scent of baby powder wafted in with him. "Where'd you put my reading glasses?"

"They're on your face." She waved a hand toward Ruby and Bruce. "Grandpa, I'd like you to meet—"

He stuck out a hand. "Old man Granzer. That's what they call me."

"What would you like us to call you?" Bruce said after clasping the man's hand.

"Ricardo," the older man said. "What do you think? I said 'old man Granzer.' I won't put up with Grandpa from you."

"Grandpa and I, we have a surprise for tonight." Deborah's eyes were bright, and she squeezed her hands together.

"A surprise? This is plenty surprise already—" Ruby said.

"Ding ding!" old man Granzer said. "I'm going back to the kitchen. A real sweetheart with a five-star heinie is unloading canapés." He toddled off.

"Does your grandfather live here?" Bruce asked.

"Used to. When Louie and I married, he bought a condo on the waterfront. Loves it. He knows the names of all the boats that go by."

Louie Granzer might not have made it, but having old man Granzer tonight—that was a real coup.

"Let me get you two a glass of wine," Deborah said.

"You wouldn't have a beer, would you?" Bruce said.

"Yes, we do—"

"Honey, a glass of wine is just fine. Beer is for baseball games." Ruby patted Bruce's arm. She knew at least five members of the Carsonville Women's League would be there that night, possibly including the League's president. "Thank you, Deb. I had no idea you'd—you'd had such a vision."

"I just got started, and I don't know what happened. One thing led to another. I had a talk with the florist, then the caterer, and, well—" Her eyes widened. She was, Ruby saw with some relief, still the same Deb. "But don't worry about the cost. Louie and Grandpa are paying for the whole thing. Besides, I sold another fifty tickets."

Ruby smiled. Tonight was going to be something special, she could feel it. Those biddies who hustled to her salon, then bragged about slumming? The ones who wouldn't let her join the Women's League? They'd see who had class. Her mother would get that plaque yet.

***

Deborah's gaze swept the crowded room. She smiled. She'd spent way too many evenings alone in the big old house, and the riot of noise, color, and people jostling their way through the entry hall to the dining room was surprisingly soothing. People seemed to like it here. She'd already had half a dozen people ask her who'd painted her entryway.

And she loved her new haircut. It was terrifying at first. She'd insisted on the haircut right away, not even going home to change. They drove straight to Ruby's salon. Her heart pounded as chunks of hair fell to the floor. When, at last, Ruby spun her chair to the mirror, a thrill rocketed through her body—a thrill much bigger than lifting a Rolex from a half-drunk businessman.

She felt light, free. What happened when Louie came home and found their house transformed, she didn't know. But tonight it was as if she'd been reborn, and this time into the right world.

"Oh, Mrs. Granzer—" started a thin brunette with an improbably placid forehead.

"Call me Deborah."

"Deborah, then. I just love your house. What a wonderful party. Why haven't we seen you down at the Women's League?"

"I'm not much for clubs, although I'm sure yours is nice. Besides, I'm already part of the Booster Club."

"Let me give you my number. We could have lunch at the League, and you can tell me about this Booster Club. I'll show you around, introduce you to the girls." The woman rummaged through her purse and drew out a small gold pen. In the background, old man Granzer's voice roared something about engine size.

"Deborah," said another woman, this one with white-blonde hair. "Louie has been hiding you away. Where is the son of a gun, anyway?"

"Birdwatching," Deborah said serenely. "If you'll excuse me, I need to see to the caterers." The caterers were fine. She just wanted the excuse to step away and luxuriate in the moment. She'd never hosted anything this big before. Louie had insisted on a small wedding, and they rarely had guests for dinner.

If only he were here. He'd be so proud of her, and if he really thought about the Rizzio kids, he'd understand why this was all so important. A hand flew to the short hair at the nape of her neck, and uncertainty set in. As long as she hadn't gone too far.

In any case, the guests were enjoying themselves. Not surprisingly, Claudine hadn't arrived yet. She'd probably slip in at the last minute and stake out a spot near a wall. Again she wondered what Claudine's night job was, when she wasn't at the Scent Shoppe. Carsonville wasn't far from San Francisco or even Los Angeles by plane. She might jet down and carry off a few hits. Bringing guns on planes was nearly impossible now. Maybe she used poisoned darts.

"For Christ's sake," a voice behind her said. Deborah turned to see Joy Ellen, ex-beauty queen and Grandpa Granzer's occasional consort, resplendent in rhinestones and a frosted wiglet. "I feel like I landed at a convention of Cougar Barbies. Have you ever seen so much Botox in all your life?"

Deborah suppressed a giggle. Now that she'd mentioned it, the ladies of the crowd did cast an air of aging sorority house. "Did you get yourself a drink?"

"Right here." Joy Ellen tapped a glass sitting on a nearby table. "I love what you did to your hair. Suits you. Me, I try to maximize my 'do. The volume works to balance the girls, you know what I mean?" She looked down at her chest.

One of the so-called Cougar Barbies, this one with shoulder-brushing earrings, crossed the room, dragging the arm of a more elegant woman, this one wearing a pearl necklace and pristine white pantsuit. "There you are. Come here. You've got to meet Louie Granzer's wife. Deborah, right? This is Eleanor Millhouse, president of the Carsonville Women's League."

Deborah shook the new woman's hand. Something about this woman's laser gaze unnerved her. She pulled her hand away and managed a weak smile. "Pleased to meet you."

Someone else jostled for attention. "I'm Amy, and this, come here, honey—" She pulled a dazed man forward "—is my husband, Ned Rossum."

"Commissioner Rossum," the long-earringed woman added.

Deborah stood, stunned. The evening's thrill drained out of

her like water from a tub. She had this man's watch in her basket upstairs.

* * *

Claudine hesitated at the door as a maid took her coat. Hugo had already been to the house, and he ambled to the living room, undoubtedly to search out a waiter with something to feed him. They were a bit late because Father Vincent couldn't find a clean collar when Claudine picked him up to go to the firehouse to babysit. The kids insisted they didn't need a babysitter, even without Hugo, and it took Claudine another fifteen minutes to convince them otherwise. Then Hugo wanted to stop at a burger place on the way.

She stared at the colorful hall before slipping into the living room. The hall wasn't at all like that on her last, surreptitious visit weeks before the Booster Club began. She remembered a coat rack and silk Persian carpet, but that was it. She checked the gilded mantel clock, a 1940s reproduction of a Louis XVI not valuable enough to lift. If the evening was on schedule, it should be about twenty minutes before they made their pitch. Ruby, her husband at her side, paused her rounds to come over. Her husband was just what Claudine had anticipated: plump, good-natured, and clearly devoted to Ruby.

"Hi, Ruby. Hugo's getting something to eat," Claudine said. "You must be Bruce."

He extended a hand and glanced with adoration at his wife. "This sure is a nice event. I'm so proud of you, honey."

Ruby, searching the room, didn't respond.

Claudine stepped in. "I wish I could say I had something to

do with it. Ruby and Deborah planned it all."

"I sold a lot of tickets, but most of these people won't take the time of day to say more than hello to me," Ruby said.

"Who cares about them? You got them here, didn't you? This is about the kids, remember," Bruce said.

Claudine smiled. That's right, Bruce didn't know about his wife's extracurricular activities and likely didn't know about the Rizzio kids' heritage.

"I'm going to get a drink. I saw a tray on the buffet." Claudine turned toward the dining room, then stopped short. Standing between her and the dining room was a couple, both wearing regulation architect eyeglasses and pointing to the spray-painted flowers in the entry hall. She forced a smile and nodded at them as she passed and reminded herself that they didn't know her. She'd done a job for them the year before where she'd stolen a Cy Twombly and a Pissarro for the insurance money. As always, Larry the Fence had made the deal. Claudine only knew them from their wedding photo in its place of honor in their living room.

There must be a hundred people tonight. Nice turnout. A hundred people times a hundred bucks a ticket was a cool ten thousand dollars for the kids. Not bad. Across the room, Deborah appeared to be trying to edge away from a short man with an Amazonian wife. One of the county commissioners, if she wasn't mistaken. More interesting was Deb's new short haircut. It suited her—emphasized her elfin features.

Claudine felt a tap on her shoulder. "Hey, babe, is that real silk velvet?" asked an elderly woman with enormous hair and a halo of White Diamonds perfume.

"It might be." Of course it was. "I'm Claudine." First name only.

"Joy Ellen. Pleased to meet you. I used to have a silk velvet

cape to match my tiara. I was a pageant gal before I married
Winston, rest in peace. Queen of the Cattleman's Court in
Norman, Oklahoma. Nineteen-fifty-five." She gazed into the
distance and smiled. "All the Cattleman's Court married well
that year. What do you do?"

She might have used Hugo as an excuse to escape, but he
was engrossed in the corner popping shrimp hors d'oeuvres in
his mouth. "That sounds fascinating," Claudine said. Distraction. "Tell me about it."

"Oh, no, darling. I asked you what you did. Who wants to
hear about an old beauty queen?"

Claudine downed the rest of her champagne and deposited
the glass on a side table. "I work at the Scent Shoppe. Boring.
I'd better check out what Hugo is up to—"

The woman grabbed her arm. "The Scent Shoppe? You
don't know that charming Mexican man, do you? Don't tell
Granzer" —she lowered her voice— "but he slipped me his
number."

"Attention, everyone," came Ruby's voice from the living
room, accompanied by a brief squeak of the microphone.

"I'd better go," Claudine said.

She hurried to the living room. Ruby and Deborah stood by
the fireplace with Hugo, a sausage roll in one hand, next to
them.

"First, I'd like to welcome everyone tonight. I wish Louie
could be here, but he had urgent business out of the country,"
Deborah said.

Ruby took the microphone. "We'd especially like to welcome special guests Commissioner Rossum—"

The commissioner took a bow from near the front of the
room. Although Ruby had introduced him, he kept his gaze on
Deborah.

"—and the president of the Carsonville Women's League, Eleanor Millhouse."

Eleanor Millhouse's chignon glinted as she turned to face the audience. Perfect teeth mirrored her perfect pearl necklace.

Heat, then cold, washed over Claudine's face. The risk of running into a robbery client faded into the background. Here was Eleanor Millhouse, or, as Claudine had known her, Ellie Whiteby. The girl who had ratted her out in high school.

***

"Step up, Hugo," Ruby said.

She looped an arm around the boy, who was wiping crumbs from his fingers with surprising delicacy. Deborah was at their side. On cat's feet, Claudine had settled in the corner, near the entrance to the hall, as if she wanted to be able to make a quick escape. Her face was gardenia-white against the dark paneling. Something clearly bothered her.

Deborah spoke first. "Can I have your attention?" Even with Deb's soft voice, remarkably, the room quieted. "Welcome, everyone. Thank you for coming. I hope you're enjoying yourselves tonight."

Leaving Hugo leaning against the fireplace, Ruby stepped forward. "I'm Ruby Reed. Deborah and I, with the help of others in the Booster Club" —she barely looked toward Claudine— "plan to establish a shelter for families and kids. A dear friend recently passed away, and her four children were sent to foster homes. Different foster homes. The children had just suffered an awful loss, and now they stood to lose each other, as well." She turned toward Hugo. He kept a stoic expression. Deborah took his hand.

"It's hard to believe," Deborah said, "but there's nowhere kids can stay together in Carsonville. Sure, some families foster a few children, but it's almost impossible to find someone to take more than that. Maybe you saw the story on the news earlier this week."

A murmur rose. Brenda, in full anchorwoman make-up, nodded. She'd dropped by after the five o'clock broadcast.

"We're going to do something about that. We intend to buy the old firehouse in the warehouse district and convert it into a family shelter," Ruby said. She wouldn't mention that the Rizzio kids already lived there. No use attracting the attention of Child Protective Services.

Deborah gave Hugo a little push, and he stepped forward.

"Hi. I'm Hugo, and it's me and my brother and sisters Ruby and Deborah are talking about." He gave the fact a moment to sink in. "When Mom died, we needed each other. We didn't have a home together in the foster care system, so we made our own place on the street. Now the Boosters want to turn the firehouse into a home for people like us."

A voice came from the rear of the room, not far from Claudine. "Who are the Boosters?"

Ruby straightened. "The Booster Club is a group committed to the public good. Deborah and I belong." She touched Deborah's arm and smiled. "Other members prefer to remain anonymous. Unlike some organizations, the Booster Club isn't about making a public show, it's about changing Carsonville for the better." Let them chew on that, suckers. She leaned against the fireplace and crossed her arms in front of her chest.

"It was through an exhaustive search that we located the firehouse as the site for our shelter," Deborah said. Dang it if she didn't discreetly cross her fingers.

"So you kids just ran away from your foster homes?" some-one asked.

Ruby's glance shot to Hugo, but his expression remained placid. "We didn't have a choice. I owed it to Mom to take care of all of us. Given our options, this was the best of a bad situation." The kid had real talent for this sort of thing.

"What about adults? Don't you have adults to help you— you know—make decisions and things?"

"I'm an adult," Hugo said. "I'm eighteen."

"The point is," Ruby rushed in before anyone could ques-tion his age, "the land belongs to the county now. The structure needs work, too, obviously. We—the Booster Club—plan to buy it, once we have the county commissioners' permission."

"And to that end," Deborah said, "I have a special an-nouncement." The crowd parted to let her stand behind old man Granzer on the couch. She placed her hands on his shoulders. "Do you want to say it, Grandpa?"

"Save the firehouse," the old man said. "I'm ninety-six years old. That's no joke."

"And?" Deborah prompted.

Ruby watched with rapt attention. They would take her seriously now.

"One million dollars," he said. "Ding ding!"

"What Grandpa means is that he's pledging up to a million dollars to turn the firehouse into a family shelter. We're hoping the county will grant the land to us. Then we'll use the money for renovations and staff costs. Grandpa's pledge means that the shelter can become a reality."

"Firehouses are the backbone of a town," Grandpa Granzer added. "Everything burns down, you got no town. Fire engines are fine vehicles, as well. Take for instance the 1974 Mack pumper. They call it the 'bulldog' of fire engines. One thousand gallons of water that truck holds. One thousand." He shook his head in amazement.

Deborah patted his shoulder. Next to him, Joy Ellen beamed.

"Waiter," Deborah said. "Champagne for everyone." Three wait staff, already holding trays of full champagne flutes, fanned through the room.

Ruby rushed to Deborah's side, and they hugged. "I can't believe it. He's serious, isn't he? I know you said he'd make a donation, but I never expected this much."

Deborah was flushed with happiness. "Oh, yes. The Granzer men are passionate about their hobbies. Grandpa has been obsessed with fire engines for years. He's a little, well, outspoken at his age, but he's very serious about money." Deborah nodded toward Claudine, still near the wall, and smiled. "I wish she didn't have to hide."

"She might have more reason to than we have." Ruby swiped the champagne flute from Hugo's hands just as he was lifting it to his lips. "Not for you, my friend."

"What do you think she does?" Deborah whispered.

A voice cut through the celebration. Eleanor Millhouse, president of the Carsonville Women's League. Ruby straightened. "I applaud your efforts." Where Deborah's sweetness had silenced the crowd earlier, Eleanor's commanding tone silenced it now. If Ruby ever made it into the League, she'd talk to Eleanor about trying a more youthful hairstyle. She was too young for pearls and a chignon. "But you can't renovate a firehouse you don't yet own. Commissioner Rossum is here tonight. Why don't we see what he has to say?"

On the face of it, Eleanor's words were harmless, but they sent a chill through Ruby's body.

Eyes shifted to Ned Rossum, whose gaze, in turn, was fixed

on Deborah. Deborah looked unusually nervous about it, too. Ruby glanced at Rossum's wrist. Deborah didn't...no, couldn't have. Rossum's wife nudged him, and he snapped to attention.

"Oh. The firehouse. Yes, well, we can't ignore the needs of Carsonville's youth." A murmur of appreciation swept the room. "And yet, the firehouse's land is valuable, set as it is on the edge of the warehouse district. The county could sell the property to a developer. In fact, we're entertaining a proposal right now."

Ruby's jaw clenched. This was it. The developer Brenda had mentioned. "Who wants to buy it?"

"They want it for a business. Or condominiums. I can't remember. Anyway, it's an offer the county can't afford not to consider." A solemn look came over his face. "Of course, our city's youth are our number one priority, and we have a moral responsibility to look after them."

"I can't help but express my concern that children are living alone, too," Eleanor said. Ruby wondered why the woman's champagne hadn't frozen in its glass. "Something should be done about that now."

"Something is being done," Deborah said. "We're taking care of them."

"That's good," Eleanor said. "We wouldn't want them to have to steal to get by. We don't need to be nurturing juvenile delinquents."

Only now did Hugo look to be losing his composure. Ruby put a hand on his shoulder and forced a smile. "You can be sure we've taken care of their needs. With the generosity of Carsonville's residents, other orphans won't suffer the same. And now," she added to cut off further discussion, "we'd be happy to collect donations to supplement Grandpa Granzer's pledge."

Eleanor nodded once and sat down. Ruby couldn't help but

notice Claudine stiffen, and if it were possible, melt even further into the background. What was with her?

Jocelyn, the client Ruby had run into at Klingle's, pulled a twenty dollar bill from her purse. "Here. It's not much, but my budget is tight. Those kids—" She sighed and looked at Hugo. "I don't want to put down what you've done here, but this seems like something the mayor should deal with."

"They don't have anywhere to live together," Ruby said.

"You could work with St. Jude's and build a brand new shelter," she said.

"Grandpa won't donate unless it's the firehouse," said Deborah, suddenly at her side.

It would be years before a new shelter could be built, Ruby knew. If it were built at all. The county would be more than happy to kick that can down the road. Jocelyn, for all her expensive clothing and European vacations and business connections, was starting to look cheap to Ruby.

Jocelyn nudged her bag higher on her shoulder. "I guess I should get home. Thanks for the lovely evening. Oh, I almost forgot. Do you think you could get me one of the new Lanvin chokers wholesale? The one with the ribbons and baroque pearls?"

Ruby's stomach turned. Jocelyn had only tossed a Jackson into the kitty, and now she wanted a deal on expensive jewelry. Ruby looked at the crumpled twenty dollar bill in her hand. Dirty money. "I don't think so."

***

Deborah watched nervously as guests swarmed around Ruby and Hugo. A few guests had already left, but not Commissioner Rossum.

It had to happen sometime, Deborah thought. At some point she had to run into one of the guys she'd duped. But she'd been so careful to choose out-of-town businessmen. How could she know one of them would be a county commissioner? She should pay more attention to politics, she guessed.

Ned Rossum sent another flirtatious smile her way, although when his wife tugged his arm he shut the smile off. As far as Deborah could tell, Rossum didn't recognize her. Thank goodness for the haircut. And, of course, he'd never expect to find a hotel hooker in the mansion of one of Carsonville's most distinguished families.

She kept her distance and nodded politely at Rossum's wife as they passed into the hall for their coats. Just a minute more now, and she'd be in the clear.

As a crowd clustered in the entrance hall, the front door burst open. Who'd be coming at this hour? The party was practically over.

Then she saw. A smile spread over her face, then froze. It was Louie. Oh, my God. She was so happy. But so much could go wrong right now. The hall, her hair. She hadn't told him about any of it.

"Louie," said a tall, thin man Deborah remembered as married to one of the Women's League members. "Haven't seen you down at the golf club in ages."

A curvaceous brunette grabbed his arm. "Deborah said you couldn't make it tonight."

Louie set down his suitcase. The taillights of a cab faded into the distance through the windows. "Where's my wife?"

With a mixture of delight and terror, Deborah stepped forward. It was as if she'd left her body and were watching herself in a movie.

"Hi, chickadee." He stood for a moment in complete silence. The crowd in the entry hall quieted, too, watching the couple. Louie raised his head to take in the spray-painted flowers, his wife's shorn hair. His mouth was locked into a frown. Then it widened. And smiled. "Hi, honey," he said. "You look great."

Within seconds, the crowd in the hall became liquid again. People took their coats and waved goodbye and shook Hugo's hand. The Rossums passed through the front door, with Ned casting a final goodbye glance.

"You made it, Louie. You made it to my event. I'm so glad." She rushed forward to clasp her arms around her husband's neck. He looked more tan, but relaxed.

"I knew this was important to you, so I scrambled to get an early flight back. Besides, the weather was crappy." A maid took his suitcase upstairs. "Could you get me a cola and milk? I'm parched," he told Deborah.

As she passed the living room in a happy haze on her way to the kitchen, she saw Ruby and Bruce gathering checks in an envelope while Grandpa lectured them on hook and ladder trucks. The caterers quietly collected the remains of the evening's drinks and hors d'oeuvres.

The Booster Club was a success after all.

***

What a disaster, Claudine thought. What a freaking disaster. Claudine barely noticed the commotion until she saw the stubby guy in a safari get-up with a suitcase. Deborah's husband. Had to be with the way Deborah had her arms wrapped around him.

After another glance at the hall, Claudine turned to Hugo. "Shall we see what the caterers have left us, then get you back home?"

"Okay," he said.

They passed through the dining room to the kitchen where the caterers were loading carts into a van. Claudine placed a hand on a server's arm. "You saved the extra, right?"

"Right here," the caterer nodded at the counter.

"Do you have any more of those brownie things?" Hugo asked. "Those were really good."

A few minutes later, Claudine left the kitchen with a box of foil-wrapped food. "Take this to the car. I'll check in with Ruby, then I'll be out to meet you."

Ruby was in the entry hall with Bruce. Otherwise, the main level was almost empty. Claudine had no idea where Deborah and her husband had gone.

"Oh, it's you," Ruby said. "I thought it was a successful evening, didn't you?"

"Grandpa Granzer clinched it," Claudine said.

"I felt bad for you hiding out all night. I'm sure it would have been fine—"

"Thanks, but it's better this way," Claudine said. "What do you think about Ellie Whiteby's comments?"

Ruby looked puzzled a moment, then relaxed. "Oh, you mean Eleanor Millhouse."

"I knew her from high school, and it doesn't look like she's changed much."

"I'm not sure what to make of what she said. And the competing offer on the firehouse. That's not good."

"Definitely not good," Claudine agreed. "You're going to

need—I mean we are going to need a plan."

"You girls have plenty of moral standing. That's what matters," Bruce said.

Ruby didn't respond. Maybe she was right not to agree, Claudine thought. What kind of moral standing could a trio of crooks have? "And now we have the money to buy the firehouse and a good start on the cost of renovation."

"Yeah," Ruby said, but didn't sound convinced. "We just have to figure out our next steps."

The fight was not over. "I'll see you tomorrow at our meeting," Claudine said. "We'll figure this out. I'm taking Hugo home."

The car was cold when Claudine opened its doors. Hugo hadn't even touched the box of food.

"So," Hugo said. "What do you think's going to happen next?"

Claudine directed the car down a winding street from the hill where the Granzer mansion nested among other rangy old houses. "I'm not sure. One thing I know, though, is that we've got people talking. And they've heard your story." Damn that Ellie Whiteby—Millhouse—whatever.

"Yeah, but what does that mean? Will they let us have the firehouse? Not everyone seemed to think it's a good idea."

"So they disagree. Enough people see it like we do, though. All we have to do is get the commissioners' votes." Claudine glanced in her rearview mirror. "Can you read the license plate number on that car behind us?"

Hugo craned his neck, the foil package rustling in his lap. "The gray one? Looks like the same one behind us on our way here."

Claudine's face grew cold. "What?"

"Yeah. It picked us up after the burger stop. Why? Do you

know him?"

How had she missed it? After he'd run the license plate, Mickey had told her the car was part of an insurance company's fleet. In other words, someone was on to her. How it had happened, she had no idea. She'd always been so careful, and Larry would never rat her out. It would mean the end of his career—or worse, depending on who heard the news.

She dropped a hand to the gear shift. "Hang on, Hugo. We're going for a ride."

Chapter Nine

Claudine edged the Accord to the stop sign at the end of the street. The gray sedan followed half a block back.

"Seatbelt on?" she asked Hugo.

"Uh-huh."

She launched the car to a sharp left, accelerating through second, third, and fourth gears down the road that circumnavigated the hill. Hugo erupted into shrieking laughter. The sedan held the trail, although it lost another half block. Just as suddenly, Claudine yanked the Accord left again and climbed the hill on a narrow street, a dirt-and-gravel connecting alley at its top. The neighborhood might be grand, but it was old, its streets originally cut for buggies, not sedans. Thanks to her work, she knew every back alley in Carsonville.

This time she pulled the car right. The car's underbelly hit a pothole that slowed it a millisecond while it spun gravel into the brush lining the alley. Hugo hooted with glee as the car rocked. Where the alley met the paved road, she turned left once again, burning up the hill a block, then turning into a bush-lined driveway and cutting the lights. A few years ago, she'd had a kill switch installed that not only instantly turned off the headlights but every other light from the dashboard to the license plate at the same time. The gray sedan roared past them up the hill.

Amateur. No professional would have fallen for that move,

but it was all she had. She flopped her head against the seat and regained her breath before continuing down the other side of the hill at a more relaxed pace, using side streets, and periodically checking her rearview mirror.

Twenty minutes later, Claudine pulled the Accord in front of the firehouse. The block was dead quiet. Her heart still beat erratically.

Hugo hadn't stopped laughing. "Where'd you learn to do that? Will you show me?"

"Upstairs. Next time, if you see a tail, say something." She watched until Hugo waved from the firehouse's second story window. Father Vincent appeared on the street, his vestments covered with dog hair.

"How were the kids?" Claudine asked.

"Just great. We played Old Maid. Lucy's got a good hand with the deck."

"I hope you didn't—"

"No, child. No monkey business. We stuck to Old Maid, although I may have improved Lucy's shuffle." The priest took in the dashboard with an expert eye. "Standard four-banger? I could retrofit it with a Pontiac eight-cylinder I got down at the Villa. They think all you can do is crawl, then—boom!—you're a Maserati."

"I'll keep that in mind." She pulled into the street.

The priest's hand twitched as if he were shifting. "You taking Main? This time of night, Taylor will be wide open. You'll shave one-point-five, maybe two minutes off your time."

"I had a tail on the way home." She knew the father would understand.

His face turned grim. "How'd you shake him?"

"I was up in the Heights, narrow streets."

"And winding."

"So I did a toad-in-the-hole."

Father Vincent nodded. "Fell for it, did he?"

"Amateur," they both said at the same time.

"Who'd be following you home from a social engagement? I don't get that," the father said. They pulled up to the Villa. "You be careful," he added as he slid out the passenger side.

"Thank you, Father. And thanks for babysitting, too."

The late night streets were quiet. When she arrived home, she rested a moment in the darkened garage. She'd have to be more careful, and she'd definitely talk to Larry the Fence to see if any of their deals had soured.

She opened the car door to the quiet sounds of a late autumn night: wind, the occasional car on the boulevard. It had been an exhausting evening. First, the event and seeing Ellie Whiteby again. She never had been great with crowds, and her feeling toward Ellie had only fermented over the years. Then shaking the sedan. If he'd known she'd be at the fundraiser, how long would it be until he showed up at her home? She'd been smart to keep the Accord garaged.

At an upward glance from the street, she froze. A faint light burned in her apartment above the Scent Shoppe, its yellow glow barely reaching the window. No burglar would have left a light on, and no one had a key to her place, except André. Someone had been in her apartment—or was there now.

She paused only a moment before easing her key into the lock on the ground floor. On cat's feet, she mounted the steps to her apartment. As she'd expected, the front door was unlocked. She flattened her back against the wall and reached for an old-fashioned blackjack she kept behind the coat rack.

Ready to swing, she tensed her muscles.

"Deanie," came a voice from the couch.

Claudine's breath caught in her throat. Lounging full length, taut-limbed and beautiful, was her ex-husband. Damn.

"Oz," she said.

He smiled slowly and pulled himself to a sitting position. Every muscle in his torso and legs seemed to ripple as he moved. "I thought you'd never get home."

* * *

Claudine awoke tangled in bedsheets. After a confused second, her eyes flew open. She patted the space next to her. Empty. The bed creaked as she sat up.

"In here, babe," came Oswald's voice from the living room.

Claudine groaned. What had she done? She was smarter than this. After the turmoil of last night's event and the gray sedan, she'd been too worn out to resist him. Not that he'd be easy to resist on a good day.

She pulled on an old kimono as a robe. Cup of coffee at his side, Oz was at her laptop. He had a notepad next to him, and her cat purred in his lap. She pursed her lips. So that's what he wanted all along. She swished by him to the kitchen and lifted the coffee pot. Empty. Figured. He'd made only enough for himself. If she ever had a daughter, her first words of advice would be to target a nice accountant for a boyfriend and stay far, far away from con men.

She leaned against the kitchen doorway and folded her arms. "That laptop is personal. Nothing there is any of your business."

Frustrated, he leaned back. "Come on, babe. What's the password?"

"Nothing doing." She returned to the kitchen to make more

coffee. She'd bolster the locks. He wasn't breaking in again.

He followed her and sat at the tiny table that served as her dining area. "Your dad said you were working on a heist. A big one. 'Historical,' he said."

Ignoring him, Claudine put the kettle on and filled the Chemex filter with ground coffee.

"You know I can help out. I have new connections."

"From the joint?"

"Sure, but elsewhere, too. Whatever you're doing, I can help. You can't do a big job alone. I know you're putting together a team. Let me in on it, Deanie."

Claudine shook her head. When the kettle boiled, she poured the hot water over the grounds.

He took a different tack. "Hey, babe, it sure was great to see you last night. I've been thinking about that for a long time. It got lonely out by the river."

She lifted an eye. A smile had spread over Oswald's face, and against her will, her heart tugged. He reached up and stroked the sleeve of her kimono. His eyes shone warm amber with lashes thick as a puppy's. That fraud. He had the con man's gift of having every smile look genuine. Whatever he said next, you believed. The Oz was a force of nature.

She pulled her kimono from his grasp and took a chance. "I bet you were thinking quite a bit about Natalie, too."

Oswald stiffened. "Ah, Deanie. She's no you."

Bull's eye. Natalie had probably been waiting for him at the prison gate with a pocket full of condoms. Claudine took a mug of coffee into the living room, and Oswald followed. She sat in the armchair and drew up her legs.

"I need to get on my feet again. You can use my help with this heist. You can trust me. You know that."

"Trust you. Right." The coffee was too hot yet to sip, but

the scalding on her tongue kept her on track. Maybe Oswald was right in that she could trust him, in ways other than romance, that was. He knew the code of the craft, and he'd worked on a few big heists, although in a tangential role distracting guards and pinching security codes. The thing is, he'd also been caught. If he were arrested, this would be strike three. Who knew whom he'd sell out to shorten another prison stay?

"Why don't you tell me a little about the heist? Just the overview." He'd settled himself back into the chair at her desk, and one hand absently stroked Petunia. The cat closed his eyes halfway. Claudine knew just how he felt under those long fingers. "Your dad is worried about you," he continued. "He knows you're good, but I think he'd like me around to keep an eye on things, you know? He'd never say so to you, of course."

Her father would worry about her, as proud as he was of her skills. But the Oz was a liability.

"I don't know. The risk is simply too great for both of us. I'll have to think it over. Now, you need to leave. I have a busy day ahead." A lie, but he didn't know that. "And never break into my apartment again. Never. Do you hear me?"

Oswald looked away and drummed his fingers on the desk for a moment. "Fine," he said finally. "I'll give you time to think about it."

The phone rang. Claudine turned her back to her ex-husband and took the call in the kitchen. The elm out back had lost nearly all its leaves. "Yes, this is she. My father?" She whirled and looked at Oswald in panic. "Of course. I'll be there as soon as I can." She clapped the phone into its receiver and took a deep breath. "Dad. They think he's had a heart attack."

She'd throw on something to wear and be out of the house in five minutes. It was another ten to the hospital. Please,

please, let him be all right.

"Deanie." Oswald grabbed her shoulder as she rushed toward the bedroom. "Your father?"

"We'll talk later. I have to go now."

"I'll drive."

* * *

"Five minutes," the woman in scrubs told Claudine. "He needs rest. You have five minutes."

Claudine had been fidgeting in the hospital waiting room for more than an hour while they ran tests on her father. Gilda called every ten minutes or so to check in. While Claudine had picked up, then tossed down magazines, standing and pacing, then sitting, Oswald sat relaxed and calm.

Finally, a doctor had given them a brief update. An EKG showed that her father had had a heart attack. Two of the arteries near his heart were clogged, and he'd need bypass surgery. "You can come back tonight before the surgery," the doctor told her.

But she had to see her father. Now. Had to. "All I want is a minute with him. I just want to tell him I love him. He'd appreciate that."

The doctor was already flipping ahead on his chart and turning away. "You'll have to wait until later this afternoon."

Claudine started down the hall after him, but Oswald grabbed her arm. "Wait. Let me see what I can do."

At the nurse's station, a man and woman sat behind computer terminals. Oswald leaned in and smiled, showing his dimple, focusing on the woman. Claudine couldn't hear him, but the woman resolutely shook her head "no." The man seemed much more interested in Oz's story. While the woman continued to indicate "no," the man touched the woman's shoulder. By God, he was pleading Oz's case to her. Finally, the woman shrugged, and the man rose to get someone else. Oswald returned with a confident smile.

"They'll take care of it," he said.

"What did you tell them?"

"What does it matter?"

The woman in scrubs gave her five minutes with her father. Oswald followed her down the hall and into the room.

"Dad," Claudine said.

Her father lay pale and inert, surrounded by monitors. One tube ran from his nose and another to his forearm. His breathing came hard and jagged, but he opened his eyes. "Deanie. Too much French food, eh? Those damned cream sauces."

"Dad, don't talk. I just wanted tell you I love you. You have to rest now. I'll be back before your surgery. Everything will be all right."

How often had her father told her the same thing—that everything would be all right? He'd said it when her mother died. He'd said it when Ellie Whiteby derailed her plans for college. He'd said it when Claudine filed the papers for her divorce. Now she understood that the words had probably brought him at least as much comfort as they'd brought her. She'd give anything to make him better.

"Deanie, you've got to take care of yourself."

"Don't worry, Hank," Oswald said, putting an arm around Claudine. "I'll make sure she's fine. You just focus on getting better."

"You know I can take care of myself."

Her father patted the bed sheet, and Claudine clutched his

fingers. "You let him help you."

A monitor next to the bed blipped regular beats. "Dad." She couldn't say anything more.

"She'll be fine. I'll be with you on your big heist, right, Deanie?" Oswald said.

Claudine opened her mouth to snap "no way" when a glimmer of a smile lit on her father's lips. He actually wanted Oswald in on the heist. It was hard to believe, but he thought Oz would be an asset. She knew better, but couldn't argue with him now.

"Sure. Sure, he'll help me." There had to be some minor thing she could throw Oswald's way. She'd worry about it later.

Chapter Ten

Ruby held the theory that people are more like Chihuahuas than they would like to recognize. The pack system, for instance. Some dogs are happy to let others lead the pack. They look to their peers for direction and rarely break out on their own. Deborah—darling as she was—fit this mold. As Ruby waited at the tea house this afternoon for her and Claudine, she saw most of the other patrons as submissive dogs, smiling for the host's approval.

Beta dogs were the most annoying. They constantly struggle to prove they're better than the pack's leader, and they pick fights and snarl at their pack mates, faking their importance. They have no idea how weak it makes them look. Commissioner Rossum was a beta.

The alpha dog, though—the alpha was calm and commanding. The alpha decided who sat on Bruce's lap and who ate first. The alpha didn't need to snarl or pick fights, because he was firmly in charge. Eleanor Millhouse, president of the Carsonville Women's League, she was an alpha. Whatever she wanted done would get done. Ruby took a sip of water to quell the warning tingle in her stomach.

What about Claudine? Claudine was confident, too, but she didn't need a pack to boss around. Claudine was a rare thing, a genuine lone wolf.

As if on cue, Claudine arrived with Deborah right behind her. With the change in weather, the tea house seemed to have picked up business. Steam from teapots and conversation frosted the front windows.

"Well," Ruby said after the women sat down. "We raised a grand total of" —she waved her hands with a flourish— "ten thousand in ticket sales plus a couple of thousand in donations. Plus the million from old man Granzer." She beamed.

"That's marvelous," Deborah said. "I'm so proud of us." Her skin glowed and she seemed happier, more relaxed than she'd been in recent weeks. Having her husband home must really agree with her, Ruby thought.

"Does that include the cost?" Claudine asked. She seemed to have absorbed all of Deborah's former melancholy and more. Circles darkened her eyes.

"No, it doesn't, but even with—" Ruby said.

"Louie said he'll cover the catering and the valet," Deborah said. "So what we got at the fundraiser is all for the kids."

Ruby flashed a smile at Deborah but focused her attention on Claudine. "Is everything okay?"

Claudine examined her coffee cup. "I'm sorry. It's just—it's just that—"

"You can tell us," Ruby urged.

"Yes," Deborah said. "Whatever it is, we can help."

She sighed. Lines deepened around her mouth. "My father's in the cardiac care unit at Memorial. He had a heart attack this morning. I just got back from visiting him."

"That's awful. I'm sorry." Poor girl, Ruby thought. She was always so quiet. Yes, a real lone wolf. Ruby had long passed attributing Claudine's silence to snobbery. She knew it was on account of her work, but it had never occurred to her to wonder what the rest of her life was like. She never talked about her family or relationships.

"I'm so sorry, too," Deborah said.

"Don't worry about it. I shouldn't have even brought it up—it's not your problem." Claudine laid her hands flat on the table. "Let's talk about what we're going to do for the shelter."

Ruby and Deborah exchanged glances. It would be useless to try to drag anything else out of Claudine. She'd made it clear she didn't want sympathy.

"All right," Ruby said. "If you're sure."

"I'm sure."

Ruby nodded once. "How were the kids when you dropped off Hugo?"

Claudine might have flinched for a moment, but if so, she quickly regained her equilibrium. "It, uh, took us a little longer than normal to get home, but everything was fine."

"Tinkerbell helps, I bet, with safety," Ruby said. "Chihuahuas are great for barking, but not so scary." She cast a meaningful look at Deborah.

"What worries me is the idea that someone else wants the firehouse," Claudine said.

"I had the same thought. Any chance old man Granzer would fund a shelter somewhere else?" Ruby asked. "I mean, if the firehouse doesn't come through?"

"Not unless it's another firehouse. It's pretty much all about fire engines for him," Deborah said.

"The county commissioners' meeting is exactly a week from today," Claudine said.

"I was surprised they fit us in so quickly."

"I hear the governor sent a letter." Claudine averted her eyes.

"If the governor cares, we stand a good chance," Deborah said.

"I don't trust Commissioner Rossum," Ruby said. "But I don't know what we can do about it this late."

"At this point, we work on our presentation and hope for the best," Claudine said.

"If the mood at the fundraiser was any indication, we stand a good chance." Ruby added more sugar to her tea. "Sure, someone wants the land. Overall, though, the crowd seemed pro-shelter. I mean, didn't you think so?"

"Of course they'll sell it to us. The person who wants the firehouse can buy something else. There are plenty of old warehouses available, but we need the firehouse," Deborah said.

"Just because it's the right thing to do doesn't mean the commissioners will do it," Claudine said.

Ruby shot her a glance. "Honestly, Claudine. Lighten up."

Deborah set down her spoon suddenly. "I have an announcement." She pulled herself up straighter. "I'm done stealing things. Louie's home, and that part of my life is over."

"Louie's staying home for good? Are you sure?" Claudine asked.

There she was again, Ruby thought, raining on everyone's parade. "Claudine, this isn't really our business."

"I think he is," Deborah said. "Things feel different this time. This is fun, but I'm going to cut back on the Booster Club once we get the firehouse settled. Louie needs me."

"He said that?" Claudine, again.

"He doesn't need to." Deborah sat upright.

"Claudine, we have—" Ruby started.

Deborah turned her face away from Claudine. "I don't like it when he goes away. Why would he like it when I go away? Even if it's only for a few hours."

"Well, there's the fact that every time he jets off on one of his birdwatching trips, he's putting distance between you. He doesn't seem to mind that."

"Honestly, Claudine, leave her alone." How dare Claudine rile up the poor girl? Sure, her father was in the hospital, but that was no excuse. "It's not for us to question her marriage."

"My marriage is fine," Deborah said. She turned her head away from the table and raised her chin. "You're not married. You don't understand."

"I used to be," Claudine said.

Deborah and Ruby swiveled toward Claudine. The table fell silent. This was interesting. At last, a crack in the armor.

"It didn't work out." Claudine rose and shrugged on her coat.

"Why? What happened?" Deborah said. God bless her innocence.

Claudine looked down at them, the low light streaming in the window behind her. "You might say it was birds."

* * *

"Dang it." Ruby lifted a branch from the flat plaque that covered her mother's grave. "Sorry, Mom," she added. "I meant to get down here earlier and tidy up."

Ruby and her sisters Pearl and Opal had chosen the Lone Oak cemetery because they loved its vast canopy of trees—pines, elms, and more than one lone oak for sure. They also loved that the county owned it, so the cost of a plot wouldn't break the bank. The downside was that maintenance wasn't as frequent or thorough as in the private cemeteries, and the recently interred residents weren't particularly upscale. Gravestones engraved with the images of Slavic and gypsy families sat above the unmarked graves of Chinese laborers from the turn of the nineteenth century.

Ruby wiped her mother's plaque clean. Then she pulled an airline bottle of Cointreau from her bag and emptied it where she estimated her mother's mouth would be. Heat sparked in Ruby's chest, gathering and radiating throughout her body. She mopped her brow. "Mom, how did you handle hot flashes? Did they wake you up at night like they do me? Jeez, I swear it's every fifteen minutes as soon as I get to bed. It doesn't help that Bruce is a regular furnace."

Ruby didn't remember her mother complaining about menopause. Then again, it paled against cirrhosis of the liver. She winced, remembering her mother's last days in the county hospital. They had no money. Ruby's father had been long gone, in Palm Springs with a new wife and kids and little desire to remember his first family.

She put her hand on the cool marble of the plaque to trace its letters, then quickly pulled it away. Her mother was fifty-five when she died. The same age Ruby was now. The exact same age.

"Mom," she said. Did she look as old as her mother did when she died? Maybe because she never had children, she had the sensation of cruising through life at the age of, oh, thirty-five. But she'd started to notice her neck's tendency to crinkle like tissue when she tensed, and the lines around her eyes were harder to plump with eye cream.

"Mom," she repeated. "I have a plan to get the monument you deserve. The Women's League is warming up to me, but I guess there's some history to overcome." Like finding her mother passed out drunk in the League's coat room when, as president, she was supposed to be opening the annual garden party fundraiser.

Ruby leaned on her elbows and watched the shadows move with the breeze. "Anyway, I have some new friends, and we're helping a group of kids get a permanent home. They're orphans—not my friends, the kids. They kind of got stuck in the same situation we did. They're siblings, four of them, and they want to stay together. The Women's League is impressed."

Ruby could almost hear her mother wonder about the kids. Why didn't they have someone who'd take them in? What were they doing on their own?

"Oh, Mom. Their mother, well, she had an untraditional career. I won't lie to you, she was a hustler. She'd pretend to trip and get hurt so she could get insurance money. She died in jail."

And you're helping them out? her mother seemed to ask.

"Of course. You would, too. After you died—" Ruby paused. Did her mother know what their life had been like? "After you died, the girls and I had nowhere to go. It wasn't like the Women's League was going to take us in."

So you stole.

"I only shoplifted because I had to. For us. We did okay though, right?"

Then why do you still do it?

So she knew. "It's for you, Mom. To please those snobs. Once I'm in the League, they'll have to give you the gravestone, don't you see?" Besides, I'm good at it, Ruby thought. I'm good at hair, too, but that's less impressive.

You're good at relationships. You and Bruce have a good thing going. Don't mess it up. What about these friends of yours?

"We're doing it straight, all by the book, Mom." Well, mostly. "We're going to buy the old firehouse the kids are living in, fair and square." She pulled herself into a full sitting position. "My friends—we call ourselves the Booster Club, isn't that funny?—are great. Deborah is rich, she married the guy who owns the Granzer grocery stores, but she's really sweet. She likes Patsy Cline, and she loves the dogs. The other one, Claudine, is more aloof. Honestly, I'm not sure what to think of her, but she has solid judgment, and she really seems to care about the kids." Ruby's throat closed. She could only manage a whisper. "I hope you'll be proud of me, Mom."

I'm proud of you already, Ruby.

Chapter Eleven

Claudine picked up the phone. She just wanted to check one thing with Ruby. If she was right, they knew their competition for the firehouse. The phone rang through to voice mail, and she left a message.

Oswald—who had behaved like a guest, thank God, and actually rung the doorbell this time—fidgeted in the armchair. Petunia purred in his lap. He drummed his fingers on the chair's arm, then dumped Petunia on the floor and went to the kitchen, probably to look for a beer.

As she pressed "end," Oswald's voice from behind her made her jump. He held a beer by the bottle's neck. "I don't know why you're wasting so much time with those kids. You should be focusing on the big job. D day is coming up."

"I just want to make sure they're okay. Anyway, the Cabrini heist is planned. At this point, it's all about execution."

She'd let Oswald take over managing the ground crew, and her only job would be the actual break-in. He was right. It had been a relief to let him handle the scheduling, and as far as she could tell he'd done it well. He'd built on her map of the museum, written up a character profile for the niece, and had the offshore bank accounts set up to handle payment. All she'd have to do is fly to San Francisco, play the part of the bereaved niece for an after-hours visit to set up the strike, then return when the streets quieted to collect the jewels.

"Babe, I'm worried about you." He cracked open the beer. "We're planning a huge job here, and you're not focused."

"I'm focused. Everything's set up. All we have to do is wait, and we're on."

He shook his head. "It's not about the plan, it's about your state of mind. You have to be calm. In charge. But you're all over the place."

He was right, and she knew it. She was so immersed in her father's illness and saving the firehouse that she was forgetting about what was important. Not that her dad wasn't important. But in less than three weeks she'd be pulling off the heist of her life, then giving up the lifestyle for good. If she wasn't completely sharp about it, she'd be spending her "retirement" behind bars.

"Listen. Trust me. I've known you a long time, Deanie. I've seen this look before."

"I'm just tired, that's all."

He moved a step closer. "When you're on, no one can beat you. You're a step ahead. I've seen it since you were in kindergarten and a kid tried to beat you at jump rope. By the next day you could cross and double-cross and knew those jump rope songs better than anyone else on the playground."

Funny he'd remember that. She barely remembered it herself until now. "You're right, Oz. I need to focus on the San Francisco job." She leaned against the door. Dear God, she was tired.

"No more messing with this firehouse business?" He pulled her gently by the wrist.

"There's a county commissioners' meeting next week. I have to go to that." She could let Ruby and Deborah put together the testimony. She planned to stay in the background, anyway.

"But you're just going to watch, right? No more trips to the firehouse?"

"No. Definitely not. Just the meeting."

"Good girl." He placed an itinerary on the computer. "Here's your ticket. All in Linda Cabrini's name."

Linda, Rosa Cabrini's niece, was conveniently in an Indian ashram for the next month. "The costume's done," Claudine said. "Honestly, unless something falls through, we're set."

"I ordered the exhibition catalog, too," Oz said. Claudine opened her mouth to speak, but he cut in. "All anonymously, of course. No one could trace the credit card or mail box."

"I was going to say that I know every one of those jewels by heart. I did lots of research before handing off the files to Otto for the dupes."

"It's a nice reminder, though, isn't it? A little incentive?" Oz leaned over the desk and opened the catalog. "Look at that. The Maharajah's necklace. Insured for eighteen million dollars."

A twenty-three carat yellow diamond, cut in a teardrop, dangled from an equally brilliant collar of diamonds the size of Chiclets. It had been first made for an Indian princess over two hundred years ago. It was the star of Rosa Cabrini's collection, but it wasn't Claudine's favorite. She flipped ahead in the catalog to the item she loved most.

"I thought you'd like that one," Oswald said. "It reminds me of you."

The photo showed a Cartier panther brooch studded with diamonds and sapphires, familiar to anyone who'd perused photos of Wallis Simpson. It was one of the least valuable items in the collection, but the flicker of blue light in the panther's eye mesmerized her. The quiet, graceful panther.

Oswald touched her arm. "Here. Keep it as a reminder not to get distracted by those kids. They'll do fine. Hell, they're already doing fine. They obviously got you hooked." His voice was soft, caressing. "It's you I'm thinking about. I don't want anything to get in the way of your success."

It would be so nice to believe him, believe that she was his primary concern. But Oz's primary concern was always the Oz. She'd learned that lesson the hard way. He was right, though, in that she had to keep her focus on the heist. It would be her final job. Her future was riding on it. Once the jewels were liquidated, she'd be free, even after Oswald took his cut. But it didn't mean she'd let go of the firehouse altogether.

"As I said, we're in good shape," Claudine said. "Thanks. I'm going to make an early night of it, visit Dad at the hospital. He's coming home tomorrow."

"I thought maybe we could get some dinner, you know, spend time together." The lamp cast shadows over his face, emphasizing his full lips and the dimple on his chin. He touched her arm again, but this time pulled himself closer. He gave off the warm scent of soap and spice.

Claudine slipped from his grasp and made her way to the front door. She opened it and gestured toward the stairs. "Stay warm. It's cold out there."

His mouth flattened in disappointment. "Oh, I will. Don't worry about that."

***

Later that night, Claudine leaned back from her desk and stretched her arms. Despite telling Oswald she was going to bed early, it was well past midnight and she was reviewing the Cabrini plans once again, making up for her inattention.

She rose, putting her hands in the small of her back and pulling her shoulders forward to loosen them. In the kitchen, she took a glass of water to the back window and rested against its frame for a moment.

Once she was set financially, what would she do? She'd been a thief for so long. And not just purses and dresses, like Ruby, or secondhand watches, like Deborah. She'd stolen millions of dollars of jewels, artwork, and historical artifacts. Once she even lifted a Louis XIV bergère on its way to the Frick Museum.

From her second story perch, Claudine had a clear view into the backyards of the houses on the next street. In the house just to the right, a pale light switched on. A man's silhouette appeared against the light. He was holding something—a baby. Over the summer, she'd seen the man's wife grow bigger with child as she puttered in the garden or rested on the patio with a glass of iced tea. Claudine let the curtain drop. Her little apartment felt so quiet.

The Cabrini heist would seal her place as a world class criminal for the rest of her life. It would also be her ticket to freedom. And a curiously blank future. She set down her glass and leaned against the window frame. Ellie Whiteby—Eleanor Millhouse, now—had certainly settled her own life. Upstanding husband, pillar of the community—not a crack in that façade. Ellie, and her questions about the firehouse.

She stood straighter. All those questions about the firehouse. On a whim, Claudine went to her laptop and searched for Eleanor Millhouse. Yes, there it was: Eleanor Millhouse, CEO, Fine Properties of Distinction. She was a property developer. A chill ran down her arms.

The trill of her phone shattered the silence. So late. Could it be about her father?

"Private," the caller ID read. Nearly everyone she knew

blocked their ID, but not many of them would call this late at night.

"Hello?" she answered breathlessly.

"Deanie, it's Mickey. You were right to put someone on the firehouse. My guy just stopped an intruder."

Claudine sucked in her breath. "The kids. Are they all right?"

"Everything's fine. For the moment, at least. Jojo was keeping an eye out from the building next door when he saw someone pull up and park down the street, quiet-like, with his lights off."

Claudine's breath left in a gust. "What happened?"

"He started nosing around the firehouse. Had something in his hands, too, might have been a fuel can and rags."

The kids. "Truly?" She wouldn't.

"My guy's been getting attached to the kids. He was tempted to beat the living sheisse out of the stranger but thought it might be more useful to figure out who he was. So he made some noise, like he was a bum coming up the street, and the other guy beat a hasty retreat. The thing is, his license plate was mudded up. No way we could get the number."

"He'll be back," Claudine said. This was getting a lot bigger than she'd imagined. She put a hand to her face.

"Yeah. He'll be back," Mickey agreed. "I've doubled the patrols, but you're going to have to secure that building properly. Or give it up altogether. I am not joking."

Chapter Twelve

When Claudine showed up at Ruby's back door the next morning, the rising sun cast pink light over the driveway and the row of yellow pansies planted in the kitchen's window box, complete with the wooden cutout of a Chihuahua pretending to take a leak. The house was a cheerful yellow with cream trim, giving the place the feel of a raucous cupcake. Claudine hadn't been to Ruby's Crafty Cuts before, although she'd driven past it scores of times.

The flounced curtains on the windowed back door moved. Ruby gestured for Claudine to come in. "Bruce is still sleeping," she whispered. "You want a cup of coffee before we go down to the firehouse?"

"If you don't mind." From the looks of things, the one cup she'd had this morning wouldn't be enough. Something squeaked under Claudine's feet. A dog toy shaped like a hedgehog. Ruby filled two travel mugs.

Claudine's car felt instantly brighter with Ruby settling in. Ruby tucked the lilac tote at her feet, and the fragrance of her orange blossom perfume blended with the aromas of coffee and the Mercedes' old leather seats.

"A luxury car. Very nice," Ruby said. "I thought you drove an Accord."

"I keep the Accord for business. This one's for pleasure. I

do love this old girl."

Ruby turned to her with a look of mild surprise. "Funny, I believe you do. This might be the first time I've seen you smile. Apart from with the kids, that is."

Claudine concentrated on backing out of the drive. Carsonville's streets were nearly empty this early in the morning, but a freezing fog overnight had left patches of ice here and there.

"The car, you didn't—" Ruby started.

"No. Bought it. Car theft isn't my line."

Ruby sighed and settled back into the seat. "The kids. Who'd be after them?"

"That's all I've been thinking about all night. It has to be someone who wants the land. If Jojo hadn't been there—"

"Which means it has to be someone who knows we want the land. Brenda never mentioned the location in her story—"

"It must be someone from the fundraiser," Claudine said. "I can't help but wonder if it's Eleanor Millhouse. I did some research last night, and she has a development company." Ruby had an obvious fascination with the Women's League. She glanced at Ruby to gauge her reaction, but couldn't read her.

"I know. We should go through the guest list at the fundraiser and see if any of the rest of them have connections in construction, but I'm not sure it matters at this point." A few moments passed. "It's not long until the county commissioners' meeting. Once the firehouse is ours, we're golden."

The commissioners' meeting couldn't come too soon for Claudine's taste. Anyone willing to risk the lives of children wasn't anyone she wanted to go head to head with. Claudine cranked up the heater another notch.

"What are we going to do with the kids? I mean, once we convince them they have to leave," Ruby said.

"I'm not sure. I guess I'd hoped Deborah would come

through for us. She has enough room, but she can't."

"Louie—" Ruby started.

"Louie," Claudine said at the same time. "I think she was more upset about it than I was."

"I guess the kids could lay out sleeping bags in the salon at night. I wonder if Tinkerbell is good with other dogs?"

"It's not ideal. But it's only until the county commissioners' meeting."

Claudine pulled up to the firehouse. The sun had risen fully now, though the wind was shivering cold. Her travel mug steamed when she set it on top of the car. "There's a box of donuts in the backseat. Not the healthiest breakfast, but I thought the kids would appreciate them."

This earned another surprised look. What kind of heartless person did Ruby think she was?

"Hugo, especially," Ruby said.

A stocky man leaned on a lamp post half a block away. He raised a hand in a salute before moving away, presumably to circle the block. Claudine joined Ruby at the firehouse's front door. Unless there was an emergency, the sentinel wouldn't tell her anything anyway. All his reports went through Mickey.

Ruby rapped their signal foxtrot rhythm on the door and waited for two knocks in return. Silence. After a few minutes they tried again, and after finally hearing the answer, they went to the side window to be let in. Sleep lines creasing his cheek, Hugo, accompanied by a wagging Tinkerbell, greeted them. Sniffing at the pink bakery box, the dog kept trying to stand on her hind legs to get closer. Their breath hung in the air.

"Down, Tinks," Hugo said. "You showed up early to bring donuts? That's awesome."

Claudine handed him the box, and he had a maple bar in his mouth before she could reply. "Let's go upstairs. Are the rest of you up? We have some news, and it's important."

Maple bar suspended from his mouth, Hugo led them up the stairs. The kids were sitting up in the bunks. When they heard Ruby's voice, they snuggled back under the covers.

"Is it about the guard you got for us?" Hugo wiped his mouth with the back of his hand. "Because I really like the guy who came last night. He had dog treats and everything."

Smart move, Claudine thought. "It's about last night, in fact. I don't want to alarm you, but the guard caught someone trying to break in. He wasn't able to track him, and I'm afraid he'll be back."

"Wait," Lucy said. "Someone was going to get us?"

Joanie put a protective arm around Tinkerbell.

"We think someone else wants the firehouse—or at least the property it's sitting on."

"Who?" Hugo asked. Amazingly, he hadn't dived back into the box of donuts. "It was someone at the fundraiser, wasn't it?"

"Not sure," Claudine said.

"We're trying to figure that out," Ruby said.

"They want to kill us," Lucy said.

Ruby patted the girl's back. "Honey, don't let your imagination run away with you."

"It's not about you—it's the firehouse. We're not going to let anyone hurt you. Besides, no one but us knows you live here. At least, I don't think so," Claudine said.

Hugo watched them talk. Finally, he said, "Have they threatened you guys?"

Ruby and Claudine exchanged glances. "No. But it looked like he had rags and gasoline. It's not safe for you to stay here any longer."

Claudine braced herself for Hugo's resistance.

Hugo drew a breath as if to speak, then looked at his siblings, watching from their beds. "Okay," he said. "We'll move."

"Good," Claudine said before he could change his mind. "Let's pack up. Deborah is on her way. We just need to keep you safe for a week, until we have the firehouse squared away."

"Where are we going?" Scotty said.

"We're taking Tinkerbell, too, right?"

Claudine glanced at Ruby. Her house was tiny, and the thought of four kids and a pit bull stuffed into it with Ruby and Bruce and all those Chihuahuas was too much. She'd been generous to offer, and Claudine had thought she'd take her up on it, but she couldn't do it.

Claudine let out her breath. "We were thinking about Ruby's house. But I have another idea. How do you like old people?"

***

"Really? An old folks home?" Ruby checked the side view mirror. Deborah was following them, her husband's Land Rover packed with the Rizzio kids, an armchair, and the dog. The bearskin rug and a stack of sleeping bags filled the Mercedes' back seat. "Are you sure they'll take kids?"

"I'm not sure of anything. But the Villa Saint Nicholas is...well, unusual. And safe. We just have to convince the manager he won't regret it."

Claudine pulled the Mercedes into a small parking lot in front of a Spanish-style building with chunks of plaster falling from its walls. Evenly spaced aluminum windows lined one side. An arched portico extended into the parking lot. Two men in wheelchairs rested under the portico, despite the autumn cold. One of the men absently shuffled cards on a lap tray. The cards fanned and reversed direction and arched again with balletic precision. A violently red-headed woman peeked between the blinds of the Villa's front room.

"What is this place?" Ruby asked.

"I told you. A retirement home. Follow me."

The wheelchairs swiveled as they entered. A burly man covered in tattoos stood just inside the door.

"He doesn't look old enough to be retired."

"He works here," Claudine said. "Why don't you get Deborah and the kids? Tell them to mind their Ps and Qs."

Ruby reluctantly left Claudine just as the tattooed man's eyebrows came together and his scowl deepened. The heavy front door shut behind her. A glance back showed Claudine's expression as implacable as always.

"What's going on in there? What is this place?" Deborah asked. Tinkerbell squeezed out the Land Rover's back door and squatted to pee.

"Can we get out?" Hugo said from the back seat.

"In a minute," Ruby said. Then, to Deborah, "It's a retirement home. That's what Claudine says."

The tattooed man moved more lightly than his body had led Ruby to guess. He was at the Land Rover in seconds, Claudine behind him. "Kids? Really? You want kids to stay here?"

"Ruby, Deborah, this is Warren," Claudine said. "He's the manager."

"Is there a problem, sir?" Deborah looked up at him, probably having little idea of her effect. The man's face smoothed and his eyes lit up. What was it about Deb? Sure, her features were good, but Ruby tended to the heads of dozens of prettier women. It must be the sheer lack of guile, the goodness and helplessness, that drew men like babes to the teat.

"I, um—"

"They're Wanda's kids, Warren. They were squatting in an abandoned firehouse. I had Mickey keeping an eye on them, and someone tried to set it on fire. They need a place for only a week. That's it."

"They're such good children." Deborah turned to the Land Rover. "Hugo is very responsible. Lucy—that's her in the middle—is so tidy. It's amazing. Scotty is a good listener, and you won't hear a peep out of Joanie. I promise."

Tinkerbell bounded around the corner, barreling toward the tattooed man. Claudine visibly stiffened. Shoot, Ruby thought, there goes plan B.

With one hand, Deb caught Tinkerbell's collar, halting her just before she would have leapt on Warren. It was only affection, but it looked like aggression. The man, instead of recoiling in fear, broke into a wide grin.

Deborah touched the man's bulging upper arm. "Look here." She traced the outline of a crudely drawn pit bull's head. "Your tattoo looks just like Tinky. You're a dog lover." She gazed into his eyes, smiling.

Warren's face softened. He patted both his shoulders, and this time Tinkerbell leapt up, setting a paw on each side of his hips. "She's sweet as my Goldie."

The three women stood, silent. Remarkably, even the kids held their tongues. Tinkerbell licked the man's elaborate mustache clean, and if Ruby wasn't mistaken, he chuckled. Ruby's shoulders relaxed.

"All right," he said. "I guess they can stay. The girls can bunk in André's room. Your brother can share the TV room with the boys."

"Thanks so much, Warren," Claudine said. "Maybe you can put these kids to work. Help you out with the chores."

"Not a bad idea." Warren walked back to the Villa Saint Nicholas's entrance, Tinkerbell trotting behind him. "I just might, at that."

Ruby pulled Claudine back. "What's the deal? Level with me."

"What?"

"He's no regular retirement home manager. Not with that many prison tats."

Claudine turned away, then back to Ruby. "Used to be a prison warden, actually."

"Why isn't he still working in a jail, then? It has to pay better than this." She took in the row of dented trash cans, the barren rose bushes.

"He got in trouble with state corrections for passing what he thought were love letters to inmates. He's more of a romantic than he lets on. Unfortunately, one of the letters included a detailed map of the prison's HVAC system. You heard about the escape of those embezzlers five years or so ago?"

The news had been full of it at the time. The men had been locked up for draining the hedge fund accounts of Carsonville's largest bank. Two of the embezzlers were caught three states away, and the other was never found.

"Are you coming?" Deborah asked from the Villa's front door.

"In a minute," Ruby yelled ahead. Then, more quietly, "All the more reason this is no normal retirement home. Spit it out."

Claudine let out a long breath. "Everyone in the Villa is bent. To the last."

Ruby's eyes widened. It hardly seemed possible. An entire retirement home for the lawfully challenged. She pictured flatware disappearing, locks picked, and, of course, a bouquet of illegal cable connections. They might hot wire cars to go bowling. Gin rummy would enter a whole new dimension here. She smiled. Then reason returned.

"We can't let the kids live with a bunch of criminals."

"What other option do we have? Besides, the residents take a vow to go straight once they move in. It's too risky, otherwise. We could lose the whole place if anyone found out."

"We?" Ruby asked, lowering her voice. She must have caught Claudine off guard. Her eyes darted to the Villa, then the garage, then back to Ruby.

"My father lives here."

"Are you coming?" Deborah yelled once again from the Villa's doorway. Behind her, the redhead, leaning on a cane, admonished Tinkerbell to sit.

"We're coming right now. Just grabbing the sleeping bags from Claudine's car." Ruby nodded at Claudine. "Come on. But I want to hear about everything."

"I guess it's only fair."

Ruby grabbed the rolled-up bearskin rug, and Claudine pulled the sleeping bags from the back seat. Arms full, they made their way inside the Villa. Claudine bumped the automatic door opener with her elbow as the men in wheelchairs continued to look on. "Hey, Deanie," one of them said. The other, watching the women, expertly turned the deck of cards in his hand in an automatic reflex. Now it was all starting to make sense, Ruby thought.

"Dad home yet?" Claudine asked the men.

"Yep," the man with the cards replied. "Those the Rizzio brats?"

"You'll be meeting them in a minute," Claudine said. Then, to Ruby, "Let's take this gear upstairs."

Complaining the whole way, the rickety elevator inched to the second floor. Its doors opened to a hall carpeted in lumpy gray. A turbaned man stepped out from a few doors up.

"Darling Deanie," he said.

A Middle Eastern crook? Ruby wondered. He looked tan enough, but too young for a retirement home.

"What's your scam now?" Claudine said.

"Just playing around," the swami said. "I found some old sheets in the laundry room. I can't watch *Practical Hospital* with Grady all day, you know."

"He loved seeing you in the telenovela episodes, didn't he?"

"Adored them, even if he didn't understand a word. I'm afraid you'll never match my esteem in his eyes," the swami said, adding a vaguely Saudi accent.

"Ruby, I'd like you to meet my brother, André."

Ruby looked at Claudine. What was his gig?

"Pleased to meet you." The man's smile showed perfectly white teeth.

Charisma. Genuine charisma. She felt her heart warm in spite of herself. André yanked off his turban to reveal ruffled hair. The man on the street wouldn't be able to tell it was a dye job, but Ruby knew better and would suggest he try the neutral rather than cool tones next time.

"And now you're booting me from my room," he said.

"Middle Eastern sheikhs are known for camping in the desert."

"The TV room is curiously Saharan, but I'm certain it's never seen nobility."

"Then you'll just have to change that," Claudine said. "We'll drop off these things, then I'm taking Ruby and the kids to the cafeteria. I think it'd be best if we introduce them."

"They don't know about us? I mean, the situation?" André asked.

"No," Claudine said. "And it had better stay that way."

Ruby studied the exchange. She'd never call Claudine an emoter, but she gained layers of depth in Ruby's eyes as she watched her joke with her brother. Funny, somehow she'd assumed Claudine had arrived in the world unfettered by family. "Where's your dad?"

"Downstairs," the young man answered.

Claudine turned toward the elevator. "Come on. I'll show you around."

The cafeteria was as drab as the rest of the Villa she'd seen—at least, its bones were. But every chair and every table were different. A large television and shelf of DVDs anchored one end. A fireplace and entrance to what Ruby assumed was the kitchen were at the other end, closer to the Villa's central entrance.

"I thought you said the boys would be sleeping in the TV room? Is this it?" Ruby asked.

"No, the TV room is across the hall. Grady is very particular about his programs, though, so some of the residents prefer to watch in here."

"Are you talking about me?" a stooped man, possibly the oldest man Ruby had ever seen, said from his chair. Behind him, three more of the Villa's residents stood. "These Wanda's kids?"

"I thought you couldn't hear well," Claudine said.

"New hearing aid."

"Then you can turn that blasted television down now and then," the redhead said. Her voice sweetened, and she waved toward the kids. "I'm Gilda. Are you poor orphans coming to live with us?"

Joanie's eyes widened. She backed up and grabbed Hugo's hand.

"We'll be temporarily residing among you," he said. In his

nervousness, he'd lapsed into stiff talk.

"You look just like your pa," a man in a wheelchair said.

"Kids—and Deborah and Ruby—this is my father, Hank," Claudine said. She stooped to whisper something to him, and her father touched his chest and nodded.

"Which husband was that? I recall Wanda had a few," Gilda said. Then, to Ruby, "By the way, I love your color."

"It's eight golden with a touch of neutral, but I am—or was, rather—a natural redhead," Ruby said.

"Me, henna," Gilda said. She extended a shapely leg from a slit in her ankle-length gown. "A cup to a gallon of water, every two weeks."

The henna would be great for protecting her hair shafts, but if she ever wanted a decent dye job, she'd have to wear it off. It would be an eight week wait, minimum, Ruby thought.

"The older one's dad was the forger, am I right?" Claudine's father said.

"Uh, I'm not sure," Hugo said. The kids were completely absorbed in the conversation. Lucy's thumb lifted to her mouth.

"Honey," Claudine's father said. Claudine kissed him on the head.

"How are you feeling?" Claudine asked him, her voice gentle.

"Not bad, considering." The man turned to Ruby and to Deborah, who'd emerged from the TV room across the hall wiping her hands.

"Do you need anything?" Claudine asked her father.

"I'm all fixed up. Dr. Parisot's coming by later." Then, to Ruby and Deborah, "As Deanie said, I'm Henri Dupin. French, you know. You can call me Hank."

"Oh, Dad, we haven't been French for eighty years," Claudine said.

"Mais oui. We're French, all right," the old man insisted. "We only do it French. French perfume, French bread, French fries, you name it."

Claudine was still smiling, and it wasn't condescending, either. Ruby looked at her, eyebrows raised. Whatever it was that he did, criminal work was the family way.

"I love it here," Deborah said. "I've already met the most fascinating people. Grady knows simply everything about soap operas."

Ruby shot a glance at Claudine again, whose single raised eyebrow hinted that Grady might have other skills, but she wasn't talking.

"And there are these darling men, Bobby and Father Vinny," Deborah continued.

Strangely, Father Vincent wore a floor-length floral skirt with his black shirt and collar. In fact, Ruby was certain she'd used the same fabric for her bathroom curtains. Bobby was the card-shuffling man from outside. A few other residents had gathered. Claudine introduced them, but Ruby immediately forgot their names. Their professions, had she been told, she would have remembered.

Tinkerbell was glued to the manager's side, and he palmed her what looked like a scrap of ham. The manager—heck, all the men—watched Deborah like she had the fairy wand to produce beer. The kids stood, mouths agape in rapt fascination.

"Welcome, children," Claudine's father said. "We hope you'll be happy here."

"I think you all are in for a bit of a shake-up," Ruby said.

The dog belched.

Chapter Thirteen

R uby glanced at her watch. An hour until the hearing. She unclamped the curling iron.

"You're not done yet," Gilda said. "Finish me. This weather makes my hair all flyaway."

"I've got just a minute before I have to leave for the county building." Gilda was right, though. Humidity mounted in the air. Summer was trying one last stand, but all its heat had condensed into black clouds that had darkened the afternoon enough that Ruby clicked on the overhead light. She pulled her silk shirt from her damp chest.

Gilda pouted in the mirror Ruby had set up in the retirement home's dinner room. "That curl by my ear isn't long enough. It needs to be longer. Look at the photo. What do you think, Hank?"

Claudine's father looked up from the book in his lap. The book was some kind of exhibition catalog for jewelry—at least, a diamond- and ruby-studded tiara was on its cover. His perusal seemed half-hearted. Really, she was surprised he was downstairs instead of taking one of his many daily naps.

"Looks beautiful, hon," he said. "You're a real magician, Ruby."

Ruby grabbed a comb and skimmed it over Gilda's hennaed head. Where were the kids, anyway? During the week, Deborah had enrolled them in school. Thanks to resident Villa expertise, it was easy to forge birth certificates. Deborah insisted on buying them backpacks and school clothes. She'd told the school's staff that the kids had just moved to Carsonville, and she was a cousin helping them get enrolled while their parents were at work.

But school should be out by now. Ruby lifted her head from the curling iron and found Scotty near the fireplace chatting with Eddie, who was hooked to his oxygen tank. They seemed to be focusing on something between them. A board game? The man moved three small shells. Shoot.

"Just a minute, Gilda." Ruby dropped the comb and charged toward them. "You," she said to the man. "What are you teaching this child?"

The man put up his hands in mock surrender. "What? It's just a game."

"Just fraud. Come on, Scotty. Pay him no attention." She hadn't had a moment's rest since she'd arrived. Maybe when they'd moved in, the residents had to sign an oath that they'd leave their professions behind, but they still considered it sporting to practice. She'd be lucky if she had tires on her car when she left.

"Hmm." Gilda lazily scratched between her breasts.

Ruby's eyebrow went up. "Hand it over."

"What?"

"Whatever you stole from my bag. Where'd you put it? Your bra?"

Gilda sniffed and pulled from her blouse one of Ruby's best lipsticks, a Dior she'd boosted from Klingle's.

"Thief," Ruby muttered.

"Look who's talking," Gilda retorted.

"Sit back and shut up. I'm almost done with your hair, then

I've got to leave."

"Hi, Ruby. Hi, Gilda." Deborah breezed into the dinner room.

"There's our sunshine," said Eddie from the fireplace. He'd put away the shells and now had a well-worn copy of *True Crime* in his lap. "The sunshine of Villa Saint Nicholas."

When Deb hadn't been at Ruby's helping her work up a statement in support of selling the firehouse, she'd been at the retirement home with the kids. She and Lucy had sewn curtains for the TV room, both to give the boys some privacy and to cheer up the décor. She'd even started training the dog. Tinkerbell could roll over on command, especially if she got a belly rub mid-roll.

"You look very professional," Ruby said.

Deborah smoothed a hand over her wool dress. "Thanks."

"Listen, after the hearing we need to talk about what to do with the kids. I saw Lucy taking apart a lock yesterday, and Hugo's been spending too much time in the garage with Father Vincent. They don't need to pick up any bad habits."

"I've been worried, too." Deborah examined her feet. "I asked Louie again if we could take them home, just for a little while, but he needs his quiet."

"The house is so big, though. Couldn't he just shut himself up in the den?"

Deborah's gaze stayed on her feet.

What Ruby thought about Louie wasn't worth saying aloud. "Anyway. How are you feeling about tonight?"

"Nervous."

"Honey, you'll be great. We practiced, remember?" She unplugged the curling iron and turned to Gilda. "Your curls look fine."

Thunder rumbled in the background.

***

"I'm still really nervous," Deborah said. She'd given only one presentation in her life, and that was to sell Girl Scout cookies at a church potluck. These stakes were a lot higher.

"And wet." Ruby shook rain from her Chihuahua-patterned umbrella. On their drive to the county building, the sky hung leaden until the moment they reached the parking lot. Then it burst like an over-filled water balloon.

"Where should we sit?" Deborah asked.

The county commissioners' hearing room was laid out like a small baseball diamond, with the commissioners' dais at home plate, and chairs for the audience in the outfield. A desk for a recorder and another for witnesses were stationed where batting cages would be.

"Close to the front. Not many people here," Ruby said. A few men, street people, maybe, lingered toward the back, perhaps waiting for free coffee to come out. Four people in suits sat closer to the front. One snapped open a briefcase.

Deborah nudged Ruby. "Look. Who's that?"

"Whoever they are, they have money. And are getting paid by someone with even more of it." She squinted. "Public relations. That's my guess. Or lawyers."

Lawyers. She was no match for lawyers. Ruby handed her a water bottle, and she took a long draw.

They settled a few rows behind the suited team. Ruby pulled out her leopard-print cheaters and glanced at the photocopied agenda on her seat. "Looks like we're on about halfway through the meeting, and another witness is right after us." She looked at Deborah, her eyes curiously magnified behind the lenses. "Must be them." She nodded toward the suits. "For the developer who wants the place. Then the vote."

"The vote," Deborah repeated. Her stomach churned with nerves. Why had Ruby and Claudine decided she should be the one to read the testimony? Commissioner Rossum might listen more closely, they'd said, but she doubted it. They told her it would be easy. Read the statement, smile. That's all.

Deborah's phone chattered with birdsong. Louie? Maybe he'd texted to wish her well. He knew this was an important day. Too bad he couldn't make it, but the Carsonville Warblers Association was meeting. She glanced at the screen, and her face fell. Ruby raised an eyebrow.

"Ned Rossum sent me a text," Deborah said.

"Rossum the Possum. Well, what does it say?"

"Nice2CU cutie."

"Weenie the size of a gherkin pickle, you can count on it," Ruby said.

Deborah smiled wanly toward the dais, then turned toward the door, mostly to avoid any further eye contact. Claudine arrived, close behind a group of other people. Somehow, she looked like she'd walked in from an old movie. She seemed to be drawn in cream and gray, like the photos in Grandpa Granzer's album, always watching, always thinking. She nodded toward Ruby and Deborah, then settled on the other side of the audience. As they'd agreed, she'd remain anonymous.

"Alert at eleven o'clock," Ruby whispered.

Commissioner Rossum was bearing down on them. "Deborah." He put a hand on her shoulder.

She was tempted to peel his hand off, but she knew she had to make nice—at least until the hearing was over. "Hi, Commissioner. This is my first public meeting. I can't wait to see you in action." She forced a smile.

"I'm glad you could make it. I look forward to your testimony." He glanced at his watch, a low-end Rolex, and Deborah froze. It was nearly a duplicate of the one she'd stolen. She wondered if it had the same engraving on its back, "Faithful for all time."

"We'll get started in a few minutes."

"Cutie," Ruby mumbled, then cleared her throat and pretended to cough.

Rossum straightened his tie. "I keep thinking I know you from somewhere, but I can't place it."

Deborah's heart leapt to her throat. "I don't know how. I don't know a lot of important people like you."

"Well, then. Back to work." He strode toward the dais, stopping to shake hands with the suits seated near the front row.

A moment later, Deborah's phone chirped again. Louie? Rossum again, letting her know he was free after the meeting if she wanted to get a drink. She glanced up at the dais to find him staring fixedly at her. Shoot. He was going to make her too nervous to read. At least the testimony was tucked in her bag, safe and reviewed a dozen times.

"Relax, honey." Ruby patted her hand. "It's all going to be fine. Eventually."

* * *

Claudine settled into a seat near the back. Maybe a few dozen people had turned out for the hearing, probably because of the news piece, but the room was far from full. Deborah kept glancing at her phone, then sticking out her lip in exasperation. Judging from Commissioner Rossum's fixed stare from the dais,

Claudine would be willing to bet he was texting her. Ruby fanned herself with the agenda.

Toward the front was the developer's team. Couldn't be anyone else. Likely it was a PR person or two and a lawyer. There was a good chance the developer wouldn't even show up tonight. Why should he—or, thinking of Ellie—she? His well paid team—from the cut of clothes and quality of shoes, that much was evident—would take care of business. They spoke the same language as the commissioners.

If the developer were Ellie, she'd be there all right. She'd never miss a front row seat to potential victory. Claudine just had to hope that the Boosters' appeal to social responsibility with a touch of emotion tossed in would be more powerful.

People trickled in, and all of the commissioners' seats at the dais were occupied. The chair, an older woman with a long history in local politics, sat in the middle, with the four other commissioners, each representing a different area in the county, beside her.

A couple slipped into the room. Claudine could see only the backs of their heads. The woman was tall and dressed in pearls and a meticulous dove-gray wrap dress that would flatter either a businesswoman or a lady-who-lunched. She lit on a chair at the opposite end of Claudine's row. Claudine leaned forward to catch her profile. Ellie Whiteby. Claudine drew a quick breath. Ellie Whiteby was here. That sealed it.

The man—her husband, probably—was equally crisply dressed. He seemed to be holding—could it be?—a book of crossword puzzles.

The chair rapped her gavel on the table. "I will now call the meeting to order."

"Bobby, don't run over my skirt," a woman said.

Gilda? Claudine cursed under her breath.

Her father was right behind Gilda. He should be at home, in bed, so soon after his operation. Bobby pushed Hank's wheelchair into the hearing room, and Gilda followed, gripping her walker, but still managing a seductive sway to her hips. Father Vincent, fully tricked out in long black priest's attire, took up the rear.

Claudine half rose from her seat to tell her father to go home, then lowered herself when she met his disapproving stare. Serve the family by serving the job, it seemed to say, and at the moment this was the job. She hesitated, then turned her attention to the front of the room. Maybe, she convinced herself, just maybe they'd come simply to watch. Maybe they were here to support her, and they'd be quiet. At least they'd left the Rizzio kids at the Villa.

"Holy Mother of Christ." Father Vincent's voice boomed through the room. "Could you walk any slower?"

The whole crowd turned to watch the foursome make their way to the handicapped seating area at the front. Smiling, Gilda looked right, then left as she traversed the room. If it weren't for the firm grip on her walker, she'd probably be waving. Claudine had to admit that her hair looked fabulous—nightclub-ready. Father Vincent's robes still emitted a hint of incense, along with the stench of the cigarillos he smoked. Bobby's cap was low over his forehead as he pushed Hank's wheelchair.

Her father. His face looked shrunken and colorless, but his eyes held that steely determination. He breathed shallowly. Her heart flooded with concern—and warmth that he'd come to support her.

"If everyone is settled," the chair said, "we'll get started."

Chapter Fourteen

During the meeting's business drudge—the approval of the minutes, a budget modification, a mind-numbing proposal by the county attorney on proposed tax law changes—Claudine's attention ping-ponged from Eleanor Millhouse and her husband, to her father, to the crisp-suited team. The hearing had all the ingredients for a fine explosion: fuel, air, and a spark. If only they could be kept separate.

Rain drummed on the windows as the meeting slogged on. At last, the firehouse came up. Claudine sat up straighter. This was it.

"The county calls Deborah Granzer to the stand," the chair said.

Deborah, dropping her phone into her purse after an exasperated glance at its screen, grabbed her folder. Ruby patted her arm. Commissioner Rossum's head swiveled to follow her. Deborah had only three minutes for her statement. She and Ruby had practiced over the past week, she knew, but Claudine hadn't heard it yet.

Deborah took the lectern and smiled. One thing Claudine could say about Deborah was that she was engaging. She might spend most of her time cleaning house, but when she was on the stand, no one could look away. She radiated sincerity.

Claudine stole another glance toward Ellie and her husband.

With a calm smile, Ellie watched Deborah. Her husband scratched through a puzzle, barely pausing.

Deborah looked down at her prepared testimony. Her smile morphed into shock. Claudine held her breath. Something wasn't right. Deborah glanced up at the audience, then back to her papers before pushing them away.

"Thank you for the opportunity to support selling the old firehouse. Over the past few months, I've gotten to know some young people who turned to the firehouse for shelter. They'd been split apart in foster families, but after their mother's death, they wanted to be together. I think it's all right to talk about it now." Her voice was gentle, honest. Persuasive. But she wasn't reading. She was winging it, Claudine was sure. "Just like how the firehouse was used in the past to save people's lives, even as it sits abandoned it continues to do good."

Claudine noticed the public relations team listening attentively. One of them made a few notes in a legal pad. Ruby, sitting, behind them, seemed mystified.

"A group of us—"

A very small group, Claudine added silently.

"—called the Booster Club hope to buy the old firehouse in the warehouse district and renovate it as a family shelter. The firehouse is structurally sound, and its layout is already largely suitable. We have a donor willing to pay for the building, and we've collected a solid sum toward renovations. Right now, there's nowhere in Carsonville a homeless family can stay together." She swallowed. "Say you're a mom and you lose your job. You can't afford to pay the rent. You don't know anyone in town with a house big enough to take you in. Well, right now in Carsonville, you're on the street." Rain thrummed on the hearing room's windows. Thunder rumbled like a growling mastiff. "Worse, say you're kids, and both your parents are gone. In that case, at least there's foster care. But most families can't take in more than two kids, so you get split up. You've already lost your parents. Now you lose each other."

Deborah glanced toward the lectern. "I had a bunch of statistics about how families who stay together are healthier and more successful, but I must have grabbed the wrong papers. So I guess that's all I have to say. But please, commissioners, vote to grant us the firehouse. It's the first step toward doing something important for Carsonville's families—especially the children."

The audience was silent. Someone may have sniffed. Lightning flashed outside.

"Do the commissioners have any questions?" the chair asked.

A bald man whose campaign materials boasted "Carsonville Cares for Calvin" said, "Say we sold you the firehouse. Say you managed to fix it up for families. How would you get the money to operate it? Shelters are expensive to run."

Claudine knew Deborah had prepared this answer. "Should the sale go through, the Booster Club will incorporate as a nonprofit and raise funds throughout the year."

This was, in fact, how the Villa ran. The criminal community pitched in two percent of its earnings, and Art Weinstein invested the proceeds. Any of the tithers who retired and were willing to abide by the Villa's no-crime rule were eligible for an open spot.

"The fact that we can raise enough money to buy and renovate the firehouse in the first place shows we're more than capable of funding its operations," Deborah finished. "We'd contract with the county, of course."

Ned Rossum leaned toward the microphone. He beamed over the audience as if expecting applause. The few dozen people present looked on dully. "I'd also like to congratulate you on such a worthy mission. That's remarkable." Again a pause, and again no reaction from the crowd. "There are many ways to help families, though, and one way is to provide jobs, not services. We want to offer a hand up, not a handout."

Isn't that original, Claudine thought. A regular Shakespeare, he is.

"You mean we should put the children to work?" Deborah asked, her face all innocence. "I thought that was against the law."

Gilda tittered, as did a few people in the audience.

"No, I mean we give the parents jobs, then they can afford the rent."

Deborah looked perplexed. "How do you give a dead mom a job?"

Bobby guffawed from his seat between Gilda and Hank.

"Never mind," the chair said. "Any other questions from the dais? No?"

Not bad, Claudine thought. From her seat, she couldn't see the audience's faces, but the shushed attention they paid Deborah spoke volumes. When she stepped down, Ruby clapped, and so did the crowd from Villa Saint Nicholas, with Gilda stamping her walker on the ground. Deborah lowered herself in her seat, and Ruby turned to her asking something. Deborah shrugged her shoulders and handed her the testimony, which Ruby held at arm's length until she slipped on her reading glasses.

"Next we have Marcus Pickering from Pickering and Pickering public relations."

A suited man with the bearing of a game show host took the stand. "Thank you, Madame Chair, and thank you to the representative of the Booster Club, who expressed so eloquently the group's deep care for Carsonville's families and youth. We at Pickering and Pickering speak for our client as well as ourselves when we say that we share your concern. After all, children are our city's future." He smiled.

Claudine knew a con man when she saw one, and Mr. PR had flimflam coursing through his veins.

"That's why we're doing something vital for the community as well. Our client has already purchased parcels of land surrounding the firehouse with the goal of creating a riverside district offering vital public services."

Ruby's hand shot up, but the PR man studiously looked away. With a calm flick of his wrist, he turned on a projector. "Would someone darken the lights, please?"

The next few minutes were spent on slides showing a glass and steel building with marble floors and lush landscaping. The "vital public services" appeared to include a salon, penthouse condos, and a cocktail bar with stiletto-clad women drinking from martini glasses. The last slide, a marvel of architectural beauty, morphed into a shot of the firehouse as it stood now, with boarded-up windows and ferns growing from its brick walls.

"I think you'll agree that the high-rise complex, including Carsonville's new spa, the Shangri-La Too, is a vast improvement over an aging and unsafe firehouse." The PR man's smile turned to a sigh. "Sadly, the children who lived at the firehouse seem to have abandoned it. Or perhaps they've been picked up and sent to juvenile detention or—we can only hope—foster homes."

Damn it. Could that have been why someone tried to break into the firehouse—to get the kids to leave? They hadn't thought moving them to Villa Saint Nicholas would hurt their case. More importantly, how had they discovered that the kids already lived there?

"Of course, we were concerned for the children's safety," the man continued. "Right away we tracked down their foster care files to see if we could find relatives who might care for them." He paused for dramatic effect. "The children's mother, Wanda Rizzio, had died in jail. She was a criminal, I'm sorry to say. Insurance fraud. She bilked law-abiding business owners out of tens of thousands of dollars."

Claudine shifted in her seat in a combination of anger and disappointment. She wanted to smack that smirk right off the PR man's face. She knew that every cent of Wanda's earnings had gone toward keeping her family healthy. When she died, her bank account was nearly empty.

"Do the commissioners have any questions?" the chair asked.

As before, the bald commissioner was the first to raise his hand. "Do you already have funding lined up for the project?"

"Thank you, commissioner, for that insightful question. Why, yes, we do. The developer is investing her own funds. We're not relying on outside funding at this point. Purchases against the businesses will fund half of the project."

Rossum glanced at a note card. "Is it true that this project will provide nearly fifty jobs for Carsonville residents?"

Claudine rolled her eyes. How did this man stay in office? He had "business patsy" written all over him. Handy how he already knew the job count.

"Thank you, commissioner. You've put your finger on one of this project's greatest benefits. It's an economic engine. Yes, besides the hundreds who will participate in building it, the complex will employ janitors, security people, beauticians, and more. Those people will take their paychecks into Carsonville to buy groceries and other goods, which will, in turn, help businesses throughout the city."

A few more smarmy questions like this bandied between Mr. PR and the commissioners. Claudine felt sick. Ellie was going to win. There was no stopping her. And the children would be left without a home.

The chair pulled the microphone forward. "Do we have any questions from the audience?"

"Yes." The deep voice came from near the front. Father Vincent. He took the microphone beside the dais. His black robes swished as he moved.

"Your name, please."

"Father Vincent Samboni, Madame Chair."

Claudine's family hadn't been much for going to church, and she'd never experienced Father Vincent at the pulpit. Seeing him now, stately in his crisp collar, she practically heard the organ music.

"Commissioners. Fellow citizens of Carsonville. In this room tonight, we have the opportunity to do something good. Something moral. It our chance to be merciful and care for our flock, just as the Lord cares for us."

There was no soothing organ music, no altar brimming with flowers, but the audience seemed more alert. Even the rain calmed to a gentle patter. Claudine began to relax just a little. Given his bearing, she wasn't sure why Father Vincent wasn't Pope, or at least a cardinal.

The priest's voice reverberated through the hearing room. "Tonight, I heard a poor woman denounced because she had strayed from the path of the Lord. Her children's bond was deemed unimportant. We don't know their mother's circumstance. We don't know the choices she faced. We don't know the goodness she contained within herself." He lowered his voice a touch for dramatic effect. "We don't know the grace

God bequeathed her."

Perhaps he was laying it on just a bit thick, Claudine thought. The audience, though, sat enraptured.

"Let me remind you that in this world, there's book law and there's God's law. Those who profit while others suffer will face their judgment at the final reckoning. But tonight we have the opportunity to be merciful." He paused once again. "A city's goodness is not in its pocketbook but in its mercy. It is by giving to others that we become a true community. By giving the firehouse to the community to protect those of us less fortunate, you are truly doing God's work. Bless you." He stepped down, and moving with the dignity of a papal cortege, retook his seat.

The commissioners' expressions were unreadable. Eleanor Millhouse's face was equally placid. Claudine could only hope Father Vincent had swayed just enough votes their way.

One of the commissioners who had been quiet so far, a plump brunette, asked, "So you're saying it's okay to break the law? Is that what I hear?"

"Or maybe it's better to pass laws that line your pockets?" Gilda shouted.

Claudine cringed.

The PR man cut in. "I'd like to make an announcement."

"Yes. Please proceed to the microphone."

"The father's words were very moving. On behalf of our client, we would like to present a check for $25,000 toward a new family shelter built elsewhere. With the Booster Club's obvious resourcefulness, they'll quickly find the perfect location."

Anger burned slow and steady through Claudine's bloodstream. They—Ellie—had this planned, just in case.

"That's quite generous," the chair said. Ned Rossum leaned

back, the worry erased from his forehead. "If there aren't any other comments, we'll vote."

"They called Wanda Rizzio a criminal. Well, I'll tell you who the baddie is. It's them." Gilda, near tears, stood at her walker. Deborah knelt at Gilda's side and placed a hand on her arm.

Commissioner Rossum studiously kept his eyes away from Deborah. "Transforming a dangerous eyesore into an engine of beauty and prosperity serves all of Carsonville's citizens. We're lucky to have a developer willing to take this on. We cannot vote any other way." He spoke as if he'd memorized the words.

Claudine bent her head. It was no use listening to the commissioners vote. She knew how it would turn out.

"The ayes have it," the Chair concluded. "The county has made a preliminary commitment to sell the firehouse to" —she read from a card— "Eleanor Millhouse of Fine Properties of Distinction. We'll meet again in two weeks when papers are drawn to finalize the sale. The meeting is adjourned." The chair banged her gavel one last time.

Safely hidden in the crowd, Claudine glanced again at Ellie and her husband. Ellie's calm smile hadn't changed the whole evening. She knew she'd get what she wanted. She'd never doubted.

Two decades of rage surged through her system. Ellie was not going to get away with it this time.

Chapter Fifteen

Let's meet at your place. Claudine's text flashed across Ruby's phone as she and Deborah crossed the parking lot. What could Claudine have to say at this point? Ruby wasn't particularly interested in wallowing in their loss. Not when she could be getting even instead. She set her purse on the car's roof and unlocked the door.

Deborah appeared to be near tears. "The kids."

"What happened to the speech?"

"I don't know. I had it in my bag—I saw it at the Villa. But when I took it out it was a flyer for Mighty Mart." Deborah slid into the seat next to her. She'd left her car at the Villa, and they'd driven downtown together.

Ruby slapped her forehead with her palm. "Your bag was in the cafeteria, right? Where Eddie was showing Scotty card tricks?"

"You don't think—"

Ruby backed out the car. "Not think. Know. Scotty is now skilled in 'the drop,' and our speech is probably on an end table. All by accident, of course." She groaned. "Claudine wants to meet at the salon. Mind a detour before I drop you at the Villa for your car?"

"Maybe she has a plan." Deborah dug in her purse for a tissue. "But I don't know what we can do. We lost the firehouse. And the kids...."

When they arrived, Claudine's car—she was driving the Accord, not her Mercedes, this time—was already idling in front of the house. She cut the engine just as Ruby pulled into the driveway.

They came through the kitchen door, on the side. The muffled sound of gunfire erupted from the TV set in the den. Three Chihuahuas barreled into the kitchen, sniffed everyone's feet, then scampered back toward the den. Ruby grabbed a bottle of tequila from a cupboard and looped her bag over her arm. "Bruce is watching Diehard again. We have plenty of time to talk. Let's go to the salon. It's quieter."

Claudine took a seat in one of the two hairdressing stations, and Deborah pulled up a small side chair. Ruby had to admire the way Claudine looked so regal and removed in the salon, like a tiny corner of the salon was playing an old noir movie. Ruby poured them each a shot.

Claudine downed her tequila in one go and set the glass on the vanity. "We know the developer for sure now."

Ruby dug into her bag and waved a file folder in the air. "Yep. I liberated this from the PR lady's briefcase when she was snickering at Gilda." Ruby unfolded her reading glasses. "Eleanor Millhouse, Developer of Fine Properties and two-timing fink President of the Carsonville Women's League." She looked up. "That last part wasn't on her card."

"But should be," Deborah said.

"Yes. Ellie Whiteby," Claudine said. "I knew her in high school. She was everywhere. Homecoming queen, champion equestrienne, class president, valedictorian."

Ruby refilled Claudine's glass.

Tequila untouched, Deborah stood at the front window staring at the lights of the traffic moving down the hill. "What does it matter now, anyway?"

"We should have anticipated she'd make sure she had the whole thing sealed up tight before she even made a move to buy the firehouse." The second shot of tequila streamed through Ruby's blood. Lauren Bacall, that's who Claudine reminded her of. Lauren Bacall in *Key Largo*.

"She definitely has Rossum sealed up," Claudine said. "Tight. Ellie always had to be right. She got mad that we nearly squelched her plans for a spa. We almost bested her. There's no way she'd let us get away with that."

"So what?" Deborah said. Ruby didn't think she'd ever heard her raise her voice. "So what? Why are we here? Why don't we just go pack up the kids and send them back to foster homes?"

"Is that what you want?" Claudine said.

That tone—it was unrelenting. Lord, that girl was competitive, Ruby thought. "I get it that you carry a grudge against the developer, but what can we do? With the way she's been moving, she'll have bulldozers down there before breakfast."

"You heard the chair. The sale isn't final for two weeks," Claudine said. "She's counting on us walking away. Is that what you want to do? Split up the kids and give in just because of one hearing with a greedy developer?"

"I don't see what we could do at this point," Deborah said. "We gave it our best shot."

Squealing cars sounded from the television in the next room. Ruby shut the door between the rooms.

"We have skills," Claudine said. "She doesn't know I'm involved yet, either. And everyone has a weak spot. All we need to do is find that weak spot and exploit it. We tried playing clean, and it didn't work. Now it's time to try another way."

Could it be Claudine's tequila talking? She'd only had one

shot. Ruby'd had to drag Claudine into the Boosters kicking and screaming, and now she insisted on following through. "I seem to remember that you weren't so hot on the whole idea to start with."

Claudine ignored her. "Are you two in?"

"What do you mean about 'another way'?" Deborah asked.

"It's like Father Vincent said," Claudine replied. "There's the government's law and there's God's law. We're in the right here. We want to do something for homeless families. Ellie Millhouse wants to make money at their expense. We just have to find another way to make it happen."

"I'm in," Ruby said. "If you really think you can find something, I'm behind you all the way. I don't appreciate this kind of disrespect."

Claudine turned. "Deborah?"

"They talked bad about the kids and their mom. It was awful. Practically called them juvenile delinquents."

"They might be, if we don't help them," Ruby said. The truth was, they might be delinquents, especially if they helped them. But there was a vast world between the righteous but self-centered do-gooder and the kind-hearted person who bent the law a bit. Witness Eleanor Millhouse.

"Then you can count me in, too." She sighed and dropped into a chair. "What are we going to tell the kids?"

"Dad and Gilda might have already taken care of that."

* * *

The next morning when Ruby arrived at Villa Saint Nicholas with Deborah riding shotgun, Claudine was already there.

Ruby had been dreading seeing the Rizzio kids. Even though the battle for the firehouse wasn't over, last night's decision wasn't a great first step. When Ruby pulled in her Volvo, the Villa's front door burst open, and the Rizzio kids came running out. With smiles on their faces.

"I knew you could do it," Lucy said.

"I was worried when I saw I'd forgotten to put back the real speech, but Deborah did great, anyway," Scotty said.

"I wouldn't—" Deborah started.

Claudine stood outside the door, hands on hips. "They told the kids the sale was delayed, but that it was only a matter of time before we got the land."

"Uh-huh," Ruby said. "I see." A setup.

After checking the back seat for a donut box, Hugo joined the group. He looked purposefully from woman to woman. "This means a lot to us. There's no way you can understand just how much."

Ruby knew exactly how they felt. When her father left, he disappeared so completely that she found him again only when she was in her late thirties and had the money to hire a private investigator. By then her father had Alzheimer's and didn't recognize her. Her dreams of revenge, of how she'd tell him about their mother's death, then how they lived on the streets, were quashed.

"Poor darlings," Deborah said and leaned forward to hug Joanie. Tinkerbell thumped her tail against the car's bumper.

"Now if that isn't the sweetest thing I've seen in years," Gilda said from behind them.

Gilda. That fink. "Nobody asked you to butt in last night."

"What do you kids know about show business, anyway?" Gilda rattled her walker. "Deb's statement was dull. Poor little kids, blah blah blah. Nice firehouse, blah blah blah. You needed some pizzazz."

Ruby pulled her into the Villa, away from the kids. "Yeah, well, it might have cost us the firehouse, that's what. The commissioners weren't real interested in hearing about the good reasons for breaking the law."

"You lost that firehouse yourself," Gilda said. "The developer hired himself a pack of high-end snake oil salesmen. You didn't stand a chance."

"Herself. The developer's a woman, Eleanor Millhouse."

"Eleanor Mill—you mean Ellie Whiteby?"

Ruby nodded. "You saw her."

"I didn't put it together." Gilda cackled. "Oh, yes. You'll get that firehouse all right. Claudine won't let it go any other way. Ellie Whiteby. She's so clean she probably poops cotton balls." She turned toward the TV room and yelled, "Hank, get in here. Wait until you hear who the developer is."

Eddie ambled up, trailing his oxygen tank. "Hello, Ruby. Gilda here tell you you're in luck? We talked it over. We're going to help you get the firehouse."

Chapter Sixteen

Claudine stuck her head into the TV room. Hugo and Scotty's sleeping bags were rolled up and stowed in a corner, but the boys were nowhere to be seen. As she'd anticipated, the room's only occupant was Grady, dwarfed by his recliner.

"Hey, Deanie," he said without taking his eyes from the screen.

"Hi. I'm going to come down in a minute to talk to you. I need your help."

"No can do. My shows are on."

"I might have an incentive."

He rolled his head in a "maybe yes, maybe no" motion. "Later. After my show."

Upstairs, Claudine knocked once, then let herself in. Her father was lying in bed, looking over the neglected vegetable garden toward the school yard. He seemed smaller, somehow. The overcast sky filled the room with gray light.

"Deanie," he said. "Come sit over here and talk to me." He patted the chair near his bed.

"You don't look so good."

"It's nothing," he said. "It's just taking me a while to recover from that operation." His words came slowly. "I was sorry to see about the firehouse. I know you really got invested in those kids."

"How are they doing? You see them much?"

"Joanie, she brings up my breakfast most mornings. Doesn't say much, but she's a sweet girl." Hank swallowed. "The kids are okay, but they can't stay much longer."

"Are they getting in the way?" Having four kids and a dog around would turn the place upside down, but she hadn't heard many complaints.

"No. That's not the problem. I think Vinny's giving them a lesson on chop shops. In the garage. I don't know that they need to be like us. The life has its drawbacks."

"Dad." Claudine noted his pale skin, his shrunken hands. "I've never heard you say that before."

He turned to the window. Leaves blew from the oak tree in the schoolyard. "The hearing last night got me thinking."

Claudine watched him without replying. She'd expected him to launch into his usual lecture about how they stole from people who had more than was good for them anyway, about how the home security industry and the police owed their jobs to them, about how the criminal element had been a part of society since the saber-toothed tiger stole from the mastodon. This time he surprised her.

"I regret not getting you into college."

"You didn't have a choice. I was caught stealing, remember?"

Hank shifted and turned back to Claudine. "André found his way. He found his niche. We could have got you into college. We could have had some references made up—heck, we could have got you into Harvard if we'd wanted."

This time Claudine didn't reply because her throat was choked with emotion.

"The truth is—the truth is, Deanie, that I didn't want you to go away. I missed your mother a lot. You remind me of her. If you'd gone off and done something else with your life, maybe you wouldn't have ever come back." He put a hand on hers. "Or you'd have been ashamed to."

"Dad," was all she could manage to say for a moment. Claudine plumped his pillow, then sat in the chair next to him.

"I'm sorry, sweetie."

"Don't be sorry. I'm happy for every moment I have with you." Her father's expression tightened. Claudine abruptly changed the subject. "Well, we haven't given up on the firehouse yet. I'm going to see if Grady can help me dig up some dirt on the developer."

"You be careful."

"Of course I'll be careful," she replied absently. All these years later. She might have gone to college after all. She looked at his hand speckled with liver spots. But she would have been away from family.

"I mean, you're doing this for good reasons, right? Not just out of pride. Not just because it's Ellie Whiteby." Her father's gaze drilled into her. "I know you never forgave her."

She looked away. "We're doing it for the Rizzio kids."

"Not that I blame you for holding a grudge. From the looks of it, she hasn't changed a bit. Wound up tighter than a duck's hind end. Always has to win."

"Honestly, Dad."

"Because if you were doing it out of pride, then you're no better than she."

Claudine wandered to the window at the foot of her father's bed. The school bell rang, an old fashioned clanging quickly followed by kids yelling as they filtered into the school yard. How much did pride motivate her? Maybe it didn't matter. The cause was good.

"I know," she said.

"Anyway, tell me about the heist," her father said. "Saw the Oz the other day. Sounds like everything is moving ahead."

"Yeah, we're in good shape. Less than two weeks now." Claudine kissed his cheek.

Her father studied her a moment before turning again to the window. "Honey, I'm tired. You go roust Grady."

* * *

"Whatever you're selling, I ain't buying." Grady kept his gaze on the TV. "And you can take those danged kids with you."

Claudine rolled her eyes. "How was your last visit to the doctor?"

Grady shot a quick glance toward her before returning to the dancing cartoon characters extolling the virtues of frozen pizza rolls on TV. "All right, I guess. Not getting any younger. I got the usual complaints."

She manufactured a sigh. "All those special diets the doctors want you on these days. How you bear it, I just don't know."

Grady shifted in the recliner, his bones jutting beneath his skin. "You're telling me. At ninety-two years old I should be able to eat whatever the hell I want. So my cholesterol's a little high. So I don't get a lot of exercise. When I was a bookie, I sat at the phones all day, and I was in great shape. Besides, I'm thin. Look at me. Skin and bones."

Claudine knew that despite his low-salt diet he was allowed a weekly treat, and she also knew the cook wasn't given to making a lot of exceptions. Cook had enough to do to juggle the diets of fourteen elderly residents as it was. Plus the kids, now.

"Too bad about that, because I just happen to have some frozen macaroni and cheese. And beef stroganoff. They're starting to get a little soft. I should get them in the oven soon."

Grady swallowed. "Hungry-man sized?"

"You know it."

He stared at the screen. A blonde with a nurse's cap slapped a stethoscope-carrying doctor. "You idiot," he told the TV. "Don't you know he's carrying on with the Meisenheimer twins?"

"Stroganoff and mac and cheese."

Grady looked at her, then looked at the TV. "They take one hour and twenty minutes to cook with both in the oven. I'll give you that much time, but that's all."

"I'll meet you in your room."

When Claudine arrived upstairs after her visit to the kitchen, Grady's door was ajar. She pushed it open to reveal a room resembling the control tower of an airport. A desk with a computer and three screens dominated one wall, and a shelf with more computer equipment, including his own server, took up another. He'd shed his housecoat and settled at the desk.

"All right. Lay it on me," the ex-bookie said.

Claudine told him about Ellie. She explained how finding some kind of dirt on her could help them save the firehouse.

"You didn't tell me this would get those kids out of the house. I might have helped you out for only a chicken pot pie. Give me spelling and approximate year of birth. You say she's lived in Carsonville all her life?"

"She may have gone away for college, but she lived here in high school and lives here now."

"Yeah. In a real sweet place on Silver Ridge." Grady's fingers had been working the keyboard while she talked, and two of the screens were full of information.

When Grady had retired from bookmaking, he'd discovered computers. The same brain that could juggle the odds across scores of sports teams turned out to be well suited to computer hacking. Claudine's father had told her Grady was now a legendary cyberpunk. Other hackers thought he was a sixteen-year-old Croatian and probably didn't pick up that his online moniker, Britney Wilson, was a nurse on *Weeks of Our Lives*.

"Looks nice," Claudine said of Ellie's home. Photos from a design magazine's website showed white shag carpeting and a marble entryway with a chandelier. A mirrored wall reflected puffy white furniture. It was immaculate, like Ellie herself.

"Looks like a set from *The Young and the Nervous*," Grady said. "Anyway, that's just the public stuff. Let's see what we get if we dig around in back. Have a seat." He gestured toward a chair covered with back issues of *Soap Opera Digest* and one of *Arthritis Today*.

Claudine sat silently while his knobby fingers clacked the keyboard. Every once in a while he took a note in his shaky hand before returning to the keyboard. The computer screens glowed almost blue in the dim light. Oswald would be waiting for a message from her to finalize plans for the heist. Soon she'd be finished with stealing. What she'd do next, she didn't know. Spend more time with her father, that's for sure.

"Not getting much," Grady said finally. "Excellent credit score, no priors, dean's list at college. Longstanding member of her church. She's had a subscription to Gracious Living for ten years." He turned toward her. "Frankly, she sounds like a real pain in the ass."

"She is. Kind of a control freak. Nothing on her business?"

"Looks like she specializes in buying properties, demolishing whatever was on them, and putting up something new."

"Anything in particular?"

"Lots of different stuff. Apartment complexes, big houses. Here's a strip mall." Grady scrolled down the screen. "Huh. Here's something. Nothing illegal, mind you. But it's interesting."

Claudine stood. "What?"

"She's been buying condemned houses for a good price, then selling the lots as a plot. This sewage treatment plant, for instance." He tapped the screen. "She bought seventeen houses condemned by the county. According to property tax records, she got them at about half price. The old property owners weren't too happy about it, either. Here's a news story from a couple of years ago, part one, but it looks like the reporter never followed up. No part two."

I bet, Claudine thought. She pulled up a chair. "Where are these properties?"

"East side. Poorer neighborhood. Unlucky sods," Grady said. "Probably had the county pull their houses right out from under them."

"And with those minuscule buy-outs they'd never be able to afford another place." Claudine would bet it all that Ellie had something going with the county. They'd condemn properties and value them low, and she'd sweep in and buy them just above the county's offer—probably with a little something for particular election campaigns in return. Like Ned Rossum's. The people they displaced didn't have the money to hire a lawyer and fight it. The county could claim it as economic development.

"You know, they carp on and on about crooks, and then you find something like this," Grady said.

"Can't be legal, but can't be proven."

"But their mothers would be ashamed." Grady massaged his

hands. The typing must be bothering his arthritis. "Let's see if we can dig up something on the girl's husband."

"Thank you, Grady." She'd load the freezer with frozen dinners the next time she visited.

After another ten minutes of switching between screens and mumbling, he swiveled toward her. "The husband, a Roger Millhouse, got a divorce about ten years ago. The wife filed for alienation of affection."

That was something. Maybe Millhouse cheated on wife number one. That would mean he might be tempted again. "Anything else? What does the husband do?"

"From what I can tell, he's an investor. Eleanor was wife number three. He must have had some ironclad pre-nups, because the guy still has two cents to invest." Grady pushed back his chair and pulled off his thick spectacles. "Otherwise, he's as clean as her. Spends a lot of time in puzzle forums, and kind of an expert crossword puzzle guy, but that's it. Pretty boring."

"Are you sure?"

"What I'm sure of is that my mac and cheese is ready. Let's go."

Claudine didn't move. She slowly tapped a pen against her arm. "Could you give me the names and addresses of the houses that Millhouse bought out last year?"

"I already told you about them."

"Just the names and addresses, Grady. Please."

With a sigh, Grady returned to his keyboard. "Here." He tapped on a screen to a block of text in an enlarged font. "I'm sending it to the printer. Get it and meet me downstairs. I can taste those noodles now."

Chapter Seventeen

Claudine stared through a chain link fence at the edge of a wet pit. Churned earth spanned at least five square blocks. "Carsonville Sewage Treatment Facility Coming Soon," a sign wired to the fence read. This was what Ellie bulldozed all those homes for. "Coming Soon" appeared optimistic. At the bottom of the pit was a lonely bulldozer, but otherwise construction appeared halted. Waiting for spring, maybe.

The autumn-stripped trees and bare earth didn't make the most of the neighborhood, but it hadn't been a ritzy one to start with. The sidewalk edging the construction site was cracked and streets pitted. Many of the nearby homes were boarded up or had windows hung with tattered curtains and bent blinds. Beyond the houses on one side slogged the murky river.

She'd never spent much time in this part of town, where the industrial area had encroached on a residential neighborhood that had probably followed the river since Victorian times. Her work certainly didn't take her there—no one had anything worth stealing. Her father had always made sure they lived in a firmly middle class, nondescript neighborhood.

She released the cold fence. Where to start? She looked at the list Grady had printed out the day before. She'd already called—or tried calling—the phone numbers Grady found in a reverse directory. Most were out of order, and one that rang through went to voice mail. She'd have to knock.

Green asbestos shingles covered the first house she approached. A pit bull—not as friendly as Tinkerbell—was chained to the front railing. The living room curtain briefly parted, then fell shut again, and no one came to the door. Pass.

At the next house, a duplex fashioned out of an already modest residence, no one answered her knock upstairs or down.

At the third house, a plump woman with wide eyes greeted her from the top of the stoop before Claudine even made it to the door. It was hard to pin down her age. Her upswept white hair and stooped figure put her in the senior category, but her unlined skin glowed. She smiled as if Claudine had been expected.

"Come in. What a nice surprise," the woman said.

"But I'm—"

"Oh, you don't need to explain. Now come on in, I'm not going to keep the door open all day. We don't own the electric company, you know." The woman turned to the living room and clearly expected Claudine would follow her.

She paused only a moment. Why not? The older woman looked harmless enough.

"I'm Letty." She bustled into the kitchen and put on a kettle. "We'll have some tea, and you'll tell me what's on your mind."

"Claudine Dupin." Claudine stuck out a hand, but Letty was busy settling into a pink armchair with a clear plastic slipcover. The vague scent of gardenias hung in the air.

"Have a seat," Letty said.

Claudine lowered herself onto the sofa, also covered with clear plastic, facing Letty. Elasticized plastic covers shielded the lamps. Beyond Letty, through the pristine picture window, yawned the muddy pit of the construction site.

"Now, what can I tell you?" Letty said.

"How did you know I wanted to talk to you?"

"You were going door to door, weren't you?"

"Yes, but I could have been selling something."

"No valise or clipboard." Letty smiled in satisfaction.

"Or worse. It's not safe to let just anyone in your house," Claudine said.

"Now listen to you." Letty dismissed her with a wave. "You're not packing heat. Not in that slim jacket, and your purse is too small. Besides, you were looking at a list out there by your car. I'd guess you've come to see Madeleine."

Madeleine? The kettle in the kitchen began to whistle, but Letty showed no sign of rising to get it.

"Shall I?" Claudine offered.

"If you don't mind. Thank you."

In the kitchen, Letty had laid out a tray with two pink ceramic tea cups and spoons on a fresh paper towel. Claudine filled the teapot and carried the tray to the living room. She made sure to stay on the clear plastic strip that made a runway into the next room.

"Madeleine isn't here. Not now."

"I'm not sure who Madeleine is," Claudine said. "Actually, I came to talk to you about the sewage treatment plant."

Letty tittered. She leaned forward and lowered her voice. "You don't have to make excuses with me. I could see it in you when you walked up. You're looking for a little extra help finding someone special, aren't you? Madeleine got all the glory, but I have the gift, too, you know."

"The gift?"

"They're telling me you'll find your direction. And soon."

"They? Who're they?" She'd made a mistake coming in the house. Letty might be able to take care of herself, but a screw was loose somewhere in there. "Look, thank you for your time, but I'd better get going." Claudine grabbed her purse and rose.

"Wait," Letty said, teaspoon in the air. Her eyes darted to the side for a second. "They're telling me you're right. There was collusion." She frowned. "What's collusion?"

Claudine lowered herself to her chair again. "A kind of conspiracy. Are you talking about the sewage treatment facility? Condemning all those houses?"

"Oh, that was awful," Letty said. "One afternoon last spring everyone across the street and for the next few blocks got the same letter. Madeleine got one, too. She used to live right across the street, you know. In a little blue house with a yellow door. I thought it was the cleverest thing to paint the door yellow. You don't often see that, probably because of the marks you can get on it. Use your foot to push open the door, and you've—"

"What did the letters say?"

Letty poured the tea. "I can show you, if you'd like. We received one, Madeleine and me. Maybe I've been saving it for you."

"The both of you?"

"Yes. We lived together. Have for a good forty years. When the house was condemned I moved here. The people who lived here didn't want to be across the street from a sewage facility. I wanted to stay nearby. So many memories." Her voice weakened, and she looked away.

"I'd love to see the letter, please."

The older woman still smiled, but the light behind it seemed to have gone out. "Oh. Yes." She wandered down the hall and past the kitchen.

Claudine picked up a photo on the side table. It showed two young women, one of whom looked like Letty but with thick black hair. The other woman had equally black hair, but short, and huge eyes. Doing jobs, she'd been inside a lot of houses, read a lot of life from dishes left in the sink, bedside reading, framed photos like this one. One thing was for sure: no matter the value of your stock portfolio, everyone had people they loved—or used to love. They passed holidays, happy or busy or alone. They celebrated births and feared death. It's just that some did it over Aubusson rugs. Here it was 1960s molded carpeting with vinyl runners.

"Here it is. The letter." Letty arrived with an envelope the familiar pale gray of county correspondence.

Claudine glanced through it. An address, presumably Letty and Madeleine's, was printed in large type on the top. The rest of the letter looked to be boilerplate about how the property was needed for critical functions, and how the property owner would be remunerated at—was that all?—a price far below what Claudine would have guessed, even given the neighborhood. The last paragraph gave information about where to petition the letter.

"Did you follow up with the county at all? You know, follow the instructions to petition?"

Letty kept her gaze fastened on the teapot as she refilled her cup. "I told her it was a bad idea. I told her no one else was getting anywhere with it, but she insisted." She lifted the cup to her lips and looked toward the window. "It was the darlingest house. Little yellow door."

Claudine gave the woman a few moments to respond before prompting her. "A bad idea?"

"Oh yes. They'd never let her get away with it. They wanted the property. And then...."

Another moment passed. Claudine couldn't tamp down her urgency. "What happened? With Madeleine?"

"Oh." Letty set down her cup. "I guess you didn't know.

She killed herself."

* * *

Letty's staunch expression melted into tears. "I told her we should have taken the offer. They warned us when they came around the second time. But Madeleine said no, that we weren't going to take it, even if we were the only house left standing on the block."

Had the women been sisters? Lovers? Simply friends? Whatever it was, when Madeleine died, Letty lost family. "She took her own life because of it." Claudine said it as more of a question than a statement.

"She was fine at first. Oh, she was mad, but fine. Then he came again."

"Who?" Claudine found herself perched at the edge of the couch.

"I don't know," Letty said. "Madeleine wouldn't tell me. But she wasn't the same after that." The rosiness had drained from her cheeks, and her hand trembled. A dog barked down the street, bringing the silence into relief.

"What about the neighbors? Did any of them back you up, do the same?"

"What?" Letty swayed a bit in her chair.

"The neighbors. Did they sell or try to hang on to their houses?"

"Well, let's see." She ticked off her fingers. "The Titos refused at first, but they seemed to change their minds awfully fast and sold. Barbie Stanton was planning to go live with her son, anyway. The house next to her was a rental, and I don't think the landlord cared. The Krugers…." Her voice trailed off. "They're all gone now."

"Letty? Are you okay?"

"Is it Wednesday yet? I have to go to the doctor on Wednesday."

"Tomorrow. Can I get you something?" She shouldn't be living here alone.

"I'm fine. They say it's all right."

Talking to spirits again. "You're not feeling well. I shouldn't be pushing you like this. I should go," Claudine said.

"No. Stay. Just a few more minutes until this passes. I'm all right. Ask me another question."

"If you're sure." At Letty's nod, she said, "Then tell me about the first offer on your house," Claudine said. "After this letter, right?" She held up the letter from the county.

"Oh, no. A young man came around about a month before the letter arrived. He said he wanted to buy our house."

This was getting interesting. "Did he say why?"

"No. Only that his firm was looking to buy out that whole side of the street for a big project. Madeleine told him we wouldn't do it. He had a shadow over him." She looked at Claudine with meaning. "He said this was the best offer we'd get, then he left."

"The condemnation letter came later. But the man wasn't from the county?"

"Oh, no." Letty's chest rose as she inhaled deeply. She let it out in one long sigh. "Oh Madeleine. I told you we should have left it all alone."

"But you say you had two visits."

"We did. By the same man, but he wasn't very gentlemanly the second time."

"Let me make sure I understand. You got a visitor with an

offer to buy your house."

Letty nodded.

"You declined the offer. Then you received this condemnation letter from the county. Shortly after that, the visitor showed up again and offered to buy the house at a price just above what the county proposed."

"Yes."

"You declined that offer, too."

"I told Madeleine just to let it go, not to pay attention to his threats. For a little while, she was fine—and then…."

"He threatened you?" Claudine spoke more sharply than she'd intended.

"He said he'd tell everyone—something," she whispered.

"Letty." She clinked her tea cup into its saucer to punctuate the word. "Do you happen to remember the name of the man who visited you?"

Letty pulled a cream business card from the pocket of her housecoat. "I thought you'd want it."

"Fine Properties of Distinction," it read.

Chapter Eighteen

At the tea shop the next day, Ruby scooted her chair closer. Claudine seemed a bit more animated, more vivacious than usual. But frustrated, too. "That's all? You couldn't find anything? They got Al Capone on a tax charge. Isn't there something like that?"

"Eleanor Millhouse is ridiculously clean," Claudine said. "Immoral, but clean. Grady scoured computer records. Couldn't even get a parking ticket on her."

"But what about trying to break into the firehouse?" Deborah said. Her hair was molded into 1920s-style finger curls, like Betty Boop in the old comic strip. It had taken only half an hour with the curling iron before their meeting, but Deb had been thrilled. Ruby thought it was like having her little sister around. "You know we can't be the first people who got in her way."

"If she crossed the line with someone else, there's no record of it."

"So blackmail's out of the question," Ruby said.

"I'm not sure about that. Not entirely, anyway. On a hunch, I went to visit her last big property sale to the county. It's out by the river, south of town."

Claudine told them about Letty and Madeleine, and about Madeleine's death and the property sales. Claudine pulled a notepad from her bag and tapped her pen on the page at each point. "I had Grady chase down the Fine Properties sale to the county, and compared to what she paid the homeowners, she made heaps of money."

"So," Ruby said. "Eleanor tried to buy out the neighborhood. For the property owners who didn't fall in line, the county condemned their homes. Then she came in with a slightly higher offer."

"Condemning the property doesn't do her any good though," Deborah pointed out. "That means the government gets the houses, right? There's no money in it for her."

Ruby nodded. Got it. "But Fine Properties can't sell the land to the county without a contiguous plot. A few stubborn home owners could sour the deal," she said. Ingenious. But there was just one problem. "How did Eleanor Millhouse know the county would want the property, anyway? And how did she coordinate with the condemnation letters?"

"Exactly," Claudine said and locked eyes with Ruby.

"Exactly what?" Deborah asked.

"Somehow Eleanor Millhouse knew about upcoming county projects. Then she's the one holding the land they need." Ruby explained. "If she can assemble a large plot, she can sell for a good profit."

Claudine nodded.

Ruby continued. "If a homeowner doesn't sell, she strong-arms them into it."

"But that's not fair," Deborah said.

"Fair and legal aren't always the same thing." Ruby lifted the teapot. It was empty. The women held their silence a moment while the host refilled the teapot with hot water. Wonder of all wonders, he actually smiled as he placed it on the table.

"If Ellie had some sort of privileged information, it wouldn't be legal," Claudine pointed out after he left.

Ruby shook her head. "If she was getting the inside scoop on county construction projects, you know she scrubbed her trail good and clean."

"What about the lady you talked to—Letty? Couldn't she tell her story to the police?" Deborah asked.

"I thought about that. I believe her, but she wouldn't be a reliable witness. Besides telling me about her and Madeleine, she, well, she talked with ghosts while I was there. They'd call her batty, and that would be that." Claudine shook her head.

"I have to wonder how the firehouse factors into all of this," Ruby said.

"So do I," Claudine said. "It could be something completely different, a vanity project. Maybe she's just stubborn and can't bear that she wouldn't get what she wants."

"Or maybe she knows something we don't," Ruby said.

Claudine didn't reply. She seemed to be contemplating something but hesitated to bring it up, Ruby thought. What? Finally, Claudine said, "The kids seem to be doing well in school. Grady built them computer work stations in the cafeteria. You were great to get them enrolled, Deborah."

Ruby was momentarily confused, but Deborah's face lit up. "I knew it was the right thing. Education is the best way to get ahead."

"Apparently, Hugo is showing a real aptitude in auto shop. Father Vincent has him working on his Corvette," Claudine added.

"And Joanie gets a real art teacher," Deborah said.

Claudine was buttering them up for something. "Out with it," Ruby said.

"Well, there's one way we might be able to convince Eleanor Millhouse to see the light," Claudine said.

Ah. Here it was. "Well?"

"Roger Millhouse's first two marriages ended in divorce for alienation of affection."

Ruby caught on immediately. "Do you think Deb would do it?"

"What? Do what?" Deborah said.

"She means to set you after Roger Millhouse and manufacture something we can use to blackmail his wife. We'd have to do it soon, though. Get her to pull out before the next commissioners' meeting."

"Oh." Deborah toyed with her napkin.

"It's not as bad as all that," Claudine cut in. "Millhouse meets at the Presbyterian Church's basement every Tuesday for game night. You show up, and convince him to go somewhere more quiet. I'll be around to take photos. All we need is enough to edit into something to threaten Ellie Millhouse with."

"I don't know any games." Deborah said. "All I know is Euchre. Besides, what if his wife is there?"

"She might be. It's a chance we'll have to take. And come on, it's only games. How hard could it be?"

"But you want me to come on to this Roger guy, right? Like, try to get him to touch me?"

Claudine exchanged glances with Ruby. "Well, yes. That's the general idea."

"It's coming up soon," Deborah said.

"Uh-huh," Claudine replied.

"I don't know, Claudine. Things have been going really well with Louie. I put his suitcase in storage and everything."

"Games in a church basement?" Ruby said. "That hardly sounds threatening. In fact, it sounds pretty wholesome, if you ask me."

"But you're not asking me just to play games." She bit her

lip. "I thought we agreed to do everything legally. Straight. All this sounds so underhanded."

"And cheating a bunch of people out of their homes isn't?" Ruby said.

"Deborah." Claudine laid her hand on the young woman's. "It's our only chance at this point to save the firehouse. I know it's asking a lot of you, and if you don't want to do it, I understand."

"I know. But why can't you or Ruby do it, instead?"

Ruby held up her hands in mock surrender. "I have my own charm, but I don't see the gents going wild for it."

"But you're so pretty. And what about Claudine?"

"I'm afraid I don't have the personality."

Ruby knew it was true. Claudine would disappear in a full room, and not many men would have the patience to get to know her better. Certainly not over one evening playing games. She had a glamour about her, though, if you were patient. But Deb was the sure thing.

Deborah focused in the distance toward the steamed-over front window. Her fingers tapped the tabletop. "I'll tell you what. I'll think about it, okay? That's all I can promise."

Chapter Nineteen

Claudine stretched and rubbed her eyes. The laptop's screen had become a blur. She rose and went to the kitchen window to look into the night and give her eyes a rest. The windows at the house across from hers were dark. The baby was probably asleep by now.

She returned to the computer. Next to the laptop was a printout of the warehouse district. So far, she'd discovered that four of the seven properties surrounding the firehouse were already owned by Fine Properties of Distinction.

The apartment's buzzer squawked. It had to be nearly midnight. Claudine went to the front window to see who it was. A tall, broad-shouldered man, arms folded over his chest, leaned against the doorjamb at the foot of the stairs.

Oswald. Shoot. With all the stuff with the Rizzio kids, she'd completely forgotten to get back to him.

Oswald took the stairs two at a time and pushed past her without saying a word. Once they were inside, he turned to her. "Where the hell have you been? You said you'd get back to me today about the plans. It's all set up hour by hour."

"Look, Oz, I'm sorry. I had other things to deal with, okay?"

He tossed his coat on an armchair. "No, it's not okay. This job is your number one commitment right now."

"Calm down," Claudine said. "Like you said, it's all planned out. We'll be fine."

Oswald's jaw was set tight. "Even though the jeweler in Antwerp was busted this morning?"

Claudine was struck dumb. The Antwerp connection was essential to getting the jewels on the market. Without him, they couldn't be reset and cut down before going to the fence in Switzerland. They might as well just forget the whole heist.

Oswald nodded slowly. "That's right. If you'd checked in today—as you should be doing regularly, I might add—you'd know about it."

"He didn't reveal anything about his—?"

"No. They got him on a specific job, something else, and as far as I know our names are out of it."

"Well, I'll get in touch with Roget, and we'll get another jeweler lined up. There's a—"

"Never mind. I took care of it."

"Who?" It was her job to manage team members, not Oswald's.

Oz paced to the back window in the kitchen and returned. "I'm going to be honest with you. I don't know if I should tell you. You haven't been focused. Think about it. If our positions were reversed, you'd wipe me from the job."

He was right, of course. This was a complex heist worth millions of dollars. They had to break into a highly protected museum, smuggle out the jewels, leave the country, sell the jewels, and launder the proceeds. The team was good—the best—but every one of them needed to be watched every step of the way. One tiny misstep, and the whole deal would fall apart. This heist was her ticket out of the trade. All she had to do was focus a bit longer, and her life would be hers. Hell, she'd have enough money to build the kids a shelter herself.

Her father had warned her not to let pride get in her way.

She wasn't making smart choices. She had to focus.

"You're right," she said simply.

Oswald studied her a moment. "Are you sure?"

"Yeah. I'm sure. Tell me where we are."

"I'm not sure I trust you, Deanie. You said this before, but you dropped the ball."

She could tell him about Ellie Millhouse's land deals. She could explain that the kids, like she and André had, needed a home. She could tell him about her own confused feelings. But she didn't think he'd get it. "It's Dad. I'm worried about him, that's all."

He began to relax. "You got a beer?"

"Help yourself."

Claudine opened her laptop and closed out of the land records. She started the encryption program.

He pulled a chair up to the desk next to her. "You know, your dad would be really proud of you right now."

* * *

Ruby was still awake with the small lamp next to the bed on and a book open. Bruce snored next to her. She didn't know if she could sleep without that snore droning so soothingly. Sometimes she toyed with the idea of taping it in case something happened to him so she could play it back like a lullaby.

She rested the book face down on her chest. If Deb didn't agree to lure Roger Millhouse into a compromising position, she didn't know what they'd do about the kids. They couldn't be turned out onto the street again, and they refused to go to foster homes. When she and her sisters had been homeless for a few months, it was terrifying. The way people had looked at her. Worrying about where they'd eat, lying to their teachers. The condescension, the pity, and, occasionally, the blatant fear. They had to find the Rizzio kids a home.

Claudine really seemed to have come around. She was doing an amazing job digging up info on Eleanor Millhouse, although it didn't seem to be coming to much. Ruby had to give her props for getting the retirement home to put up the kids. She sighed. Hopefully the kids would come out of there without misdemeanors on their records.

And Deb. Ruby didn't care what she said, Louie wasn't worthy of her. But you can't tell other people how to live their lives. She'd figure it out eventually. Everyone did.

Ruby reached over and clicked off the light. Bruce snored on.

***

The Granzer mansion's grandfather clock ticked in the darkness. The clock was as tall as a man, with a walnut cabinet and a heavy brass pendulum. When Deborah had first moved in, Louie had told her the clock was the first thing Grandpa Granzer bought when he started making money. He'd disabled the chimes since the clock was near their bedroom, but the ticking never stopped. Like a good wife, she wound it every week. During happy times, the clock was barely a distraction. Other times, like when Louie was away, it was a relentless reminder of every second she was alone.

"Go back to sleep, hon," Louie said.

At her husband's voice, warmth washed over Deborah. She

could ignore the clock tonight. It was wonderful to have Louie back. She was busy all day taking care of him—doing the laundry, cleaning his binoculars, keeping up the stock of cola and milk. She hadn't thought about the watches once. The Rizzio kids had been on her mind, though.

"Sorry for waking you," she whispered.

Louie turned toward her and drew her in. "You're worried about those orphans, aren't you?"

"I can't help it." She slipped an arm over him and talked into his chest. "That developer bought the firehouse. Grandpa won't donate unless it's to renovate a firehouse. They don't have anywhere to go."

"You're so sweet to think about them," he said.

"I can't help it. Oh, Louie, you should meet them. They're such good kids." She'd been wrong to worry about Louie. He was dedicated to her. He loved her. He was showing it right now.

"I don't know what I'd do without you," he said. "You're a natural mother."

At his words, a flicker reverberated deep in her chest, a click like a final puzzle piece snapped into place. That was it. She was a mother, that was who she was. Taking care of the Rizzios had been the most rewarding thing she'd done since she married Louie. She thought of the house, the six bedrooms, two living rooms, and library. And it wasn't like she had a lot to keep her busy. It was a far better solution than the Villa Saint Nicholas.

She played with a curl of Louie's chest hair. "Would you—would you consider having the kids here until we found them somewhere else?"

He rolled away. "Honey."

"We have so much room. The boys could stay in your old bedroom, and the girls could sleep in Grandpa Granzer's old room."

Louie didn't respond.

"Or we could put them in the apartment above the garage, although I'd much rather have them closer."

Louie heaved a breath. "Like I told you before, it's not the best idea, honey."

"I thought when you said I was a natural mother, you meant you'd" —she sat up, wide awake now— "unless. Unless you mean having our own kids."

Louie stayed on his side, faced away from her. The grandfather clock's ticking seemed to gain speed. "Honey, I'm your baby. I'm the one for you to take care of."

Her fingers clenched, then released. "I love taking care of you. Sometimes you're gone, though. It's such a big old house."

"You've never complained before." He rolled back toward her. "That's one of the things I love about you. You're not one of those women with a me-me-me attitude. You let me be myself."

Now she understood. He didn't want children. Not just the Rizzio kids, he didn't want their children.

The clock's ticking gathered until it swarmed in her brain like hornets. She put her fingers in her ears. "What about me? When do I get to be myself?"

"Honey, what's eating you? This isn't like you."

Deborah threw the covers aside. Her feet hit the floor with a thud. "What do you know about who I am?"

Louie sat up. "What's got into you?"

She threw the grandfather clock's front open, rattling its glass window. The scent of the lemon oil she'd used to polish it month after month wafted into the dark hall. She yanked the clock's pendulum, hard. With an off-key clatter of chimes, it gave way. Deborah threw the pendulum over the banister, and glass shattered somewhere in the entry hall. At last there was silence.

Chapter Twenty

Tuesday night, Deborah hesitated in the church's parking lot. When she went to hotel bars to steal watches, the hot burn of anger fueled her. This was different. And more important. Claudine and Ruby—and the kids—were depending on her. They had confidence in her. If only she had that kind of confidence in herself. She steeled herself and made her way to the church's side entrance.

The church basement was homelier than the upstairs chapel's stained glass windows and red carpet. Down here, a built-in kitchen occupied one end, and card tables with folding chairs covered the checkered linoleum floor. Just like in her parents' basement.

"You here for game night?" a plump woman just inside the door asked.

"Yes, please," Deborah said.

The woman handed her a stick-on name tag. Good, Deborah thought as she scrawled her first name. Name tags should make finding Roger Millhouse easier. Claudine had shown her photos, and he'd come to the county hearing with his wife, but there'd been so many people.

"We've got bridge over there." The woman pointed to two tables. "Cribbage here and pinochle over there. Punch and cookies are on the side table."

More games she didn't know. Someone put a scratchy Dolly Parton album on the stereo. Deborah wandered toward the punch bowl. She filled a paper cup with neon green punch and scanned the crowd. She'd deliberately arrived a little late hoping Millhouse would already be there, but she'd be darned if she could find him. Maybe Grady was wrong. Maybe he didn't come to these things after all.

At a movement at the door, Deborah turned. It wasn't Roger Millhouse but Claudine who entered. She stopped to talk to the woman inside the door. Ruby really had done a great job on Claudine—no one would recognize her with that short blonde wig and all the makeup. And the clothing. Ruby said they were going for "ex-hippie, New Age stockbroker," and laid out the exotic print skirt and fringed boots—all from the couture department at Klingle's—and the diamond-inlayed hoops. Claudine's normal look was so much more simple, she realized. Nice quality, too, as usual. In her parents' dry cleaning shop, she'd seen all sorts of clothing, and she could tell Scottish from Chinese cashmere from across the room. Claudine wore Scottish.

Claudine made brief eye contact before pretending to look for a table to join. Deborah had better hurry up and find Roger Millhouse so Claudine could settle in nearby with her purse camera.

"Lots of new people here tonight," a man's voice from behind her said.

Deborah swirled around. The man wore khakis and a polo shirt and had the bland face to match. His smile was friendly, though, and luck of all luck, his name tag announced him as Roger M.

She smiled. "I'm Deborah."

"Yes, of course, Deborah Granzer. Roger Millhouse." He

extended a hand. "I met you at the fundraiser at your house. You like games, do you?"

His tone was innocent, but Deb couldn't help gasping, "Games?"

Roger quirked an eyebrow. "You know, cards, board games, all that."

"Why, yes," she said and let out a breath. "Games. Of course. I wanted to find something wholesome to do in the evenings, so I thought I'd come check out game night."

"Very wholesome. Wholesome indeed. You like bridge?"

Dang. "I'm afraid I don't know bridge."

"How about pinochle? Or cribbage?"

She gave a weak smile. "I don't know those, either. I'm just a beginner." Out of the corner of her eye she caught Claudine pretending to examine the notice board posted near the kitchen.

"What games do you play, then?" He filled his punch cup.

"Well. Not many. Yahtzee."

"That's a game of chance," he said. "No strategy. Anything else?"

"I do play Euchre."

Millhouse's face lit up. "No kidding. Euchre, you say? It's been years. I've been dying to play some Euchre, but no one else will do it. Maybe we could get a Euchre game up tonight. Hey, Joan," he yelled to the woman at the door. "We're doing Euchre at table six."

He put a hand on the small of Deborah's back to guide her to the table. Deborah noticed Claudine turning, purse pointed at them.

"May I join you?" Claudine was at their side. Deborah gave an expression she hoped showed no recognition. She'd never been good at acting.

"You bet, and we'll need a fourth. Sylvia? Sylvia will join us, won't you?"

A keen-eyed octogenarian nodded. "After this hand. We've just about got it wrapped up." She shuffled the deck like a Vegas pit boss, almost as well as Bobby did at the Villa.

Claudine took the seat directly across from Roger. Deborah snagged the seat to his right. She scooted her chair a few inches closer to him, hoping they would be in line with Claudine's purse, which was maneuvered with its top just above the table.

"How is your firehouse project going, the family shelter?" he asked.

Deborah's pulse leapt. "I thought you knew. Your wife is buying the firehouse."

"That's right." Roger arranged the cards in his hand. "I don't give her business much attention. Just an investor. I'm sure Carsonville's citizens will step up to do what's right."

Deborah had rehearsed a response with Ruby and Claudine. "It's a shame we won't be able to buy the firehouse, of course, but the gift from Fine Properties of Distinction was very generous, and we hope—" Hope what? She couldn't remember the rest of her speech. She glanced at Claudine, who mouthed "very soon." Oh yeah. "We hope very soon to begin to explore other suitable properties." She latched eye contact with Roger Millhouse and smiled.

"Quite sensible," he said. "It's fine that you're thinking of the children's lives. Glad we could help."

Deborah rested a hand on Millhouse's sleeve. "Thank you. And thank you for letting me join you," she said in her sweetest voice.

"No problem." He seemed not to register her touch at all. "I'm just glad to see ladies who enjoy wholesome pleasures. So many people would be spending the evening at a bar. Or they might be gossiping, besmirching each other's character. Me, I never drink. Or gossip." He shook his head. "I just don't get it."

Deborah pulled back her hand. She might not live a thrilling life, but this guy was a real snooze. "I bet your wife is really special."

"What? Oh, yes. We see eye to eye. I was lucky to find her." He chuckled as if remembering something funny. "Every morning we have our coffee, and she circles the errors in the newspaper with a red pen. At least once a week I bundle them up and send them to the editor. He said we're—and I quote—'unique citizens.' Yes, she's a pip."

"Quite," Claudine mumbled.

"You're a unique man yourself," Deborah said. Millhouse smiled blandly in response. She'd swear he didn't even notice that she was a woman, even though she'd taken Ruby's advice and positioned herself so he could look down her sweater. Claudine said Roger had been married three times. Maybe none of them were good enough for him. Or his wives got bored and left. "Does she—your wife, I mean—come to game night, too?" She held her breath.

"Oh, no. It's important that we pursue separate interests from time to time. Keeps things interesting. She has the Carsonville Women's League, and I have my games." He adjusted his shirt collar. "What about you ladies? What do you do in life?" he asked.

Sylvia had joined them and pulled a deck of cards from her needlepoint bag. Claudine raised an eyebrow. "Retired," Sylvia said. "Used to groom poodles."

"And you, Ms. Granzer?"

"Me? Call me Deborah, please. I'm just a housewife."

"Never say 'just a housewife,' Deborah. Housewife is one of the world's chosen professions. That's my one regret, that my wife keeps so busy with her work. And you, Mary Ellen?" he asked Claudine after glancing at her name tag. "You're a quiet one."

Deborah saw Claudine bite off a smile. She'd been watching Sylvia roll her eyes at "world's chosen professions." "I'm a stockbroker," she said. "Possibly not one of the world's chosen professions."

"But a vital one indeed and essential to the economic growth we need for a healthy community."

Sylvia mouthed the words "vital one indeed" and bent to her cards when Millhouse looked over.

"How about if I deal?" Deborah said. It had been a long time since she'd played Euchre, but after several years of playing it at family holidays, she hadn't forgotten.

"Does everyone know the rules?" Millhouse asked.

Sylvia nodded and handed over her deck.

"I'm a fast learner," Claudine said.

"What do you say we put a little money on it, huh?" Sylvia said. "Say, a nickel a trick?"

"Now, Sylvia, you know gambling isn't permitted," Roger said.

The older woman rolled her eyes again.

Deborah dealt the cards. Within minutes, they were deep into the game, trading tricks and calling trumps. After a hand or two, Claudine seemed to do remarkably well. Sylvia, on the other hand, picked up a sour expression, especially at Claudine's plays. Every once in a while Deborah would pull a card to toss in the kitty, and Claudine would press her knee under the table. When Deborah reached for another card instead, she let up the pressure.

Deborah had forgotten how much she loved playing games. Her family used to rent a cabin on a lake some summers. While her mom fried up trout, Deborah and her cousins did jigsaw puzzles or told scary stories or played cards. Louie promised they'd join them some summer, but it hadn't happened yet. Maybe next year.

Too bad she wouldn't be able to come back to game night once they set up Millhouse. But it was for the kids, she reminded herself. She smiled and touched his hand. "Would you like another punch, Roger?"

"No, I'm fine, thank you." He shook his head in amazement. "I can't remember when I've had such a marvelous time."

"Me neither." Deborah beamed. She wasn't lying, either. Maybe Louie wouldn't mind playing games once in a while. They had Sorry at home somewhere. Claudine's purse shuffled at the edge of the table.

"For chrissakes," Sylvia said and tossed her cards on the table.

"Language," Roger said.

"I'm going to see if I can catch a game at one of the other tables." Sylvia hoisted her needlepoint bag to her shoulder and left.

"Cutthroat, then," Roger said. "You ladies up for it?" He glanced at his watch, a Chopard with a scratched crystal. Not bad. "Oh, my. The evening has flown. I've been having such a terrific time. One more hand. My wife will be here soon."

Claudine lifted her chin and stared at Deborah. Deborah should have drawn more out of Millhouse, but her advances seemed to bounce right off him. She drew a breath and tried again. "Oh, Roger. I've had such a wonderful time tonight."

"As have I." He patted her arm.

"Couldn't we—I don't know. Couldn't we continue somewhere else?"

Claudine excused herself and walked toward the hall, presumably where the restrooms were. Deborah looked forlornly after her.

"Don't you need to get home to your husband?"

"Oh." Deborah put a palm to her chest. "He's out of town. He often is. He's—he's never played Euchre with me in his life. Never."

For the first time, Millhouse met her gaze full on. "Oh, you poor girl. You'll have to ask him to come to game night."

"I'm not sure he'd like that. He's stubborn about his interests."

Roger leaned forward. "I know all about stubborn. I'd never cross Eleanor." He started to let out a sigh, but cut it short. "My wife. Here she is."

Eleanor Millhouse's heels clicked across the linoleum. She pecked her husband on the cheek, then withdrew quickly at the sight of Deborah.

"Honey, meet Deborah. Remember her from the fundraiser at the Granzer mansion? We played Euchre all night. She's delightful company."

"It's nice to see you. Your husband is wonderful at cards."

"Yes," Eleanor said curtly. "What a pleasure to see you. Honey, let's go." She pulled him up by the arm and led him out the door. Claudine had somehow retreated to the corner, almost melting into the paneling.

Deborah's heart sank. She knew Claudine had taken photos, but Roger hadn't proven a very willing subject. Plus, she really had been distracted by the game. Euchre. It was so fun. If she and Louie had their own kids, they could start a family tradition of playing games at holidays. He hadn't said no to children. He just didn't say yes. Well, actually, he wasn't saying much at all since she busted the grandfather clock.

Out in the darkened parking lot, she found Claudine leaning against her Honda. "I'm sorry, Claudine. I tried. I even put my cleavage on view. He didn't even look."

"Don't worry. I got some photos. We can work with them."

Relieved, Deborah turned toward the car. It didn't look like she'd be mad.

"Oh, and Deb?"

Hand on the car's door handle, she turned.

"Remind me to show you how to recognize a marked deck."

* * *

The next morning, Ruby waited in her car across the street from Eleanor Millhouse's office. The sun streamed through her front windshield, turning from icy cold to muggy as it hit the glass. She sipped her tea, being careful not to smudge the dark, frosted lipstick she'd so carefully applied as part of her disguise.

Last night when Deborah and Claudine had come home, Deborah was hardly to be consoled. She seemed to think she'd screwed up somehow, but in the next breath she was asking if they had a deck of cards. Such a sweet girl, and so gifted in some ways, but…Ruby let out a breath.

Ruby studied the sidewalk and the parking garage where Eleanor parked. Grady seemed to be able to find anything stored on a computer that had ever crossed a keyboard. A monthly deduction on Eleanor Millhouse's bank account to the parking garage settled this one. A few people, breath steaming in the cold, holding hands up to fasten collars tighter, hurried to the office building. But no Eleanor. Not yet.

Claudine didn't seem so worried about how the evening had gone. Ruby had made them all Tequila Sunrises, and they'd retired to the salon to crack open Claudine's laptop. Claudine loaded the photos from her phone-purse into the computer and started playing around with them. Ah, the magic of computers.

At first, they weren't promising. A large "Jesus Saves" banner spread behind Roger Millhouse's face. Claudine wiped that out and replaced it with a dimmed background.

"What about that cup of punch?" Deborah had asked.

"Gone. Let's make it a Martini," Claudine said.

"I see him as more of a Jack and Coke guy," Ruby said.

With a few swipes of the mouse, the church basement had become a darkened bar and Roger's punch a cocktail.

"Do you think—?" Deborah had started.

"Got it," Claudine said. She oriented the photo so that Deborah was clearly female, and Roger was clearly delighted with her, but her identity and the fact that Roger's delight was over his fortuitous hand of cards were manipulated.

After an hour, Claudine pushed back from the computer. "What do you think?"

They had three photos. One showed Roger Millhouse, drink in hand, with a stupidly happy expression on his face and a hand apparently bearing down on Deborah's chest. In reality, Roger was diving for a card in the discard pile. Another showed Roger, eyes at half-mast and lips pursed, with Deborah's blurry face in the foreground. Deborah said he was actually lecturing about tax law. The third showed Roger standing upright and advancing a hand toward a feminine derriere. This one had required some careful photoshopping to make it work. Roger had actually been reaching for his coat, but the coat was wiped out and Deborah's anonymized form pasted in. All in all, Ruby had to admit they were pretty convincing photographs.

The rest of the work was to write a note to go with them that wouldn't implicate the Booster Club, yet would make clear that "concerned citizens" didn't favor the firehouse's demolition and would make the photos public if Eleanor didn't respond by their deadline. At the bottom, they included an anonymous email address for a response. Grady had assured them it couldn't be traced.

"I just wonder—" Deborah had said.

"Yes?" Claudine said.

"Well, remember how Eleanor Millhouse looked at me? Do you think she'd recognize me from the photos?"

The chance was always there. They'd done a good job of wiping out all signs of the church basement, but that didn't mean, one hundred percent sure, that she wouldn't figure it out.

"You should be in the clear, Deb," Claudine had said. "But no guarantees."

"I sure can't tell it's a church basement," Ruby had added.

So here Ruby was to do her part. Her moment was coming up. A Jaguar slid into a parking space in the adjacent lot, and the occupant had Eleanor Millhouse's queenly posture. Ruby lifted the binoculars Deborah had provided—she said Louie recommended this brand for birdwatching—and let them fall. Yes. It was her, bundled up to the nines and carrying a soft-sided briefcase. Ruby slipped her berry tea into the cup holder and waited, one hand on her door handle and the photos firmly clutched in an envelope in her other hand.

She paused. One, two, and ready. She leapt from the car door and rushed toward the office building's lobby on a course that would surely collide with Eleanor's. Eleanor stopped suddenly to examine the sole of her shoe. Ruby correspondingly lagged and pretended to check her phone. When Eleanor resumed her stride for the building's front door, Ruby hurried forward, confident in her disguise.

"Oh," she said. "I'm so sorry. I didn't mean to bump into you. Are you okay?" Ruby backed off in mock alarm.

"I'm fine," Eleanor Millhouse's steely reply came.

"Sorry," Ruby repeated and strode past the building's entrance as if she were headed across the street. The photos and message had been dropped. Now all they had to do was wait.

Chapter Twenty-One

That afternoon, Ruby and Deborah sat in the dining room at the Villa Saint Nicholas and reviewed the kids' homework. Every few minutes, Ruby checked her phone to see if Eleanor Millhouse had responded to the note and photos they'd left. Nothing. Claudine had said she had a job to work on and wouldn't be able to join them today, but if they got any word from Eleanor, she wanted to know right away.

"I'll take the math homework," Deborah said.

"That's fine by me," Ruby replied.

"I'm good with history," Gilda said from behind them.

"Thanks, but we've got this covered," Ruby said.

"Oh, come on." She rattled her walker to a nearby chair and sat down. "Besides, me and Joanie are buddies, aren't we?"

Joanie nodded shyly.

"Come on, honey, show them what I taught you."

Suppressing a smile, the girl shook her head.

This couldn't be good. "What did Gilda teach you, hon?" Ruby asked.

"Go on, show them, little sprout."

Joanie took a deep breath and stepped back, throwing open her arms.

Uh-oh, Ruby thought.

"Oh, my man, I love him so, he'll never know—" the girl

began to sing full tilt.

Ruby had never heard her mutter more than a few words, and here she was, a regular Ethel Merman.

When Joanie finished singing, the group applauded. Tinkerbell came running from the hall and skidded across the floor, colliding full force with Gilda's walker.

"Watch it, you beast," Gilda said.

Deborah was remarkably absorbed in Scotty's algebra homework. "If a train and a truck are approaching each other from opposite directions—Scotty, I know this is about when they'd meet, and your equation is good, but, really, shouldn't they be figuring out how to avoid a collision?"

"Sure," the boy said, setting down a bagel. "They should have worked this out before the train even left the station. Of course, it could be the train was stolen. The train-jacker was making a getaway with a car full of cattle—"

"No," Bobby said. He slipped his ever-present deck of cards into a shirt pocket and took a seat. "Cattle ain't worth the boost. You got to feed them, get them to a ranch. A car full of TVs, now that might be worth it. Considering you have a getaway driver with skill in locomotives."

"Any driver worth his salt could drive a train," Father Vincent said. He joined them at the table. Today, at Ruby's suggestion, he wore a Utilikilt. A definite step up from Gilda's old hostessing skirt, and he could store his tools in his pocket.

"Not so fast," Bobby said. "This here driver got on the wrong track and is rolling head-first into another locomotive."

While the men argued and Scotty finished his bagel, Ruby stole a glance at her phone. No message yet. She was sure she'd slipped the packet into Eleanor Millhouse's briefcase. Positive. If she opened it at all, she had to have seen it. The fact that she hadn't responded could mean a number of things. Maybe she didn't care if they took out a billboard with her leering husband, holding a cocktail, reaching a hand toward Deb's cleavage. Maybe the firehouse meant more to her than her reputation.

Or, maybe she was on to them.

Or maybe Eleanor Millhouse was simply someone who didn't make rash moves. She had to think it over. And then she'd respond. It was a few more hours until five o'clock.

There was nothing to do but wait.

***

Across the Villa's cafeteria, Deborah checked her phone, too. Louie had been so attentive lately. After she busted the grandfather clock, he'd yanked his pillow under his arm and stomped to the guest room. He'd kept up the silent treatment through a good part of the next day.

But since yesterday evening, he'd been sending her loving texts. In person he was a little more stand-offish—at breakfast, for instance, when he barely made eye contact. Then she got his text telling her how beautiful she was and how much he loved her. She didn't even know when he'd had time to send it. Probably when she had her back turned to butter his waffle. But later, when she got dressed, she saw it and couldn't help running to the den to give him a hug.

Louie. He pretended to be shy, but his heart was pure gold. Maybe he wanted babies after all.

* * *

Claudine glanced at her phone, too, but it didn't have to do with Eleanor Millhouse or Louie. The Cabrini heist was scheduled to take place in exactly one week. Then last night she'd received an urgent email from their man on the ground in San Francisco saying that someone had just been nabbed for trying to steal the Cabrini jewels.

Her first thought had been that Oswald had double-crossed her. He'd been amazingly reliable, but she had to keep on her guard. She was soon set right.

"Not a pro," Tyrone said. "An insider, a guard, tried to lift the emerald brooch and beat a path to Tahiti. He never made it past the break room."

The Sultan's parure. A gift to the opera singer from yet another ex-lover. "Thought he'd disappear in the commotion?" Claudine said.

"Right. With the emeralds in his shirt pocket."

"What does that mean for security?"

"Tighter, I'm afraid. Everyone's getting another background check."

"Smitty," Claudine said. He was their inside connection. It was his job to see to a few critical details—chiefly, the employees' exit alarm.

"His papers are good. As long as they don't get too deep into references, we should be solid. I'll let you know," Tyrone said. "There's one thing, though."

Claudine gripped the phone. "What?"

"They've changed the alarm code structure. It's every hour now."

Not every day. That meant they wouldn't be able to lift the

code and use it that night. "Is it on an algorithm?" A daily code might be made up by the head of security, but hourly changes were usually too much for one brain to handle.

"Think so. I'm working on it."

Claudine set the phone on her desk and absently scratched Petunia behind the ears. Just seven days until the Cabrini heist. Not long. Just long enough for something to go wrong.

Chapter Twenty-Two

At five-ten that afternoon, Ruby set her phone face down on the vanity in her salon. That was it. Eleanor Millhouse had not responded. Ruby's chest tightened. They'd have to follow up on their threat. She couldn't see any way out of it.

The bell at the salon door rang. Her next appointment wasn't until morning. She raised her head to say the salon was closed, but snapped her jaw shut. Standing in the doorway was Eleanor Millhouse.

"Ruby. How are you?" Eleanor said.

Fake calm. Ruby felt her face redden as a hot flash radiated down her neck and over her chest. "Terrific. I'm great. Can I help you?"

Eleanor smiled. "Perhaps this sounds blunt, but—"

"Yes?" She barely got out the word.

"I'd like to offer you a job."

For a moment, Ruby stared. She dropped into the barber's chair behind her. Oh. Now she got it. "My uncle's wholesale business hasn't been doing so well."

Eleanor's smile remained constant. "I'm sorry to hear about that. Unless he's a beauty expert, my job offer is for you, not him. Have you heard of the Shangri-La?"

Of course she had. While Ruby's Crafty Cuts had the reputa-

204 ANGELA M. SANDERS

tion as the "secret address" for rich ladies who enjoyed the thrill of slumming it for their color and cut, the Shangri-La Spa gleamed with acres of marble floors, piles of fluffy Turkish towels, and a team of European aestheticians. Rumor had it that a dermatologist managed an unmarked office in the rear where you could get fillers and Botox injections while pretending to be in for a massage and facial.

"I'm happy cutting hair here, thank you."

Eleanor didn't respond, didn't move.

Ruby swallowed. "Please, come in. Sit down."

Eleanor's crisp pantsuit and box purse stood out against the lime green door Ruby had painted the spring before. Maybe she should have gone with something more elegant. Bone or Dior gray or something.

"I only have a minute, I'm afraid," Eleanor said. "We have plenty of excellent stylists. What I'm looking for is someone to manage the spa." As Ruby paused to take it all in, Eleanor continued. "Jocelyn raved about your highlights, and of course I've seen the publicity about Taffeta Darling. You have quite a reputation, you know. Just the other day, I was having lunch at the Women's League when one of the ladies showed up with a beautiful curly cut. We couldn't get over how good it looked on her."

"Must be Betsy Dobber." Betsy had been blow-drying her hair straight for years, but it didn't do her face any favors, especially as age took its course. She needed to let out her natural curl. With the right cut and a few basic instructions on using gel, ten years dropped away.

"Yes, Betsy. It was quite a transformation."

Eleanor started at the noise of a Chihuahua barking from the kitchen. Bruce must have come home.

"Hi, honey," he yelled.

"I'm with a customer," she said nervously. "That's just Marty. The dog, I mean. The other one is my husband." So far Eleanor had said nothing about the firehouse. Or the photos.

"We were talking about what a valuable addition you'd make to the Women's League." She unclipped the top of her purse and withdrew an envelope. "I've written up a job description and a salary offer. I hope you'll take a look at it—I think you'll find the terms generous." Her unflinching gaze caught Ruby's. "We could use someone like you on our team. I think we'd see eye to eye."

Ruby slipped the envelope into her apron pocket. "Can I think this over and get back to you?"

"Naturally. Shall we say by" —she punched a finger in the air— "five o'clock tomorrow afternoon?"

***

Ruby took Eleanor Millhouse's job offer to her mother to read. She opened her sand chair on her mother's grave and sat facing the inset plaque at its head.

"Mom, you would not believe this. I was sweeping up after my last client for the day—another bob, why so many bobs?— and who do you think came in? The president of the Carsonville Women's League. Just like that."

Leaves rustled in the canopy above and fell around her. A couple, one holding cellophane-sheathed yellow mums, wandered in the distance.

Ruby leaned toward the head of the grave. "She brought me a job offer. In this envelope."

Are you sure? her mother's voice came to her.

Ruby fumbled with the envelope. Eleanor had been so smug. What if she had known all along and this was a threat or some kind of legal summons? She slipped two pages from the envelope and let out her breath. It was indeed a job offer. She put on her reading glasses. Her eyes widened. A job offer with a generous salary—far more than she made on her own.

Her hands dropped to her side. This job was a huge step up. She and Bruce could use the salon as a living room again. Not only would she make more money, she'd have access to the women who could clear her mother's name. They'd trust her, respect her. It was about time.

Plus, she could give up shoplifting for good. She couldn't tell Bruce about her "wholesale" deals for clients. It was hard to say which was worse: fearing Bruce would find out she was a thief, or keeping such a huge secret from him.

But what about the Rizzio kids? She couldn't tell if it was her mother or her own conscience that whispered the words. Even more pressing, what would the Boosters do about Eleanor's refusal to answer their threat?

She sat at the grave until dark fell.

***

It was definitely later than five o'clock now, but no word from Ruby, who was in charge of the "concerned citizens" email address. Her calls to Ruby had gone unanswered, too. As far as Deborah knew, Eleanor hadn't responded yet. Or had she?

Deborah was home alone. To be fair, it had been quite a while since she'd been stuck in the Granzer mansion without Louie, but she missed him. He hadn't even left a note. Her phone chirped. Deborah grabbed it.

"Meet me @ Hotel DeRitz ASAP. Must see you. XXOO. L."

She had to read the message twice. Meet at a hotel? It wasn't the usual thing, but he must be feeling romantic. And signed his text XXOO. And L. He never did that. Warmth flooded over her. He wanted to see her. He wanted her. Now.

Deborah ran upstairs and stripped off her jeans and tee shirt. Thinking of Louie's response at the fundraiser, she pulled over her head the blush pink dress she'd worn that night and brushed her teeth. A swipe of lipstick later, she was in the car.

In fifteen minutes, Deborah pulled into the parking lot at the Hotel DeRitz. Night was falling, and violet streaked the horizon. Louie's BMW with his "Traveling is for the Birds" bumper sticker was parked in the next row. Her heart soared. Louie. Things would be different between them now. They'd be so much closer, more like Ruby and Bruce.

Except for the stealing and lying, of course. But that was over now.

In the lobby, Deborah searched the plush sofas and armchairs, but didn't find him. She poked her head into the bar— one she was familiar with, unfortunately—but no Louie there, either. She approached the front desk.

"I'm Deborah Granzer. Has my husband left me a note?"

The pimply-faced boy behind the desk searched the register, then handed her a key card. "He said he'd meet you upstairs. The Marie Antoinette suite, fifth floor."

A suite. Louie had really gone all out. Maybe even ordered a bottle of champagne, although he'd have a milk and coke for himself. She waited at the elevator. What should she say when he opened the door? She could walk in the room and say, "Honey, you shouldn't have." But that wasn't true. As Ruby would have pointed out, he indeed should have. Not that it mattered any more.

Mirrored panels set in fancy wood trim lined the elevator. Click-click-click, it climbed the hotel's floors. Deborah could hardly breathe in anticipation.

The doors opened. Ahead of her unrolled whitewashed walls with gold molding and more mirrors. She knew what she'd say. She'd simply open her arms and say, "Louie, I'm so glad to see you."

She passed the Madame de Pompadour suite, the Sun King suite, and finally arrived at the Marie Antoinette suite. She rapped on the door, her heart pounding. When he didn't respond, she slid the key card in. The door clicked open.

"Louie, it's me." The room was a awash in plush carpeting, gold-framed furniture, and flocked wallpaper. "Honey?"

There he was, lying on the bed. "Louie, honey, I'm so glad to see you." She moved closer. "Louie?"

He lay on his back, hair rumpled, breathing, but dead to the world. Lipstick smeared his collar, and his shirt was unbuttoned, belt undone. Deb's stomach curdled. A sheaf of photos lay on his chest with a note.

"How does it feel?" it read.

Chapter Twenty-Three

Claudine watched the tea shop owner pace back and forth. He'd advance a few steps, his hands full of tissues, then back off as if it weren't appropriate. Finally, he charged ahead with the whole box of tissues. "Here," he handed it to Deborah, who Ruby said hadn't stopped crying since last night at the Hotel DeRitz. Once Louie had regained consciousness, he'd packed a bag and left for Peru.

"If you need anything else, you'll tell me, right?" the tea shop host asked.

Deborah clutched a wad of tissue and nodded.

Claudine couldn't believe it. Ellie Whiteby Millhouse, that evil woman. Whether Louie was drugged—as he claimed—or seduced and led upstairs, she'd hit way below the belt. Louie told Deborah that someone from the national Warblers Association called and said she wanted to meet him at the hotel to talk about taking over the local chapter. He ordered a cola and milk and couldn't remember anything else. Whatever the case, he hadn't helped matters by taking off right away to South America with someone named Trixie.

Ruby was ready to give up the whole plan, and Deborah couldn't get out two straight words, but no way was Claudine quitting now.

"I guess we have our answer," Ruby said.

Deborah sniffled.

"Blackmail clearly won't work," Ruby added. Then, to Deborah, "Darling, I'm sorry for how things turned out. But it'll be all right. You'll see."

"That's not all," Deborah said. She pulled a legal-sized envelope from her bag. "Look at this."

Claudine opened the envelope and read while the tea house host fussed in the background. "Someone's convinced Grandpa Granzer's heirs to start proceedings to declare him mentally incompetent. Has to be Ellie."

"She'll never taste another macaron here again," the host said.

Ruby glared at him until he left. Deborah's sniffles erupted into a wail.

"We've got to give this up, Claudine." Ruby put a hand around Deborah's back. "Look at the poor girl. She can't take any more of this. It's not fair. We were wrong to try to deal with this by faking photos."

"Do you just want to let her get away with this? It's not just us, either—not just the firehouse. She's run people out of their homes."

Deborah moaned. Ruby patted her back. "There, there." She looked up. "You have a better alternative? She's hell-bent on getting that firehouse. We've played our biggest cards. It's time to throw in the towel. Besides, we've only got four days until the commissioners' meeting and they seal the deal."

What was with Ruby? Claudine examined her. Something was different from the last time they'd met. "I know Eleanor Millhouse from when she was Ellie Whiteby, remember. She's smart, she's meticulous, and she's ambitious. And she believes wholeheartedly in retribution. She won't quit until she gets it."

"Maybe she's not as bad as we think," Ruby said. "Maybe

she really believes she's doing something good for the town."

Deborah snuffled into her tissue. "She's a witch."

Claudine nodded. "A crafty one, too." They couldn't pin the episode with Louie on Eleanor. No one at the hotel remembered her, and Louie sure wasn't talking. But the Boosters knew who was responsible.

Ruby's attention seemed to be elsewhere. "I mean, sure, she's a sharp businesswoman, and she knows how to go after what she wants. But we can't catch her in anything illegal. Remember?"

"Ruby, what's got into you?" Claudine said. "To get even, she destroyed Deborah's marriage. She's trying to get Granzer locked away somewhere. She led another woman to kill herself. God knows how many people she's turned out of their homes. And now she's willing to squelch a plan for a family shelter and ruin the lives of the kids."

"And to burn down the firehouse," Deborah added. "Remember, she tried that, too. She might have killed them."

Ruby stared into her tea cup. A minute passed, then two, while Claudine and Deborah watched her. "Okay," she said finally. "Okay, I get it."

Claudine scooted her chair in closer. "Let's think this through. Eleanor wants the firehouse. Badly." As the words came out of her mouth, she could hear Oz's voice telling her to focus on the Cabrini heist, let someone else take care of the kids.

"Yes," Ruby said.

"Why?" Claudine asked. "Why is she willing to go to these lengths, enough to hire a PR firm and pledge twenty-five thousand dollars for a new shelter?"

"She must be getting a lot more than that for it," Ruby said. "With her condo complex."

"Or something else," Claudine said. "If we knew more, we might be able to figure out what to do next."

"What about the land around the firehouse? It's mostly old warehouses and things, right?" Deborah's nose was still red, but she'd set down her wad of tissues. "Maybe she wants a big parcel."

Claudine nodded. "Yes. Like south of town, that chunk of land she bought up, then sold to the county for the sewage treatment plant."

"It was legal, though. All legal," Ruby said.

"Was it really?" Claudine reached for the teapot. It was empty. The host ran over to refill it. After he left, she lowered her voice and said, "Sure, that's what she'd say." Ruby sure was being quiet. "But is it the truth?"

"I guess we'll never know," Deborah said. "It's not like we can blackmail her."

"No, that was a stupid idea." Ruby was coming around again. "It was the only thing we could grab onto then, but making up evidence got us into trouble."

"We're not completely helpless. We simply need a good plan to draw out Eleanor Millhouse. A plan that will make her show who she really is," Claudine said. She signaled the waiter. "Another pot of tea, please." She turned to the Boosters again. "We'll need it. This plan must be flawless. We can't afford to mess it up."

"No more mean things, though," Deborah said.

"No. We need to set it up so that it's her own greed that gets her into trouble," Claudine said. "It's our job to lay out the noose. She can hang herself. And we're going to have to work fast."

Ruby checked the tea room's gilt clock. "I have a meeting at five, but I'm listening."

***

Ruby sat alone in Eleanor Millhouse's office at the Shangri-La. The desk was perfectly clear, except for a gold pen in a holder and a white orchid. No personal photos, not even a telephone. And everything was white. White furniture, white walls, white marble floor. You could lose your way to the door from snow blindness.

Speaking of snow, it was cold in here. She smoothed her scarf to cover more of her neck. No wonder Eleanor's skin looked so good. It was perfectly preserved in this refrigerator. How come you couldn't get a good hot flash when you needed one?

The door opened behind her, and Eleanor's heels clicked across the marble floor, a sound to which Ruby was getting accustomed.

"Nice office," Ruby said.

"I don't use it much. Just for spa business." The orchid bobbed on her desk when she sat. "You've looked at my offer?"

"Yes." Despite the cold, Ruby's hands were clammy.

"Then we've come to an understanding." Eleanor's gaze was steel-taut. She didn't need to say that she knew what the Boosters were up to, and that they'd been fools to think they'd outwit her. Just like the alpha dog, she didn't need to snarl or pick a fight. The pack knew who was boss.

Ruby swallowed. "Yes. I'll take the job."

Chapter Twenty-Four

Eleanor nodded. "So, what's the real reason you want the firehouse?" She folded her arms over her chest and leaned back.

Ruby relaxed. Claudine had been right. Eleanor believed the whole world thought her way. "I don't know if I should tell you."

"Ruby." How strange to hear her name from Eleanor's lips. "If we're working together, we must have an understanding. No secrets."

Ruby's gaze wandered the room's antiseptic furnishings, the hard floor, the orchid. Maybe it wasn't the breeze that rattled the orchid, but the poor flower was shivering. "Okay. Radium."

Eleanor raised an eyebrow.

"There's a huge radium deposit directly below the firehouse. It's worth millions."

"Radium," Eleanor repeated. "You expect me to believe that."

Ruby filled her lungs with frigid air. "You asked, I told you. It doesn't matter if you believe me, because we have the mining rights. For radium. At $25,000 a gram." Deborah had suggested the radium angle, said it was used in watches.

A faint hum told her the air conditioning was kicking in. The orchid bobbed again from its cachepot. Ruby kept her expression neutral.

At last, Eleanor nodded. A strangely incongruous smile widened her lips. "I knew it. I knew it wasn't those orphans." Her laughter sounded raw, unpracticed.

"The county would never have sold us the land if they knew about it. We had to make up something. Who would be heartless enough to deny a family homeless shelter?" Ruby hoped her smile didn't come off as sarcastic.

"How do you know about the radium?"

"Grandpa Granzer is a freak about firehouses, as you know. He'd heard stories. So we hired a scientist to run some tests."

"You and Deborah Granzer did this?" Good. Eleanor still didn't know about Claudine. "Why? Deborah has plenty of money of her own. It's an odd project for you to take up."

"She and her husband have a pretty tight pre-nuptial agreement, and things weren't looking good between them." She glanced up for Eleanor's response and saw no change in expression. "As for me, well, you saw my house. Who can't use a little extra cash? I haven't had a vacation in years." A hot beach in Hawaii sounded good about now. She resisted the urge to stick her hands under her arms for warmth. "Our first step was to get the land. We'd worry about mining it later."

"So you investigated, found out you could extract the radium somehow."

"Definitely. We hired a scientist to measure the radium vein and estimate how much it would cost to mine it."

"What about mining it? Do you have estimates?"

"That's the best part. The extraction is targeted. The university is working up a new technique with lasers." Shoot, she'd better watch herself.

"And buyers? Have you worked out the market angle?"

"No problem. There's an international market."

"There's no reason for you to lie to me."

"Oh, no." Ruby shook her head a few times for emphasis. "You wouldn't lie to me."

"Of course not. You're doing me a great favor. You'll be rewarded." She nailed Ruby again with her stare. "If what you say is the truth."

"Oh, it is." Ruby bit her lip. "But...."

"But what?"

"There's one complication. As I said, the Booster Club as a corporation owns the mining rights. It isn't up to just me."

"They aren't worth much to you if you can't use them."

"True. The radium has been undisturbed for years. It's not like anyone has to mine it immediately." Ruby wrinkled her brow in what she hoped was a hard-thinking expression. "Maybe, though...."

"Maybe though what?"

"We could have a partnership. I might be able to convince the other members that having you on board is a benefit."

Eleanor smiled again. "Of course. My thoughts exactly. But there's one thing."

Ruby drew a breath. "What?"

"I need to meet this scientist. Today."

"Today? I don't know. I mean, it's already past office hours." At last. A hot flash. Ruby fanned herself with her employment agreement. "I could call. See about something over the next few days."

"Then first thing tomorrow. I'll need to see your mining agreement and the results of the study. I can't go ahead on your word alone. I'm sure you understand."

Lord, this hot flash was a whopper. Without changing expression, Eleanor pulled a crisp handkerchief from her top drawer and handed it to her. Ruby mopped her brow. "The change."

"I'm several years away from your condition—"

A hot flash would never dare spark in her icy gut, Ruby thought.

"—but we sell a proprietary blend of Himalayan goat hormones you might find beneficial. They're dear to import, but since we're colleagues, I can offer it to you at a discount. I hear they're quite effective. Of course, you won't advertise that the Shangri-La sells them. The F.D.A. isn't familiar with this blend."

"Thank you." Lord, that woman knew how to bag her quarry.

Eleanor leaned forward. "I know we'll work well together, but you understand why I don't completely trust you yet. Certain recent events prove your resourcefulness but perhaps not your integrity."

The room's frigid air began to seep into her skin once again, transforming into a clammy dampness. "Yes. I understand. I'll set up a meeting with Dr. Heilig and his team for first thing tomorrow."

***

Ruby burst into the Villa Saint Nicholas. "Everyone! Emergency."

Most of the Villa's residents were in the cafeteria toying with the night's serving of tuna casserole, except Hugo, who'd inhaled his plate and was reaching for Gilda's. Joanie sat on the floor brushing Tinkerbell, and Lucy and Scotty were playing cards. Only Hank and Grady were missing. Ruby darted to the

TV room, grabbed the remote control from Grady's side, and urged him into the cafeteria.

"What's going on?" André asked.

"Where's Hank?" Ruby said.

"He took dinner on a tray upstairs."

"We need him down here." Ruby tossed her tote bag on a table. "We have a situation. I called Deb and Claudine, and they're on their way."

Gilda cackled. "So, it's a go. The old biddy bit on it."

"Calm down," Warren said. Tinkerbell rose and wagged at his arrival. He gave her a beef bone, and she settled again at Joanie's side, the bone clasped in her teeth.

"You can make some fresh coffee," Ruby said. "We're going to be up for a while. We need a lab, some scientists, mineral rights paperwork, and a scientific report on radium."

Hank's voice came from behind her. His wheelchair clicked over the threshold. "When?"

"Tomorrow morning."

"No problem," Hank said. "Eddie did some topnotch counterfeiting in the early sixties. Mostly I.D. paperwork, but you duped some deeds, didn't you?"

"Plus a couple death certificates and a cat license," Eddie said. He set aside his copy of *Popular Mechanics*. "I don't have my materials anymore, though."

"I got a nice printer," Grady said. "If you've got the eye for detail."

The Rizzio kids had ceased all activity. "Kids, you go up to André's room and work on your homework," Ruby said.

"Why?" Scotty said. "I'm learning a lot right here."

"That's the problem," Ruby said.

"I'll take them up," Gilda said. "Come on, kids. Just be thankful all these nice people care so much for you. Come on, you too, Hugo."

Hugo refused to budge. He'd set down his fork even though half a piece of cheesecake was left at Gilda's seat. "I'm eighteen." At Gilda's stern look, he added, "Well, practically. I'm an adult. Why can't I be part of this?"

"Don't you have some homework to finish?" Bobby said.

"What?" he said. "You're all crooks, or at least you used to be. Mom was, too. I know that."

Gilda sat down again, Joanie, Lucy, and Scotty at her side. "We don't know what she wanted for you, honey."

"You should have choices, son," Father Vincent said. "Go to college, see what you want to do. You have mechanical gifts. You might want to be an engineer."

"Or an actor," André said.

"Or a pickpocket or a cyberhacker," Hugo said.

"Stop it right there," Hank said. "Maybe this life looks swanky to you. Maybe you see our camaraderie, our fancy French food, and you think you want a part of that."

"I take issue with the food," Bobby said.

"What you don't know is about those of us who got kicked out of our families or who couldn't make homes because we couldn't talk about our work in public," Hank said. "Or who ended up in prison, like Gilda's husband."

"He's still in jail?" Lucy asked.

"Nah, got out during the Nixon administration. Hit by a bus not long after." She crossed herself. "Rest in peace."

"Your mother didn't make it," Bobby said. "I think her fall broke her spirit more than anything else."

A sniffle escaped Joanie. She clutched Tinkerbell's neck.

"I would have done it differently, myself," Ruby said. The others seemed to have forgotten she was there. "Hiding the life from my husband is one of the hardest things I've ever done."

"Maybe he'd understand," Lucy said.

"Outsiders don't get it," Hank said.

"Come on, honey," Gilda said. "We're going upstairs."

"No. I want to stay here and be part of it," Hugo said.

"That's a great attitude, Hugo, but you can help best by keeping your brother and sisters out of harm's way," Claudine said. Ruby hadn't heard her come in. She was standing behind Hank in the cafeteria's doorway.

Hugo slumped behind her, his siblings following. "Okay. I don't want to go, but okay."

At the sound of the elevator door closing, Claudine stepped into the room. "Now. Tell me what needs to get done."

Chapter Twenty-Five

Deborah arrived at the university before the others. Thanks to Louie, she wasn't sleeping anyway. It was only the thought of this morning's project that kept her from trolling for watches.

From the chemistry lab's front steps, she watched the campus bustle. Some students rode bicycles, others toted backpacks and mugs of coffee as they kicked up leaves along the sidewalk. College life had been so fun. She'd been in a sorority—just a townie, she lived with her parents and worked weekends at the dry cleaning shop—and life had been full of possibilities. She was sure she'd be a teacher and start her own family. Her mom had asked her about kids just last week. Deborah looked down at her flat stomach, imagining the swell of a baby.

Now she was on her way to divorce. At some point Louie would come home, and she'd be kicked out. She'd be lucky to wring a few cents from the divorce, even with the photos from the hotel. Plus, where would she buy her groceries?

The Rizzio kids were her only spot of hope right now. Although, even if Eleanor followed through and they did save the firehouse, Grandpa Granzer wasn't likely to write a million dollar check to his ex-granddaughter-in-law. She'd brought this up at the Villa last night, but Claudine only said they'd cross that bridge when they came to it. There were a lot of bridges between now and peace of mind.

"You sent out the notice, right? To everyone?" Deborah recognized Ruby's voice and stood, wiping the dirt from her seat. Grady and Father Vincent followed her.

"I told you I did," Grady said. "Now quit harping at me. I got a few 'out of town' replies, but everyone else thinks there's an earthquake inspection today. As long as the university keeps its department email lists updated, we're fine."

"Oh, Deb." Ruby hugged her, enveloping her in fruity perfume. "How was last night?"

"I'm okay."

"Jerk. Got no chutzpah. A real man would have stayed around to fight for you," Grady said. "Where's Deanie? She drags me out here before my morning shows are over, but she doesn't show up herself."

"We made good time," Father Vincent said. His normally frazzled hair was slicked straight, and he pulled a collapsible hand truck with a box on it. "Maybe she doesn't know traffic patterns like I do."

"I'm here." Deborah spun in the direction of Claudine's low voice. "But just for a minute, then I'm out of the picture. You don't know me. Got it?" She glanced down the college's central square. "Side door?"

"Oh. I forgot," Deborah said.

"Son of a sea biscuit," Grady said. "Bunch of amateurs." Despite his gruff tone, Deborah would have sworn he was enjoying himself.

The lab's front door opened. A bearded man in a white lab coat looked down at them. "May I help you?" he asked in a vaguely European accent.

Claudine pushed past him. "André. Nice work, but you sound more Ukrainian than Austrian. Did you get a meeting room ready?"

"No. I came in when the janitor left. I was waiting for you."

"According to the building's floor plans, the lab proper is on the east side toward the rear." They followed her confident trot through the chemistry building's halls. "Here."

"See, all locked up. I told you," Grady said.

Dark showed behind the door's frosted window. Claudine glanced up the hall, then took two small tools from her purse. To Deborah, they looked like steel manicure tools. In a second, the door was open, and Claudine was in. Deborah stepped forward, but André held her back. Claudine returned a moment later and nodded.

"The back lab is open. André should be able to break into the AV cabinet if you need it. Right?"

"I haven't forgotten everything, Deanie," he said.

Deborah watched them. Definitely a hit woman, she thought. She was in a hurry to get out, too. Probably off to take out a rival mobster. Deborah would watch the news for a report of a shooting.

"The accent is getting better, but watch your 'r's." With that, she was gone.

If only Deborah had Claudine's confidence. It was as if Claudine could do anything. She could break into buildings and climb up walls. People listened to her. If she were married, her husband would never leave her.

Ruby put a hand on her arm. "Come on, Deb. This is important. No time for daydreaming. We only have half an hour until Eleanor gets here."

***

The desk phone buzzed. "Eleanor Millhouse is here to see you."

"Thank you, Marjorie. Send her back," André said.

To Deborah, no matter what Claudine said, André sounded just like an Austrian scientist. He looked like one, too. It wasn't just his crisp lab coat, it was as if his whole body had changed. It was André's eyes and nose, but they might have been stuck on someone else.

She stood when Eleanor entered. André was flipping through some papers on the desk and seemed surprised that Eleanor had come in, even though he'd just told Gilda to let her back.

"Ah, Ms. Millhouse," André said. "Dr. Heilig." He extended a hand.

"Thank you for meeting with me on such short notice." Eleanor released André's hand and turned to her. "Deborah. Ruby has told me a lot about you."

Deborah couldn't even force a smile. Here was the woman who broke up her marriage. She'd been ready to blame it all on Louie, but now that Eleanor stood here, so superior, with that didn't-I-tell-you look in her eyes, her chest filled with anger. She and the girls had set it up so it only looked like Roger Millhouse was unfaithful. Even if Roger took the bait, Deborah would never have crossed the line with him. Eleanor—or some minion—had gone a lot further than that.

"I'm really looking forward to working with you," Deborah said. And, oh, yes, she meant it. "I know we've had some, uh, misunderstandings, but that's over now."

"I always believe in being straightforward. I think you'll find that if you're honest with me, I'll be honest with you." She gave a tight smile. "It's best for all of us."

"Am I on time?" Ruby rushed in, just as they'd planned. "Traffic was awful."

Thank goodness for traffic, the all-purpose excuse. Ruby edged near Deborah and touched her hand.

"Yes," André said. "Well, I don't have much time until I have to get back to the lab. How can I help you?"

"We want to know more about Carsonville's radium reserves," Ruby said.

"Let me handle this." Eleanor stepped forward, practically pushing Ruby back. "What can you tell me about radium in Carsonville?"

"What exactly do you want to know?"

"If there is any radium, for one thing."

André dropped his papers in shock. "What? You doubt me." He looked at Grady in bewilderment. "She doubts us."

With his grim expression, Grady appeared to be channeling an extra in *Practical Hospital* preparing to deliver a cancer diagnosis. "Impossible."

"Oh, yes," he said to Eleanor. "Yes. Quite a deep vein."

"Then why hasn't anyone found it before?" Eleanor said.

They hadn't practiced this bit. André appeared completely unfazed. "Very good question, Ms. Millhouse. Perhaps you have scientific training? No?" André pulled a marked-up geographic survey of Carsonville from a stack of papers. "Usually, radium is mixed into the earth in broad patches. Mining it means separating the mineral from the earth's substrata. It's a difficult and costly process."

"Why costly?"

"Chiefly because of the radioactive detritus. The clean-up can run into the millions, depending on how much ground must be sorted."

Eleanor paused, then said, "But it's worth it."

"At nearly \$25,000 a gram—a single gram—yes, many would say it's worth it." He nodded for emphasis. "Plus, we have an unusual situation in Carsonville, which is why the radium has taken so long to document."

Gilda's voice rose from the hall, and the unmistakable sound of brisk footsteps approached the office. Deborah grabbed Ruby's arm just as the door burst open.

"Sorry I'm late." Deborah squinted. It couldn't be—Hugo? He wore a lab jacket, and he'd cut his hair to a dark bristle.

"Leave the door open," André said, again appearing to take this unexpected visit in stride. "This is our intern, Bradley. Bradley, you can get started evaluating the samples in the lab." He shot Hugo a purposeful look.

"I thought you said you needed me to work on the files today, Dr. Heilig." Hugo pulled himself more deeply into the room, attaching himself to a file cabinet.

"Never mind that," Eleanor said. "Finish what you were going to say. About why this radium is special."

Hugo would pay for this, Deborah thought, but as fast as her anger rose, it melted into concern. The poor boy just wanted to help.

André glanced at Hugo. "Yes. Well, Carsonville's radium vein is narrow and deep. An unusual radium formation."

"I understand it can be mined with lasers."

Deborah looked up at an odd noise from Ruby's throat. André glanced at her and nodded once.

"Yes. A new technology. It's still quite damaging environmentally, but at least the damage is localized."

"I'd like to see your report," Eleanor said.

"It's quite scientific. Not written for the layperson."

"I'd still like to see it. If I'm going to invest, I want to know what I'm investing in."

André drew a deep breath. "Very well. I have only a few minutes, but come into the lab."

With Hugo at their heels, they passed into the hall and then into a room with a long, black-topped lab table in the middle. They joined Father Vincent, also in a lab coat, fiddling with containers of dirt. Father Vincent had insisted Eleanor wouldn't recognize him without his collar, and as far as Deborah could tell, he was right. The computer monitor at the room's far end quickly flipped from what looked to be a soap opera to a bunch of numbers.

"I thought you were helping with the filing, Bradley," André said, looking at Grady and Father Vincent.

"I am." Hugo didn't move.

André shook his head and handed Eleanor a bound report. "I can't let you take this from this room. It's not yet been peer-reviewed."

That's not all it hadn't been, either, Deborah thought.

"My assistant, Dr. Grady, can show you a 3-D simulation we created from our studies of the area—"

Without warning, Eleanor began jerking open cabinets and pulling out papers. She grabbed handfuls and peeled off pages with a glance at each. They fell to the floor and slid under furniture.

"Eleanor!" Deborah said. The air filled with urgency.

"Ms. Millhouse. What are you doing?" André dashed to the cabinets while Eleanor spread the papers on the lab table. Father Vincent and Grady looked on, jaws dropped.

"She doesn't trust us," Deborah said, hands on hips. "She doesn't believe you, Dr. Heilig."

"Just protecting my investment." She picked up one paper,

tossed it to the side, and examined another. She stood up. "These look to be in order. All on radium."

"Of course they are," Father Vincent said. "I don't under-stand—"

The lab door flew open. "Who are you?" A woman—a stranger—trailing a rolling suitcase stood at the door. "I just got back from the conference. I thought the faculty meeting was this morning."

Shoot. Someone didn't get Grady's email. Deborah's gaze rocketed to André. Surely he'd get them out of this.

Hugo smiled and stepped forward. "Dr. Mullins. You're back early."

"Who are you?" the woman said.

"Bradley. Remember? I had that idea for an experiment with the ultra-twenty-nine molecule? We talked about it a couple of weeks ago? Don't tell me you forgot already." Hugo turned to André. "Pardon me, Dr. Heilig." He grabbed the woman's suitcase and wheeled it down the hall. Reluctantly the woman followed. Their voices receded into the empty hall.

"One of our brightest scientists," Grady said, "But she can't remember squat."

The wall clock's minute hand clicked forward. Five to ten.

"Ms. Millhouse, I must be getting to my next appointment. If you have questions, you'll contact me, right? In the mean-time, we have some cleanup to do." He glared at the mess of papers Eleanor had spread on the table.

Eleanor hesitated only a moment before nodding once. "Thank you, Dr. Heilig."

Before Grady turned off the lab's lights, Deborah saw him slip a paper on the table. "Certificate of Earthquake Compli-ance," it said.

***

"All right. Now that the radium is verified, we'll meet at the tea house to discuss the mining rights," Eleanor said once they were in the parking lot.

Deborah glanced at Ruby. "Oh, no, we can't meet there." Deborah's pulse still raced after the scene in the lab.

"Why not?" Eleanor tugged on her pearls, the only sign of nervousness Deborah had seen yet. "It's so close."

"I never go there. The service isn't very good," Deborah lied.

"On the contrary, I find the service excellent. Ruby agrees, don't you?"

"Sure. I guess. Deb, will you give me a ride? Bruce has the car."

"You'll ride with me." Eleanor clicked a button on her key fob. The Jaguar's locks snicked open. "See you there."

Ruby and Eleanor were already seated when Deborah arrived. The host was right behind her.

"Ladies?" he said, clearly puzzled at the new alliance. "Can I get you your usuals?"

Deborah barely nodded, and Eleanor shot her a look. Ruby said, "That's fine."

Eleanor set two copies of a multi-page document on the table. "It took my attorney all night to draw these up, but I wanted to have an agreement in place for sharing the mineral rights." She set two pens next to it. "Initial each page and sign at the end."

The host arrived with Oolong tea for Ruby, Deb's usual Earl Grey, and a tea cup only a third full of amber liquid for Eleanor.

"I think you got shorted, Eleanor," Ruby said. She stirred

her tea leaves with satisfaction.

Eleanor downed the tea cup's contents in one throw. "It's from the owner's private stock. An eighteen-year double barrel Scotch." She pushed the pens. "Sign it."

Ruby picked up the agreement. "We can't just sign this without knowing what it is."

Deborah looked at Ruby anxiously. "Why do we need to sign anything?"

"Well, I'll tell you what it is." The Scotch had flushed Eleanor's neck. "It's a legally binding agreement that says that I have a share in whatever radium is extracted. You'd do the same. We don't have time before the county commissioners' meeting for me to get an independent verification of the radium. I need protection."

"Is that all?" Ruby ruffled the papers. "That's a lot of pages to say just that."

"It also says that my name will be kept out of the venture."

"But you're buying the property, and now you'll have a share in the mining rights. How can your name be hidden?" Deborah said. "That doesn't seem right. This print is awfully small, and it must be eight pages, two-sided. Ruby, I don't know if we should sign this without reading it through. How about if we come back tomorrow after we have someone look at it?" She thought about her pre-nup with Louie. Now she wished she'd read that more thoroughly.

"Eleanor will tell us what's in there, won't you? We all have an interest in this project. We profit or fail together," Ruby said.

"I don't know—" Deborah started. That marriage-busting witch. She'd cheat them for every penny, she knew it.

Eleanor pushed her tea cup to the side. "I understand why you hesitate. It's smart business. Look, I'll summarize the agreement for you." She peeled off her fingers. "One, it says that I get an equal share in the radium. Two, my name is kept out of it. We form a separate corporation. I have a team that can do that for us. Three, we go along with the family shelter ploy."

"Ploy?" Deborah couldn't help but say.

"Yes, the front you put up. At the final commissioners' meeting on Monday, they'll sign over the land to me, and I'll publicly announce that I'm allowing you to build a family shelter."

"I don't get what we have to hide, though," Deborah said. "Why can't anyone know about the radium mining? Once we have the land, that is."

Eleanor shook her head, and her pearls tipped from side to side. "The radium mining needs to be kept quiet at first."

"But it's perfectly legal—" Deborah said.

"That's not why." Now Eleanor's voice was sharp. "If the commissioners—well, one in particular—knew it wasn't part of a commercial project, he'd call off the sale in a millisecond. He's sensitive about his reputation."

"But what about jobs? The economy?" Deborah knew she was simply being perverse at this point. Ruby kicked her under the table.

"No. We keep it quiet. It will be a family shelter and part of a larger commercial development as far as anyone else is concerned."

"And the radium mining?" Ruby asked.

"Will come later. Once we 'discover' it's there. Then the profit is ours and ours alone. No sharing with government contacts. Get it?"

Ruby pressed Deborah's knee under the table.

"Now sign the agreement. I swear to you, there's nothing underhanded there. It's simply to safeguard my interests. I'm the one paying for the land, after all."

Deborah let out a long breath. "I don't know, Ruby. How do we know we can trust her? Shouldn't we have someone look at this for us?"

Ruby and Eleanor shared a glance.

"If we're going to work together, we must trust each other. All solid relationships are built on trust," Eleanor said.

Right. Deborah had trusted Louie, and look where that got her.

"We'd better sign it, Deb," Ruby said.

"Are you sure?" Deborah asked Ruby in a low voice.

"I don't see that we have a choice." She looked up at Eleanor, who made no pretense of not listening. "We have to trust her."

Deborah hesitated, then picked up the pen.

Chapter Twenty-Six

Claudine had half an hour. That was it. Half an hour to break into Eleanor Millhouse's office and get what she came for. Ruby and Deborah would spend most of the night arranging the rest, but she'd go straight to the airport for San Francisco. In the trunk of her car was a satchel with everything she'd need for the museum break-in. She took a deep breath. She'd have plenty of time. Even if the office had an alarm, this was a ten minute in-and-out job. Ruby would stop by the airport's long-term parking later and get what she needed.

Fine Properties of Distinction was on the fourth floor just to the right of the elevators. As she'd expected, the front lobby was dark through the locked glass double doors. Also as she'd expected, a smaller, windowless door down the hall opened into the offices. She slipped a picklock from her jacket pocket and was though the door in seconds.

Just inside, a noise stopped her. She flattened her back against the wall. It sounded like conversation. But with a laugh track? Staying close to the wall, she crept around the corner. Through a conference room door, she saw two of the cleaning crew, their mop and trash buckets nearby, watching TV. One of them said something to the other in Spanish. The first janitor unwrapped a sandwich.

Shoot. It was their dinner break. She couldn't pass the window without raising an alarm, and Ellie's office was almost certainly the one on the corner, up the hall. She glanced at her watch. A quarter past eight. The show would likely run until the half hour, and the cleaning crew would leave. To her right was an office. Its door was open, and the trash was emptied. It had already been cleaned. She slipped inside, closed the door behind her, and dropped to the floor to wait.

Under the desk was an extensive collection of pumps, most with creased leather at the toes and worn heels, and a grocery sack. Claudine peeked inside. Romance novels. On the desk sat two photos, one a wedding photo of a petite blonde and a meaty guy with eyes a little too close together to recommend a Mensa membership, and the other a toddler with fairy-like blue eyes and wispy blond hair.

She peeled up her sleeve again to look at her watch. Only five minutes had passed. This was taking forever. Should she risk it and crawl past the conference room? No. Chances were the cleaning crew was already on alert, knowing that they shouldn't be hanging out watching television, even if it was their break time.

Oswald would be getting antsy, too. She'd always made a point of showing up a little bit early, not blowing in to the airport at the last minute like she would tonight. Otherwise, everything was set up for the jewel heist. They'd found another jeweler, and she and the Oz had run through the rest of their plans point-by-point until every minute of the next twenty-four hours was memorized, down to bathroom breaks.

Her phone vibrated. A text. "Where are you?"

"On my way," she texted back. Damn. Still another five minutes. Listening for movement in the hall, she did a few dexterity exercises with her hands. Three minutes left.

She could leave now. If she rushed, she could make it to the airport. If she left, by this time tomorrow she'd be on another plane, a flight to Geneva with the jewels hidden among the extra set of fakes she had made as part of her second role as a costume jewelry salesperson restocking the museum shop. She'd be away—away from these stupid insurance jobs, away from Carsonville with its petty squabbles among Women's League members, away from one-horse town politicians like Ned Rossum. She could finally decide what to do with her life.

But she'd also be away from her father. She'd miss him during the months she needed to stay out of the country. Heck, she'd miss the rest of the Villa's residents, too. They were a ragtag bunch, but they really cared about her. And she for them. She'd miss Hugo's graduation from high school. The kid had the makings for something great, she knew it. That is, if he had a home and a chance for a decent education.

It was as if she were two people: one who chose to stay and see the firehouse and the Rizzio kids through, and one who couldn't believe she was passing up the biggest score of her life—the chance for another life.

She looked at the bag of shoes, the romance novels, the family photos where she hid. Realization crept over her, like a light on a dimmer switch slowly cranked to full wattage. She was already living another life. She hadn't carried out a job in weeks. The woman who worked in this office didn't need millions of dollars of jewels to live a happy, stable life, and neither did Claudine. Somehow, the transformation had already taken place.

At last the creaking of the mop bucket's wheels told her that the cleaning crew had left the conference room. She crossed her fingers that they'd already emptied the wastebaskets in the rest of the office. She didn't have a second to spare.

After an eternity—probably merely ten minutes—they wheeled past her out the side door. She crouched behind the desk until she heard the tumbler turn in the lock. She let out a breath and shot down the hall with measured but lightning-fast movement.

As she'd anticipated, Ellie's office was in the corner. The door handle didn't budge. She probably didn't trust the cleaning crew, or anyone else for that matter. Claudine's gloved hands quickly picked the lock.

A faint vibration in her pocket told her she'd received another text. Oswald. "Too late. Gone."

***

For a moment, Claudine stalled, letting the implications of the text message sink in. *Gone.* He'd left for the jewel heist without her. With a few adjustments, he was perfectly capable of carrying it out. And of cutting her out of the proceeds completely, which he would. Of course. And it was only right. Maybe he'd known her better than she'd known herself and planned a back-up. That wouldn't surprise her, either.

She waited for the pang of regret, but it didn't come. She was where she needed to be.

Which was standing in the middle of Eleanor Whiteby Millhouse's office in the dark. Imagine that.

Ellie's desk was the size of a billiards table with a polished mahogany surface, washed over by the sparse light of a new moon. A Chinese porcelain cachepot with a white moth orchid sat in one corner, and a tidy in-box in the other. Tasteful prints framed in chrome lined the wall behind her desk, including an award for Carsonville Businesswoman of the Year. Most of all she noticed the cold. She was warmer hiding in the cubicle down the hall. The air here sliced to the bone.

It took only a few seconds to pick the filing cabinet's lock and get the papers she needed. She slipped them into her shoulder bag. Now that she wasn't leaving for San Francisco, she'd take them to the Villa in person. She also had the time to do a bit more looking around. Ellie would be too smart to keep evidence of collusion, but it wouldn't hurt to look. Ten minutes later, she scanned the room to make sure she hadn't left signs of her presence. The office was still and icy. She turned to leave.

Through the glass door appeared a face. Ellie's. Adrenaline streaked through Claudine's muscles, then as fast as it had soared, it cut. Ellie's face broke into a grin, the same grin Claudine had seen at the county commissioners' hearing—and a long time ago in the vice principal's office. But it wasn't the grin that captured Claudine's attention. It was the snub-nosed handgun Ellie held waist high.

Ellie pushed open the door. "I could shoot you right now, you know."

"But you won't," Claudine replied. Her voice was perfectly calm, her pulse remained even. All those years of training paid off.

Ellie seemed surprised at her response, and her smile faltered. "Why not?"

"Because it might stain the carpet."

In two steps Eleanor reached the phone. "I'm calling security." With the gun trained on Claudine, she picked up the receiver. Then put it down without dialing. She clicked on her desk lamp. "You look familiar."

Claudine remained expressionless.

"Where do I know you?"

She didn't reply.

Ellie stared at her, and the satisfied smile appeared once again. "You're Deanie Dupin. I remember you." She laughed, a shrill, uncomfortable sound that belied her expensive trench coat and Hermès bag. "Oh, my God. This is too much. Deanie Dupin the thief. I'm not calling security at all." She looked at Claudine to see how she took that statement, but Claudine knew she appeared perfectly indifferent. "I'm calling the police."

Her fingers punched 911 on the phone. "I have an intruder and need the police immediately. Yes." She gave the dispatcher the address, all the while keeping her gaze trained on Claudine's. Claudine did not look away.

"You always were trash," Ellie said. "Thought you were too good for everyone else, but you were just a little thief. And you still are. Amazing." She shook her head.

"You've spent a lot of time thinking about me, haven't you?"

She choked off a bitter laugh. "You're not worth a second of my time. Just because you always had someone dropping you off at school, telling you to have a good day, handing you some disgusting bagged lunch…." Her smile only faltered a second.

Now Claudine understood. Ellie was jealous. It hardly seemed possible.

"And you had that hood of a boyfriend, Oswald," Ellie continued. "Just because all the girls liked him, it didn't mean he was anything special. Where'd he end up, anyway? Sing Sing?"

Claudine leaned against the window frame and crossed her arms. "I'm impressed you remember so many details after all these years."

"Shut up. What did you break in for today? Maybe you thought you'd steal the engravings. Or maybe you're working for a competitor and you want my business plans. Good thing I stopped by to pick up some work." She smirked. "What's wrong? You've got nothing to say? You can't contradict me, can you?"

"I've got something to say, all right." Claudine's temper simmered. Only sheer discipline kept it out of sight.

"Go ahead. I'm listening." Ellie's grip tightened on the handgun. The other hand rose to her pearl necklace.

"Your Kelly bag is a fake. I don't know where you got it, but the Hermès stamp should match the hardware."

Ellie's breath came in angry puffs. "I paid three thousand dollars for this bag." The gun, her finger on the trigger, waved erratically.

"I have a question for you. You were homecoming queen. You even dated the quarterback."

Ellie's breathing calmed. "Yeah. Chad. I think he's selling refrigerators now."

"You were in the honors society. You won heaps of scholarships." She didn't have long. Soon the police would arrive. "Why did you ruin my chances at college? Why couldn't you let it go?"

"What you did was wrong. I had to tell."

"And it wasn't wrong to shoot down my future?" Claudine stepped forward. "Or ruin the lives of the people whose homes you worked with the county to have condemned?"

Ellie's nostrils flared. "That's the way the world works, Deanie. There's not room for everyone at the top. It's a meritocracy. It's pretty clear who the deserving are." She raised the gun. "You know, I could shoot you for breaking in, and I'd be within the law." She cocked the hammer. "No one would miss a piece of garbage like you."

At movement in the hall, Claudine let out her breath. Blood

hummed in her ears.

"Police." Two uniformed men, guns drawn, stood in the hall, with one of the building's security guards behind them. "Drop the gun." Ellie swung her arms toward them. "Drop it!" She lowered her arm and let the handgun slide to the desk. One of the officers edged to the desk and grabbed the gun, handing it to the other officer.

"I'm not the intruder," Ellie barked. "She is." She pointed at Claudine.

Claudine could have been a burglar. She was dressed all in black—black pants, black jacket, black turtleneck—although they were street clothes. Her hair was pulled into a neat ponytail.

"I'm building security," Claudine said. "I saw a light on and stopped in to investigate."

Ellie rolled her eyes. "Please. I came in my office, and she was here getting ready to steal something."

"I'm on the building security staff," Claudine repeated. She took a leather folder from an inside pocket and flipped it open.

"You don't know her. I do. She's a thief, I tell you," Ellie shouted. "She stole in high school, and she steals now. Don't trust her."

"Her I.D. looks real," one of the officers said. The other officer holstered his gun.

"It's a phony. She probably had it made up for just this kind of situation. I've never seen her here before." Ellie's face was breaking into red splotches.

"You know her?" the policeman asked the security guard and jerked a thumb toward Claudine.

He nodded. "Sure. Claudine Dupin. Works nights. That's probably why Ms. Millhouse doesn't recognize her."

The first officer holstered his gun, too, and turned to the

front door. "Next time, ma'am, you might want to call security before you dial 911. We have real emergencies to deal with."

Claudine silently thanked M&M Security.

***

Safely in her car, Claudine punched Ruby's number into her cell phone. Her breath steamed in the cold.

When Ruby answered, Neil Young singing in the background, Claudine said, "Listen. I ran into Eleanor Millhouse tonight and—"

"Oh, my God. She was there?"

"I'm fine. It's taken care of."

A few bars of "Harvest Moon" played faintly. "You're okay, then." A pause. "I thought you had a job to do tonight. Something big. In another city."

Claudine started the car and turned on the heater. "I did. Someone else is taking it over. This is the most important thing now."

Ruby was silent, but Claudine knew she hadn't hung up because she still heard music. "Thanks, Claudine. This means a lot to the kids—and to us."

Claudine's throat thickened. "I'm here to help. For the commissioners' meeting tomorrow afternoon."

"Good. We'll need you."

Chapter Twenty-Seven

The county commissioners' meeting was unrolling exactly as they'd expected—and as the commissioners had expected. Except for one thing, Ruby noted. The crowd.

The meeting was the final order of business that afternoon, and as a sign that it was expected to be a short one, the meeting was scheduled for four-thirty. By four-fifteen, the recorder had to call for help from upstairs to log the meeting's participants. People of all sorts filed into the meeting room. Families, elderly people, kids, individuals. The recorder and her assistant were stumped. Ruby didn't know any of them, either—except for the residents of Villa Saint Nicholas.

The size of the audience didn't seem to faze Eleanor. She was as calm and unflappable as ever, chatting with the commissioners before the meeting started. Ruby snapped open her fan and flapped it at her face. Eleanor had assured them that the sale would go through just fine. If all went well, a family shelter would be up and running before long.

"Nervous?" Ruby asked Deborah.

"A little."

"About Eleanor?"

Deborah nodded. "The agreement we signed—"

"Don't worry. She won't let us down." Ruby patted the chair next to her. "Sit. They're just about to start."

The chair rapped her gavel. "I call this special session to order." She seemed to realize that the room was a lot more crowded than usual. "Welcome, citizens of Carsonville County. Today's meeting—wait, the press is here?"

"Channel Two, Madame Chair," the clerk said.

Brenda waved from the side of the room. A cameraman stood next to her.

The chair drew a deep breath. "Fine. This is a fairly routine meeting. Are you sure you didn't mean to go to next month's meeting? We're discussing school funding then."

Brenda shook her head.

"All right. Fine," the chair said again. "Let's get this over with. Clerk, will you read the motion?"

"I, Chair of the Carsonville County commissioners, move to offer for sale the warehouse district firehouse and the land on which it sits to Eleanor Millhouse of Fine Properties of Distinction at a price determined by the county appraiser's office."

"I second the motion," Ned Rossum said promptly.

"All in favor."

A chorus of "aye"s came from the dais.

"Thank you." Eleanor took a microphone from the dais. "I'm certain that the warehouse district will soon be one of Carsonville's most vibrant neighborhoods. At the same time, I know there was a movement to convert the firehouse into a family shelter that this project derailed. I would like to announce that I plan to donate use of the firehouse to the Booster Club so its members can carry out their plans."

The crowd in the room clapped, then stood and continued to clap. Ruby nodded at Deborah. Deborah joined Eleanor at the front of the room.

"Thank you so much, Eleanor. When we discussed your

plans, I can't even tell you how happy I was. Now, families won't have to be split up when they fall on hard times." The crowd was beginning to clap again, but Deborah put up a hand. "And to think that you are actually deeding the land to us is wonderful. Thank you so much."

A murmur of thanks went through the audience.

"I'm afraid you've misunderstood." Eleanor held her smile. "I'll continue to own the firehouse. I'm simply letting you take over the firehouse for a while. A lease, free of charge, of course. The firehouse will be mine. As will the land's other assets."

Ruby's heart beat double-time. This wasn't part of their deal. Eleanor planned to screw them over. Then Ruby smiled.

"But you said—" Deborah started.

"I'm sorry if you didn't understand me. It's all right here in our contract. The contract you signed." She pulled a sheaf of legal-sized papers from her briefcase.

Deborah picked up the papers. "But here, on page two, it says, 'I, Eleanor Millhouse, shall relinquish all rights to and ownership of the firehouse and its lot and transfer ownership to the Booster Club for the purpose of creating a family shelter.'" Deborah flipped ahead.

"No, it—"

Deborah interrupted. "Oh, but here's the part that really warmed my heart. 'As part of the warehouse district's renovation, I will provide twenty-five units of low-income housing for people displaced by the new sewage treatment plant.'" She pulled a similar sheaf from her briefcase. "It's in my copy, too."

Now the crowd not only clapped, they whistled and stamped their feet.

"No. That's wrong. That's not what the contract says." She yanked away the papers and shuffled through them. Her face blanched. She slammed the contract shut.

A shaggy-haired man and his wife, holding a toddler's hand, stood. "Thank you. When we were forced out of our home for the sewage treatment plant, we had to move to a one-bedroom apartment on the east side. The money we got wasn't enough for anything else. This will really help."

A Latina mother stood, her family sitting around her. "We, too, had to leave our home. Someone from Fine Properties of Distinction told us we had no choice. We were so scared. Now I have to commute an hour each way to my job."

Eleanor watched the audience with rising panic showing in her face.

"Yeah," another, younger man said. "She put the 'stink' in 'distinction' all right."

Claudine stood, a white-haired woman—Letty—on her arm. Funny, Ruby hadn't even seen Claudine come in. "Go ahead, Letty."

"I—" Letty cleared her throat. "I live across the street from where they're putting in the sewage treatment plan. In a different house than I used to. My—Madeleine died when we left that house. I feel a lot older now. Knowing that you're giving us new housing, well, that means a lot. It won't bring her back, but I think Madeleine knows even now." Letty briefly closed her eyes. A rosy glow seemed to permeate her pores.

Eleanor slammed the papers on the table and pointed at Deborah. "This isn't the contract I drew up. You double-crossed me. Both of you. You want the radium for yourselves."

"Radium?" Deborah said. She did a bang-up job of looking flabbergasted, complete with dropped jaw and intermittent blinking.

"Radium?" the chair echoed.

"You signed over the radium mining rights to me, I saw you do it. That land is mine," Eleanor said.

Deborah continued to seem puzzled. "What mining rights? I don't know what you're talking about."

"You think there's radium on the firehouse's property, am I right?" the chair said.

The commissioners looked at each other. One discreetly twirled his finger by his ear for the "loco" sign.

"They signed the mining rights over to me. They signed it. I saw." Eleanor crammed fingers into the hair at her temples. "Somehow they switched the contracts."

That was some tight chignon she'd crafted, Ruby noted. It barely budged.

"I don't know what you're talking about. This is the agreement you signed. See?" Deborah pointed at the signatures.

"Dr. Heilig has stacks of studies of the radium vein. Ask him," Eleanor urged.

"I don't know who Dr. Heilig is, but we do have the county surveyor present for the presentation of the deed." She pointed into the audience. "Leonard. Come to the dais, please. Is there radium under the firehouse?"

The surveyor couldn't tear his gaze from Eleanor. "No, ma'am. Just bedrock. There's no mineable radium within three states."

"And so many people here are concerned about the sewage treatment plant," the chair said more quietly. A look of understanding passed over the chair's face. "Rossum, the sewage treatment plant is in your district, isn't it?"

Ned Rossum smiled weakly. He didn't say yes or no.

The Latina mother rose again. An envelope in hand, she approached the chair. She withdrew a letter from the envelope and smoothed it before handing it over. She returned to her seat.

As the chair skimmed the letter, other audience members

filed to the dais, too, placing letters before the chair and rejoining their neighbors.

"They're all the same. Condemnation letters with my signature," the chair said, placing the last letter on the stack. "But I didn't sign these. Not one of them." She turned to Rossum. "You have something to say?"

Not a muscle moved on Rossum's face. It was frozen into a wide-eyed rictus. Eleanor's fist clenched her pearl necklace.

"I see." The chair reached for the firehouse sales contract. "We have an investigation to start. And restitution to make."

"You can't tie anything to me. I'm innocent," Rossum finally managed to say. "I never colluded with her on anything. Never."

"We found this list of displaced homeowners." Deborah handed to the chair the list of people whose property Eleanor had purchased under the threat of condemnation, the list Claudine had stolen the night before.

The double doors burst open, and a man in a navy blue suit entered. "Eleanor Millhouse?"

"Yes?" Eleanor gasped. She looked like she didn't know if she should panic or run to him for safety.

"Agent Satter, Federal Drug Administration. I understand you've been illegally importing goat hormones."

Unable to take the strain, Eleanor's necklace burst at last, pearls clattering over the hearing room floor.

The chair rose. "Well, ladies. It looks like you've got yourself a firehouse."

Chapter Twenty-Eight

"Did you see Eleanor's face when she figured out that we'd swapped out the agreement?" Claudine asked.

They were sitting in the Granzer mansion den later that evening, and she was sprawled on the Persian rug with a glass of Louie's best bourbon in her hand. Claudine hadn't felt so relaxed, so carefree, really, in years. Even the Cabrini heist had barely crossed her mind.

"I thought she was going to strangle herself with her pearls," Ruby said.

"I still can't believe we pulled it off," Deborah said.

"It was her own greed that got her," Claudine said. "You know that means no membership in the Carsonville Women's League for you."

"So what?" Ruby said. She truly didn't seem to care. "It was worth it just to see her face when she was busted for the goat hormones."

"Why did you want to join so bad? I never thought they were all that great," Deborah said.

Ruby held out her glass for more bourbon. "My mom used to be president of the Women's League, but they kicked her out when she got sick. I thought if I joined, I could convince them to put a plaque on her grave like they do for every past president."

"A plaque? That's it? I'll get you a plaque if that's what you want," Deborah said.

Maybe Ruby wanted revenge more than justice, Claudine thought. Or maybe she'd finally realized that what other people thought didn't matter. She didn't have to prove she was "better," because their brand of better wasn't necessarily worth having. "Or—I know. Let's go to the cemetery and steal all of the other plaques."

Ruby laughed and choked up a little bourbon. "I'm done with stealing."

"Me, too," Deborah added.

"What?" Claudine said in reply to Deborah's stare.

"What about you? Are you done killing people?" Deborah asked.

"Killing people?"

"You know, 'taking them out,' giving them the 'K.O.'."

"Deborah, I steal things. I don't kill people."

"Too bad. I was going to ask you to do something about Louie." Deborah kept a straight face for a second before it cracked into a grin.

"I'm sorry about your husband," Claudine said. "You paid a high price to get the Rizzio kids their home."

"Well," Deborah drew out the word. "At least I never have to look at another bird again. I think I'll take up eating chicken just to get rid of more of them."

"What's with you?" Ruby said to Claudine. "You look so serious."

Claudine leaned over and with effort pulled in a duffel bag. "Deb, this is for you."

Deborah gingerly unzipped it. Her expression went from curiosity to wonder. She pulled out a fork. "Our sterling."

"Larry said he couldn't get the jewelry back, but I was able to find your flatware."

"You—you mean you stole it?"

"Yes, but it's complicated. Let's just say that you can do better than Louie."

"Hey, I think it's on." Ruby pointed the remote at the TV and clicked up the volume.

Newscaster Brenda's face appeared, her rigid coiffure touching the screen's edges. "A dramatic scene at what should have been a routine Carsonville County commissioners' meeting revealed a story of long-standing corruption. Eleanor Millhouse, CEO of Fine Properties of Distinction, is known for her lavish developments, such as the City Gents condominiums and the Shangri-La Spa. Today we learned she's also the developer behind the city's sewage treatment plant and the reason dozens of families were left homeless."

The two-minute story included footage of a bedraggled Eleanor pleading with Ned Rossum, who in turn had grabbed the chair's sleeve.

"Ms. Millhouse is under psychiatric observation while officials begin an investigation into bribery and collusion. City activists say they are planning a recall for Commissioner Rossum," Brenda concluded.

Ruby turned off the television. "We did it."

In an uncharacteristically clumsy move, as she leaned back, Claudine's hand knocked over her tumbler. She grabbed the glass, but not before bourbon left a brown spill on the rug. "I'm so sorry. I'll help you clean it up."

"No biggie," Deborah said. "My new puppy will probably shred it, anyway. You're going to get me one, right, Ruby?"

***

What a miracle. What a freaking miracle, Ruby thought as she drove home. One minute everything is lost, and the next we have the firehouse. Maybe we'll put in an art studio for kids like Joanie. And a doggy day care where the kids could learn to take care of animals. Ruby still couldn't believe it.

She pulled the Volvo into the parking lot of the Quickie Mart. She'd surprise Bruce with a six-pack of diet Fresca and some snack cakes. He'd like that.

Perry Mason flicked across the screen of a small TV near the cash register. Ruby noticed that the store was well set up to nab thieves. Circular mirrors were set into the ceiling to show each aisle, and cigarettes and batteries were locked behind the counter. Not that it mattered to her. This week's trip to Klingle's was her last. She was concentrating on her salon. That's what she really enjoyed, anyway. Those rich broads could pay retail.

She set the soda and box of snacks on the counter. *The Carsonville Recorder* showed a front page article about the county commissioners' meeting with a photo of the crowd and another of Eleanor Millhouse looking crazed. Ruby chuckled and unfolded the paper. A good, long article, and the reporter had picked up on the youth shelter angle, too. Below the fold was another story. The San Francisco Museum of Decorative Arts was burgled the night before last. Thieves made off with most of an opera singer's multi-million dollar jewel collection. Fascinating. Claudine would be interested in that, she bet.

Ruby absently stuck the newspaper in her Balenciaga tote. She was barely out the door when she felt her upper arm in a vice-like grip.

"You," the cashier said. "I knew you were a booster. Knew it from the first time I saw you. I'm calling the police."

All at once, she recognized him. Her heart stopped. It was the guard she'd gotten fired at Klingle's.

Chapter Twenty-Nine

L ate that night, Claudine's phone rang. She'd been dreaming of emerald necklaces and a velvet armchair at Geneva's Hotel Beau Rivage. She rolled over in bed and clicked on the light.

The number wasn't one she recognized. It wouldn't be Oswald. She didn't expect a victory call. When the heist was over, he was on a plane, and she'd likely never hear from him again.

Claudine cleared her throat. "Hello?"

"Deanie, it's Gilda. Your father is in the hospital."

Claudine bolted upright. "Heart attack?"

"It doesn't look good, honey. You better get down here."

Within minutes, Claudine was pulling her Mercedes out of the driveway. Her fingers trembled on the steering wheel and she couldn't get the key in the ignition. Go, go, go. At last, the car started.

At the hospital, a night duty nurse told her visiting hours were well over, but when she said she was there for Henri Dupin, the nurse ushered her down the hall. Before they entered, the nurse stopped her.

"Your father had a stroke. He's on life support now. Honey," the nurse placed an arm on hers, "if you have anything to say to him, this is the time." She released Claudine and opened the door.

"Dad," Claudine whispered and put her hand on his.

"Deanie." Hank's voice was faint. If she thought he looked bad the last time she saw him in the cardiac care unit, that was nothing compared to now. His skin was waxen and his breathing labored, even with machines whooshing and beeping to help him.

André sat on the other side of the bed. For once in his life, his composure was gone, and he looked like the little boy she remembered from childhood. Gilda sat at a respectful distance.

"Don't talk, Papa." She hadn't called him that for years. "Just rest."

When she was in kindergarten, not long after her mother had died, Claudine used to wait after school for her father to stop by on his bicycle to take her home. He perched her on the handlebars in front—probably not super safe, in retrospect, but prudence was never her father's forte. He was strong, with black curly hair and ruddy cheeks. When it was time for bed, he told her stories about how the two of them would sail a ship to Africa to save the tigers, or how they would stave off a Martian army from a perch on the Empire State Building. Then he'd have Mrs. Detweiler next door come over to sit with her while he went out to "work." It was years before she understood what this work was, but he had already started her on agility exercises, and she could pinch Mrs. Detweiler's earrings with one hand behind her back.

Just you and me and André, just the three of us, her father had always said. Just us.

She laid her head on the edge of his bed. At 4:17 a.m., Henri Dupin died.

* * *

"Hi, honey," Ruby said when Bruce dropped off the bail check and led her from the jail. She wasn't a crier. Lord knows she'd had enough in her life to boohoo about, though it didn't do any good to weep. But today all she wanted was to fall into Bruce's arms and bawl.

"Hi, honey," Bruce replied.

He'd been so sweet through all of this, and, really, she'd come off pretty lucky. The security guard from Klingle's had not been happy to be demoted to cashier at a Quickie Mart, and he was hell-bent on putting Ruby away for a long time. Since she'd absentmindedly stuck the newspaper in her bag, it gave the police the right to search it, and they found a bracelet with the loss prevention tag still attached. A lawyer recommended by Larry the Fence said Ruby would likely only have to do a year of probation and six months of community service on top of the night in jail she'd already spent. As she said, she'd come off lucky.

But she hadn't yet faced Bruce. Time in jail was nothing compared to the prospect of losing him. "Are you—do you still want me to come home?"

"Of course."

They drove home, silent. Ruby's whole body thrummed with emotion. Bruce stared at the road, and she couldn't read anything from his placid expression. Did he hate her? Would he ever trust her again?

The dogs scampered at their feet when they came in the kitchen door. Bruce steered her to the den and set her on the love seat. "Okay. I'm ready."

She told him everything—how she started shoplifting, when

she did it, how and who she did it for. She told him about the ladies who came for "wholesale" deals. About trying to win a place on the Carsonville Women's League to vindicate her mother. Then she bit her lip and waited.

Bruce taught middle school. He'd mastered the art of listening without betraying emotion. Even after years of reading his face, she had no idea what was going through his mind.

"Honey?" she whispered after a few minutes.

"You're back," he said. "It's the Ruby I love and married. It's you."

She fell forward and ground through two decades of crying in forty-five minutes. She should have told him so much sooner. God, she loved him. Who cared that his suits weren't Armani and he couldn't pronounce the words on the menu at Swift's Dinner Palace? He was her Bruce—solid, caring, funny, and kind. The man was solid gold. She'd never forget that the rest of her life.

When she was finally able to talk, she said, "How are the kids?"

Bruce knew instantly she was asking about the dogs, not his students or the Rizzios. "Marty's a little off his feed. I think he missed you."

Ruby put her hands up flat, and Bruce placed his on the other side, overlapping hers.

* * *

"Grady, sweetheart, get off your duff and come in here. Watching all that television isn't good for your health." Deborah had moved the tables to the side of the Villa Saint Nicholas dining room for a low-impact aerobics class. Gilda had helped her choose the music. Many of the attendees were in chairs or leaning on walkers.

Grady slumped in and found a place toward the side of the room.

"Amazing," Gilda whispered. "He won't listen to any of the rest of us."

"He's a darling," Deborah said. "Is everyone ready? Now lift your right arm. One, two, three. That's good."

Dean Martin's "Fly Me to the Moon" filled the dining room. The Rizzio kids were in school, except Hugo, who agreed to take community college classes for two years before any of the Villa's residents would consider inducting him into the community.

Grandpa Granzer was so grateful the Booster Club exposed his heirs' attempts to declare him mentally incompetent that he pressured Louie to sign the Granzer mansion over to Deborah as part of the divorce settlement, along with a tidy annual income. "I'll show them who's nuts," he'd said. She immediately moved the Rizzio kids in.

She felt good with the kids and at the Villa. Needed. She'd become the Villa's recreation director, and Warren said they'd even pay her to get a certificate in recreation management, if she wanted. She shared Warren's office and rented a steam cleaner to freshen up the rug. She ended up cleaning the carpets in the halls, too. She'd have this place spick and span in no time.

Louie still hadn't come home, and he refused to talk to her. She was getting used to the idea. In any case, her lawyer seemed not to have a problem getting in touch with his. A week after Louie moved out, she brought the watches she'd stolen to the police department and said she found them in the park. The sergeant behind the desk looked suspicious, but since none of them had been reported stolen, he couldn't do anything about it.

"Eddie, watch that your hand doesn't hit Patty. Thank you."

Life sure was amazing. Stay positive, as Ruby said. Stay positive and all sorts of things can happen.

*   *   *

Claudine stepped from the dark church into the crisp November sunshine. It was done. Her father's memorial service was over. If she had gone to San Francisco for the heist, she wouldn't have been there for him at the end, and today at the service. Knowing this meant more than the pasha's rubies.

Father Vincent had insisted on a real church service, but he couldn't find a parish to let him officiate. At last, Claudine located a Unitarian church on the edge of town, which, for a fee, let Father Vincent do what he wanted.

It was a fine service. Claudine had ordered a Christofle silver urn from France for her father's ashes. He would have liked that. Father Vincent preached a moving sermon integrating the Sermon on the Mount with the story of Paul's becoming a disciple and his forgiveness. Gilda sang "Nearer My God to Thee" and kept the dance moves to a minimum. They all cried.

Except Claudine. She'd already cried so much that she felt hollowed out. Deborah and Ruby had sat behind her. Ruby had said she'd name their next rescue Hank.

Not only was her father gone, but André was leaving, too. He and Father Vincent won a spot on the reality TV show, *The Perilous Path*, a sort of long-distance scavenger hunt. He'd already cut his hair short and taken on a Kentucky accent. Father Vincent, playing André's father, was looking forward to doing some fancy driving and was trying to negotiate a Utilikilt sponsorship.

Wisps of snow blew over the bleak parking lot. Now it was time to recuperate, see what life had in store for her with no father, no profession.

Leaning against her car—she drove the Mercedes this time—was a man. She blinked and looked again. It was the man who had been following her, the man in the gray Taurus. She started to back away.

"No." The man stepped forward from the car. "Don't go. Please. I just want to talk to you."

Closer now, she got a better look at him. He didn't have that stiff look of a policeman. He wasn't bad looking, actually. Fit, camel coat, a bit of a beard.

"Stop there. What do you want?" she said when they were still at least a dozen feet apart.

He began to step forward again, and she held up a hand. "I said, stop. What do you want?"

"I work for Lewis of London International. We insure high-value accounts. The big ones."

The hairs on the back of her neck prickled. "And?" She glanced to the side. She could run up the parking lot to the alley behind the church. She could probably lose him in five minutes if she tried. But what she really wanted to do was sit down where she was and bury her head in her hands.

"I'm sorry to talk to you here after your father's memorial service."

He knew about her father's death?

"But I haven't been able to get in touch with you, and I've been trying for weeks."

"So?" Claudine said.

He ran a hand through his hair. It was dark and curly, just as her father's had been. She'd be arrested by a man who looked like her father. The irony. "It's just—well, to get to the point, we want you to come work for us."

"What?" She'd heard him, but the "what" came out of her mouth automatically, to buy time.

"We can pay you good money," he said quickly. "It's just that you have—well, you may have certain skills. No one can say for sure, of course." He watched her. "With your knowledge—knowledge and skills that you may have, that is, we can't prove anything—you'd make a perfect detective for the company."

She looked around. There was nowhere to sit, so she leaned against a Mazda hatchback. "I need a minute."

The man kept his distance. "I'm going to leave my card." He set a business card on the roof of her Mercedes. "I hope you'll think about it, at least." He paused a moment. "Will you?"

"Go. Leave me alone."

He returned to the gray sedan. Once he was clear of the parking lot, she got up from the Mazda. What a wild and crazy ride this life was. She slipped the business card in her purse's side pocket.

* * *

Claudine trudged up the stairs to her apartment. Every step was an effort. Although it was barely mid-afternoon, she wanted to crawl into bed and pull the quilt over her head and not come out until morning. Petunia meowed for dinner. "All right, mister. Just a minute."

She threw her purse on an armchair, then froze. On her desk was a small package. It hadn't been there before. Brown paper wrapping. No return address.

She lifted the box and shook it lightly. It wasn't heavy, but it held something substantial. She paused as exhaustion washed over her. Should she laugh—or cry? She unwrapped it. No note. Inside was a jewelry box. She lifted its lid. Lying on a velvet pad was the Cartier panther brooch, glittering with diamonds.

Afterword

Thank you to Eric Valentin, head of security at Macy's in downtown Portland, for his insight on shoplifting. Thank you, too, to the experts at Shreve jewelers who explained the world of men's luxury watches.

As always, my writing group—Christine Finlayson, Doug Levin, Dave Lewis, Ann Littlewood, and Marilyn McFarlane—was immeasurably helpful, as was the Drink & Think group, including Lisa Alber, Cindy Brown, and Holly Franko. Jared Pierce and copy editor Raina Glazener upped the novel's quality a thousand percent. The fabulous cover—don't you want that necklace?—came from ebooklaunch.

For information on my other novels, visit my website, www.angelamsanders.com. While you're there, don't forget to sign up for my monthly newsletter full of reviews of 1930s pulp detective novels, fashion tips from Edith Head, old cocktail recipes, Zsa Zsa Gabor's dating advice, and more.

CPSIA information can be obtained
at www.ICGtesting.com
Printed in the USA
BVHW071751060220
571645BV00004B/482

9 780990 413363